DOUBLE DUTY

It is an inevitable certainty, the more one hunts a quarry, the more one becomes obsessed to capture it. Many a night before drifting off to sleep, Marcus occupied himself picturing the moment in the cave with the lady. This time, he would reach across and remove the mask—gaining proof positive she and Stara were one. In the daytime, however, he kept to his original objective for coming to Hillcrest—capturing Lady Gwendolen. Yet, curse Stara, for when she was present, she distracted his aim back and forth between both ladies, scattering his shot.

After one such dalliance, Stara called him to account for his duplicity. "Is it *comme il faut,* Mr. Justus, to flirt with two ladies at once?"

Unabashed, Marcus claimed he was not flirting with the two of them. "Rather," and he paused to add this daunting gem, "I am courting one lady—her ladyship—while I am blatantly seducing you."

LADY
ADVENTURESS

HELEN ARCHERY

HarperPaperbacks
A Division of HarperCollinsPublishers

This is a work of fiction. The characters, incidents, and dialogues are products of the author's imagination and are not to be construed as real. Any resemblance to actual events or persons, living or dead, is entirely coincidental.

HarperPaperbacks *A Division of* HarperCollins*Publishers*
10 East 53rd Street, New York, N.Y. 10022

Cover illustration by Bob Berran

First printing: January 1994

Printed in the United States of America

HarperPaperbacks, HarperMonogram, and colophon are trademarks of HarperCollins*Publishers*

10 9 8 7 6 5 4 3 2 1

*In memory of my beautiful mother,
who died May 9, 1992. Carol-Calliope, the loving,
generous, adventurous woman who inspired me to
dare, and throughout her life gave all who knew
her an unreserved, unafraid, unqualified embrace of
love.*

*In dedication to the real Stara, my sister, Astera,
who dares along and dreams along with me.*

1

"I love you," he said.

The lady smiled, expecting that declaration. But another lady's voice interrupted, "So do countless gentlemen love Lady Gwendolen. The question is how much do you love her for herself and how much for her position and yearly income?"

Those were the sparkling tones of Stara Carltons, quite a contrast to the languid voice of the much praised and adored Lady Gwendolen.

The deep blue eyes of Marcus Justus, the most successful rake around town, met the challenge of Stara's dark eyes and did not flinch.

"I say, you rather underestimate your friend, what? Lady Gwendolen herself is worthy of the entire *beau monde*'s admiration. Her beauty would make a poet of the most illiterate gentleman. Her corn-silk hair. Her grape green eyes. Her berry red lips."

"You make her ladyship sound like a culinary delight. Is that your intention? Or is it just your nature to always take a bite out of everyone around?"

Marcus frowned. This young lady was obviously going to be a stumbling block in his quest for capturing Lady Gwendolen. Not only was she always present whenever he was conversing with her ladyship, but hardly reticent about making her opinions known. If it were not so necessary for his income to capture Lady Gwendolen, he would not have been adverse to toying a bit with her sparkling companion. Actually, it might have been a sparring match worth almost half of his attention. He never bothered devoting more than that to ladies. Usually it was quite sufficient to toss a few well-rehearsed compliments and advance to deep sighs. At which point Marcus would risk a kiss, perhaps several, depending on the eagerness of the young miss. Inevitably, due to his osculatory expertise, the lady was his for the asking. He had been anticipating the same easy chase with Lady Gwendolen until he discovered she rarely went anywhere without being accompanied by her finishing school chum, Stara. In truth it had been Miss Carltons who had first caught his eye, but he'd been warned by Lord Bosley, his friend, that her income was a mere pittance. Although her mother was a lady, her parents had started out in reduced circumstances that were further decreased when they deceased. After nudging his memory Marcus recollected her father was called, Samson, for his brawn and because he'd been quite a fighter in the Napoleonic wars, during which he heroically died. The prince regent himself had given the widow a medal and she'd been left with that, and a young child. Obviously, Stara. Bosley, quite a biographer, knew all the facts about eligible ladies, and he further explained that the mother had soon died, true to romantic custom—of a broken heart, leaving Stara to the kindness of a distant relative. This Mr. Pinkerton promptly put her into a finishing school, Miss Lav-

adale's, where she met and became companion to Lady
Gwendolen.

Stara Carltons was a deucedly attractive lady,
Marcus confessed, tall, well formed and perfectly fea-
tured. Yet while her dark eyes always seemed to have
stars in them, she was obviously ill starred overall, and
he was too much a gambler to accept such an unlucky
bet. Especially when Lady Gwendolen well favored by
both fortune and fate was before him. Further, it was
known that Stara was rather needle-witted, and Marcus
would be darned if he'd put up with jabs from a lady.
Then too Gwendolen was clearly this season's diamond, which meant winning her would add mightily
not only to his income but consequence. And so, as did
everyone else, Mr. Justus selected Lady Gwendolen.

Her ladyship, accustomed to having everything
handed to her, expected to have her hand sought by
every eligible bachelor, so she was scarcely surprised to
be courted by the dashing Mr. Justus. But shortly Marcus discovered this diamond had a serious flaw. She
lacked facets. She was what she was. An exalted lady to
be admired but who gave off very little sparkle. Equally
sedate were her preferences for slow, stately dances,
short strolls rather than hearty walks and always rides
in barouches than the faster-paced phaetons. Obligingly
her gentlemen suitors kept to her measure.

That flaw probably had enabled Stara, Marcus divined, to become indispensable to her ladyship. For
Stara had spirit enough for three ladies. She loved to
dance and twirl and laugh. She even took on herself the
task of concluding her ladyship's conversations. "What
do we say to that, Stara?" Gwendolen would ask turning to her friend, who would blithely supply the necessary bon mot, and Lady Gwendolen would smile and
accept the praises forthcoming as if she herself had said
it. Actually, Lady Gwendolen preferred long pauses,

and when forced to converse, usually chose her favorite hobby, gardening. So horticulturally inclined, her ladyship only blossomed at bud mots; branching out into her most flowery phrases. Along with her gardeners, she had developed a rare rose to reflect herself. It was pale yellow and quite exquisite, she claimed, without the smallest hint of modesty. Her ladyship was hoping it would win a prize at the coming Hillcrest Garden Show.

"You are the prize yourself," every gentleman was certain to insert, so Gwen began to pause in her talk, expecting that compliment. She was rarely disappointed. If the gentleman was too feeble-witted, Stara was certain to supply it and have the gentleman echoing his agreement.

Ah yes, Stara was very useful. She did not however have to assist Mr. Justus. On his own he quickly inserted not only the expected compliment but added several additional ones. After which, Marcus glanced at Stara whose eyes were twinkling at his quick grasp of the obvious.

Tonight Mr. Justus had planned to snatch Lady Gwendolen from under the nose of her principal escort, the Duke of Clairidge. It was known that the marquis favored his grace's suit for his daughter's hand. And with such sanction and her ladyship obviously not the sort to put herself out to oppose her father, Mr. Justus assumed he had his work cut out for him. But the challenge had been disappointingly spiritless since his grace was not present at tonight's ball, and Lady Gwendolen quite willing to be wooed.

For the first two dances with her ladyship, after understanding her nature, Marcus stopped chatting and flattering and allowed long periods of quiet. But he used the silence to his advantage by staring at Lady Gwendolen with such passion she found her tranquility dis-

turbed after all. And yet, yet, the boldness of his blue
eyes boring into her green ones left her heart fluttering.
She accepted a second dance, which was a marked sign
in his favor, because she simply had never felt herself so
exhilarated. The gentleman pressed her body in the
most gentle and yet titillating manner. And once, as the
dance ended, Mr. Justus had dared to breathe on her
forehead as he slowly bowed down to her, and Gwen
felt her usually calm heart jump.

Was it any wonder that she did not refuse this gentleman's request for a stroll in the garden. But she
brought Stara along. And so there they were, the three
of them, rather than strolling, accommodating Lady
Gwendolen by sitting on the veranda, under a weeping
willow tree that swung to the music with each breeze.

Lady Gwendolen found it a delight to be resting
and receiving homage from an exciting gentleman while
her dear friend supplied all necessary replies.

While flattering her ladyship, Mr. Justus kept himself peripherally amused by twirling his fob. It was his
prize one and tipped by a carved ivory head of a beautiful woman. Indeed many a lady had wished to see that
sculpture closer. And he was nothing loath to bring it to
their eager faces. "She is my goddess," he explained.
Urged to elucidate, he did so. This carving was his ideal
face and if he ever found a lady to equal it, he would
marry her on the spot. Thereupon, not a single lady
failed to see an immediate resemblance to her own features. Lady Gwendolen was certain the lips were hers.
Miss Millicent Traver claimed the nose for her own.
And so on. While Mr. Justus just smiled with maddening agreement to them all.

Only Stara had refused to play his game, not even
giving it a glance. But on the veranda, when the gentleman devoted himself to eyeing his fob with such fervor, as if neither of the two ladies present could equal

that perfection, she was roused to pierce his pride, with the comment, "I expect the artist made at least a dozen of those."

That jab went deeper than she expected, for Marcus mightily valued his lady on his fob, deeming her his good-luck piece. With his coolest blue-eyed stare, he responded, "She is an *original*. And she is mine."

"She might be original," Stara said airily, "but no lady belongs to any gentleman permanently. Further, I predict that you yourself will lose your ivory lady one day in your gambles or gambols."

"Never," he vowed with surprising intensity. "She is my fate."

At that point, Lady Gwendolen coughed and both attendants turned, recollecting their duties. Stara lightly chastised Mr. Justus for having run out of encomiums. "Surely Lady Gwendolen rates a poem or two. Lord Silverdale wrote one on the spot to the glorious beauty of her pale hair. Equated it to moonbeams, if I recollect, did he not, Gwen dear?"

Lady Gwendolen inclined her head and half smiled in agreement or just to prove she was present.

"One does not need words," Marcus quickly inserted, not to be outdone by such a fribble as Silverdale. "One is silent before *perfection*."

That found favor with her ladyship, but Stara giggled.

"What gammon! If that were so, we'd have no poems at all—not to the perfection of Cleopatra, nor to the beauty of the night itself. Why look about you— that weeping willow must recall Shakespeare's lines. I shall quote them so you may repeat them to her ladyship, for she certainly deserves the greatest compliments from the greatest source." And walking toward the willow tree, she strummed through the hanging branches while she recited raptly, " 'Make me a willow cabin at

your gate, and call upon my soul within the house . . .
holla your name to the reverberate hills . . . and cry
out Olivia!' "

"But my name is not Olivia," Gwendolen inter-
jected in confusion, and Marcus who had been caught
up by the image of Stara under the weeping willow with
the moonlight on her face, quoting the words with all
her heart, was so tickled by Lady Gwen's literalness, he
let out a whoop of laughter, only quickly to sober and
applaud her ladyship with a hearty, "Hear! Hear!"
Then turning to Stara, he further squelched that auda-
cious miss by pointing out perhaps *she* needed her name
proclaimed to the hills, but her ladyship was beyond
such blatant shoutings. "Lady Gwendolen merits quiet
appreciation. Egad, one does not shout at a rose. One is
silent in admiration, as one comes close to sniff its exquisite scent."

He came close to her ladyship who felt herself col-
oring and was grateful for the shadows. The gentleman
could not have chosen better than to equate her to a
flower, as was proven by Gwen's inviting him to her
father's estate for the coming showing of the "Lady
Gwendolen Rose." Eagerly accepting, Mr. Justus was
all delight and anticipation.

Stara took the occasion to remind her ladyship that
the duke was invited for that presentation.

"A perfect rose cannot have too many admirers,"
Mr. Justus inserted quickly. Her ladyship agreed and
made the invitation firm, as she stood up upon sighting
the approach of her next partner. It was Lord Silverdale
and she extended her hand with her usual grace and
was led back into the ballroom, well satisfied with this
evening.

Left alone, Stara and Marcus stared at each other.
The gentleman was preening a bit, feeling he had

scored over her guardianship. "Tipped you a doubler, did I not, my dear Miss Carltons?" he said with a grin.

But Stara, rather than perturbed, showed her dimples. He eyed her quizzically, and then as she merely curtsied and attempted to leave, he grabbed her hand and asked suspiciously, "What kind of game are you playing? I have the decided impression I was manipulated tonight. And that is not a sensation I am accustomed to."

Disengaging her hand, Stara calmly replied, "If you intend to be in my presence you must become accustomed to it. For indeed, you have acted exactly according to my plan. Although I gather not intentionally. That is what I most prefer—an unwitting dupe."

And laughing at his grimace, her eyes all sparkling, Stara turned to meet her own partner waiting at the doorway, she similarly well satisfied with the evening.

2

But Marcus would not allow their engagement to end with the lady having the last word.

"What are you planning?" he demanded, waving away the waiting partner, and forcing Stara to explain herself. When she would not, he drew his own conclusion. "Ah, I gather you wished me to come. And that is how I followed your lead. Correct? You are under the assumption that with two gentlemen there, one might be left over for yourself. I must rush to disabuse you of those hopes. Under no circumstance would I accept you in consolation. I have too many other ladies of wealth and power waiting for me in the unlikely event that I fail with Lady Gwendolen."

"But I am counting on you to win," Stara admitted. "You are unprincipled enough and the duke too gentle to compete successfully with you. Equating her with a rose when everyone knows of her interest, was almost beneath you in its obviousness, yet it succeeded. And sniffing her, while comic to me, seems to have been effective with her ladyship. She does not require a great deal of ingenuity, nor sincerity."

"Obviously not. Or she would not have made you her friend."

Stara laughed. "But she did not. I simply became indispensable to her. And so I have a season. But always in her shade. And if I no longer served her purpose, if I revealed what anguish I've had in my life, she would have long dropped me. She does not wish to be disturbed from the placidity and ease of her life. And so I serve as do her servants—to answer to her convenience. It is a tip I give you, gratis. Make all easy for her and she shall allow you the honor of continuing to do so. Never ask more than she wishes to give and further never give too much *to her,* lest she feel herself overwhelmed. And if you behave according to my instructions, then you shall easily win her."

Her earnestness was the clue Marcus needed to unravel the puzzle. "Aha! It is the duke you are after! Blast it, are you hoping to be a duchess! What impudence! I could almost admire you for it. By Jove, I do. From being on the fringes of society, you are seeking to rule it!"

Stara smiled softly. "What is the point of aiming for anything unless one aims as high as one could possibly reach. I certainly would not settle for an adventurer like you."

"Nor would I settle for an adventuress, like you. And yet . . ." He came closer, intrigued by the blatancy of her admission. "I might not mind a dalliance on the side."

Stara pushed away from him. "You overstep yourself, sir. I have worked long and hard for my position and I shall never permit a casual moment to prevent me from achieving it. You yourself should not allow your nature to distract you from your goal. It would be best

if we became partners and helped each other in our
aims against these pampered pets."

Feeling her seeking to direct him again, Marcus
stepped away from those hypnotic, dark eyes. "I do not
need a partner," he said sternly. "Certainly I would not
seek a *lady* partner. Ladies have only one purpose as far
as I am concerned, and that is pleasure."

Then to put her in her place, since he resented her
taking the lead, he quickly reached for Stara and pulled
her into his arms. She attempted to sway away, but he
was too nimble, blocking her every step toward the veranda doors. Next moment she found herself under the
willow tree, her body against the trunk, and he was
whispering her name to the reverberate hills. "Stara,
Stara." Gradually she was becoming entrapped by that
and the pressure of his body against hers. Next moment
she was further shaken by his kiss. So thorough was it,
Stara was sufficiently overcome to allow him to end it
to his satisfaction. Only then did she come to her
senses, remembering this gentleman's aim was dalliance. And that would defeat her life's purpose of becoming the leader of society that had so cruelly ignored
her. And all for a mere physical pleasuring of a moment. Yet, yet, she would not end this pleasure too
abruptly, savoring the sensation flooding her body. She
even kissed him back, enjoying completely the rush of
sensuality. The moonlight was caressing them both and
when she felt him lost in the passion of the moment, she
forced herself to come out of her bemusement. Leaning
against the tree, claiming she must catch her breath,
Stara reached up unto a low branch and with its aid
swung herself against him, knocking him flat on the
ground. After which she lightly stepped over and ran
for the door, laughing all the while.

"Keep your kisses for her ladyship. She will neither
return them as I did nor best you by knocking you flat.

We could have been partners. Now we're adversaries. And you'll note which one of us is left triumphantly on her feet."

Closing the door with a slam, Stara glided into the ballroom. But she had to note, with her usual honesty, that she needed to stop to gasp, for he had left her more breathless than she'd bargained. Admittedly at one point Stara had almost let him have his way with her. He was a gentleman of much physical persuasion, she owned. One could not wonder at Lady Gwendolen's responding to that rake. While she'd come up a winner this time, Stara realized she'd have to be very careful not to deal with him any further or her plans for the duke might be seriously jeopardized.

Back in the garden, Marcus rose with astonishment. This minx, this hoyden had planted him a leveler. Egad, he had to laugh at that! Not a single gentleman at Jackson's Boxing Saloon had caught him quite so off guard. And from a lady! Her lips had floored him as well. The amount of passion in that body was not to be believed. He'd not encountered its like from the most sophisticated matrons nor even all his exotic ladybirds. Upon controlling himself, Marcus Justus entered the ballroom seeking two ladies . . . now having two intense purposes: pursuit and retaliation.

Lady Gwendolen was as usual surrounded by admirers. Adjusting his cravat, he walked toward her. She was gracious enough to allow him a near place as she whispered, "Where is dear Stara? Her next partner, Lord Fitzroy, was complaining that she had left him adrift."

Grimly Marcus sought and spotted that lady dancing with Lady Gwendolen's widower father. His eyes narrowed as he wondered if Stara did not have two arrows in her quiver. If she failed with the duke, was she intending to become the marchioness? By Jove, yes,

there was nothing he would not put past this wild lady.
And then while talking to Lady Gwendolen, Marcus
found himself again and again seeking the face of her
companion. Her next dancing partner was Lord Silverdale, saying something that apparently vastly amused
her. How that blockhead could be found witty by that
discerning lady had him marveling. Or was she all pretense? Had she even been pretending passion with him?
Dash it, he refused to accept that, knowing instinctively
he had gotten past her maneuvers as she admittedly had
gotten past his. One could not easily forget the pulsing
of her eager lips, and Marcus gave himself up to recalling that moment, down to the last twinge of pleasure.

"What are you thinking about, Mr. Justus?" Lady
Gwendolen quietly inquired.

"Of you, your ladyship. Of whom else could any
gentleman be thinking—so close to your matchless
self?"

She smiled, having received the expected answer.
And she gave him her hand for the next dance. But the
waltz was a rather vigorous one, and her ladyship de-
clined to attempt it. Lord Silverdale and Stara arrived in
time for his lordship to inquire whether Lady Gwendolen would prefer to stroll through the art gallery. She
would. That left Stara and Marcus alone. The waltz
music was sweeping them both off their feet. Stepping
away, Stara sought another partner, but he grinned and
took her into his arms.

"This dance is ours," he whispered as he whirled
her round and round, holding her body so tightly
against himself that they became one close unit, silently
enjoying their sensations, until the dance was over, and
then he bowed to her, and she nodded to him.

"You'd better keep your silences and yourself for
Lady Gwendolen," Stara warned, but her voice was
rather husky from her own emotions.

"I'm enough for both ladies," he said with a grin. "You're not enough for me."

"I expect I shall very shortly prove you wrong."

Signaling the marquis, Stara was set to whirl away when Marcus whispered, "You're too much of a woman to accept such an old man for a title. Let your body lead you. Women are best when they think with their passions."

"And gentleman *only* think with their passions, since they have such a limit of intellect. Further, the more you concentrate on my passion, the more you lose your purpose. As you have now—spending time attempting to win me, while Lord Silverdale steals a march on you. Join them in the portrait gallery, you cawker, or there will be a third gentleman invited to Westwardon. And you with the least position."

He turned to note that she was correct. Lady Gwendolen was smiling and allowing Lord Silverdale to hold her hand as he led her out of the room. Marcus was torn between going after them or cutting into Stara's dance with the marquis. His instinct, his passion had him wishing to stay for the dance, but he realized she had been correct, he was allowing his passion to rule him. Yet next moment while on his way toward the portrait gallery, he stopped, realizing she had maneuvered him again. He glanced back and saw her laughing at his following her instructions to the letter. Cursing himself, he was ambivalently unable to move either way, until he recollected that his main objective was Lady Gwendolen. First, he'd best have her ladyship tied up before allowing himself to be distracted by her companion. But Stara's time would come, he vowed, and confound her, he would thoroughly enjoy giving her a memorable comeuppance!

3

During the journey to her country estate Lady Gwendolen was much peeved. She expected Stara to be with her through the long miles from Oxford to Warwick and turning before Leicester toward Westwardon, her father's district. It was rather unfeeling of her friend to stay with the marquis, in order to arrange the extra supplies and servants needed for their entertaining at Hillcrest. Naturally, Lady Gwen was not adverse to Stara taking on these extra duties, for she believed sincerely that everybody should be kept as occupied as possible. Especially in doing the tasks her ladyship should have been doing. But she did not care for Stara, her companion, to be putting the wishes of anybody else before hers. As a poor traveler, she clearly needed Stara's chatting or even reading as a distraction. Stara's one box was strapped onto the coach along with Lady Gwen's several chests, meaning her companion would have to travel with a mere portmanteau for the long trip. Thus her ladyship was not totally thinking of her own inconvenience.

But Stara was perfectly amenable to having a minimal change of clothes, having often had no more than that. Further she had long since conditioned herself to be of assistance to others. Unlike Lady Gwendolen, her happiness had never been of first consequence to anyone but herself—at least not since her mother's early demise. So Stara had to make herself essential to others —first at finishing school, where she began with volunteering to help the girls with their lessons just to win friends, and later charged for her aid when her guardian began cutting down her stipend. Year after year Mr. Pinkerton accustomed himself to taking from Stara's principal, until it had dwindled to the point that he could scarcely avail himself of any of it with any degree of advantage, which had him most resentful and writing to Stara with threats that she might soon be taken from school as it was too much of an expense. Therefore, to meet her tuition for her last year, Stara arranged to assist the teachers.

There was no end to Stara's resourcefulness. Not only did she discover ways of making do, but of making others do unto her as she would wish. She wrote a fine copperplate hand, and would volunteer to write messages to the young ladies' relatives on holidays and anniversaries and was given a share in the cakes, guineas and other little gifts sent from the delighted, long-neglected recipients.

Her greatest coup was Lady Gwendolen; she not only wished Stara to handle her correspondence to her father and aunts and uncles, but even to do most of her school assignments. In return Stara received enough pin money to order a full outfit, including a bonnet. Then too, Lady Gwendolen had so many extra dresses, she rarely had occasion to wear them more than once. Not that Stara could wear Lady Gwen's dresses, for the two were not at all of a size. Lady Gwen, so small and fragile, and Stara, rather statuesque. But certain gowns had hems of some length and could be taken down, which Stara determinedly did late of an evening. And of course cloaks and spencers and bonnets fit all ladies, after a fashion.

Following graduation, Lady Gwen had found herself bereft without Stara's services and reassurances, and so after an entire summer and fall alone, her ladyship put herself to the bother of writing with her own hand, requesting Stara visit during her preparations for a London presentation. Stara was downy enough not to return an immediate acceptance. Instead she wrote she was to be presented as well, but had to wait the convenience of Mrs. Pinkerton and also for whenever her guardian, Mr. Pinkerton, gathered together the needed funds. While sealing that note with a wafer, Stara could not help laughing. For what she did not tell Lady Gwendolen was that a lifetime might jolly well pass ere any of those events occurred. But one never bothered Lady Gwendolen with the truth, especially not about one's having no other options. It was best to give the impression to all, she found, that one was granting a favor by accepting a favor.

Shortly after Stara's letter was sent, Lady Gwendolen obligingly did as her friend had hoped—replying there was not the smallest need to disturb either Mr. or Mrs. Pinkerton, for she and her father, the marquis, would be more than willing to have Stara presented along with her, and certainly additional gowns easily could be ordered from the same dressmaker supplying hers.

And so Stara, having arranged all as planned, agreed to come. While the decision had hung fire, Stara had been all aquiver. For she so wished to be away from the Pinkertons, who not only treated her as a servant, but resented her presence to such a degree she had to apologize for her mere existence. Aware of owing her so much, they pretended the obligation was all on her side. And when Stara finally asked for an accounting of her mother's funds, she was told bluntly not a groat remained, that for the last few years, she had been supplied out of the generosity of their own hearts. Further in repayment, she owed them many years of teaching their children and mending their clothes.

So stringently was she treated, Stara frequently went to bed hungry and was forced to ride out into the meadows to steal fruits from the trees. That was Stara's one protection, she never allowed herself to sink into a decline. When pushed down, she always managed to jump back. Indeed, she enjoyed riding out her fears. For the sensation of jumping fences, having the horse sail her over all obstacles, gave her the incentive to live her life that same way. One risked. One dared much. And one landed safe and secure. And that had been her procedure upon receiving Lady Gwendolen's first note. Daringly, Stara had risked losing all by insisting on her terms, only to sail over all hurdles and land safely at Westwardon.

The first view of Hillcrest left Stara dumbfounded, for the marquis's manor was larger than any palace she'd ever envisioned. And the amount of servants rushing about not only doing Lady Gwen's bidding but hers, had her wondering at her ladyship's invitation. But soon she discovered that her requirement was not to perform physical errands. Rather, after all their years at school, Lady Gwen had become accustomed to Stara's doing her thinking.

What a marquis degree of ennui! Stara could only shake her head at one's finding it too tiresome to use one's own head.

Day after day Stara became more overwhelmed by all the advantages at Hillcrest—so much food and leisure; not to forget a fully stacked library and a room to herself. She even had the marquis's approval to take her pick of his horses for her morning rides around the countryside. But Stara's greatest delight came upon all three arriving in London when the kindly marquis treated her to a full wardrobe for her season ahead.

Never having had a dressmaker looking over her faults, at first Stara was resentful at the woman's exclaiming over her height. She continually praised Lady Gwen's dainty waist and childlike hands that needed the smallest size glove possible. But eventually, resorting to her own taste and ignoring the dressmaker's, Stara came away with a respectable wardrobe of no little beauty.

Her choice was for whites, of course, as was suitable for a lady in her first season, but she distinguished them with contrasting accents of cherry and streaks of violet or gold to give a certain dash to her appearance. For with her dark hair and height, Stara could not outfit herself as a fragile damsel in the pale pinks and light blues that so became Lady Gwendolen and other young ladies.

Stara's only physical attribute envied by Lady Gwendolen, aside from the sculptured perfection of her features, was the fullness and natural curl of her dark cloud of hair. Her ladyship's blond locks were limp and straight, and she had to suffer putting them up in rags every night to achieve the curly tendrils of her hairdo. Loud and long was her resentment of Stara's sleeping unimpeded by lumpy knots.

"Why should I have to undergo such discomfort!" her ladyship objected. And Stara who could have told her much about discomforts bit her tongue and merely shook her curly locks, adding a consoling reminder that the results were worth the small inconvenience, for Gwendolen always looked so beautiful. That soothed her ladyship somewhat, but she still watched with set mouth as Stara devised her new hairdo. In society it was de rigueur to wear one's hair up, and Stara did so, cutting the front to allow curls to riot around her head and arranging the rest into a crown of curls. Lady Gwendolen felt that style, although it showed the beauty of Stara's face and locks, should be rethought, for it also added to her already overly imposing height.

"True enough, Gwen dear, but one ought not pretend to be demure if one is not. Best go all the way with what one is."

"Yes, but you are already taller than Lord Silverdale and on a par with Marmaduke. There should be a limit, surely, to a lady's height."

Stara did not rise to her own defense. Throughout her life she had trained herself to turn the other cheek or she'd have been turned out of school, out of the Pinkertons' house, even out of Lady Gwen's, where her residency was on contingency. That explained why a home of her own was Stara's main dream. For her ladyship undoubtedly would shortly be snapped up by one of her suitors and Stara would have no home at all. She must receive at least *one* offer. And this season was her only opportunity. Each night Stara prayed to her mother to help her find a husband, which would mean a home. In addition, the practical young lady would turn to using her mind to assess her chances. Her birth was almost respectable if one overlooked her father's family in trade. Her person and personality all a gentleman could wish. But she had not even a pence of an independence. And thus she must seek a gentleman with no need of extra income. That not only crossed off her list every gazetted fortune hunter, every younger son, but even lords whose income or estates needed to be buttressed by a lady of means. Leaving very few. There was of course, the marquis's own choice for his daugh-

ter, Marmaduke Melton, the seventh duke of Clairidge.
It might not be cricket to attempt to cut out Lady
Gwendolen, but her ladyship's heart was not engaged,
and further she had no need of either title or money,
having been born with an abundance of both. So Stara
set her cap for that capital choice, his grace himself.

Marmaduke was most gallant, but not given to
chitchat, he explained to Stara. She did not take it as an
affront as he was equally monosyllabic with Lady
Gwendolen. Actually the two together sounded like one
long pause. And so Stara valiantly had to carry on the
conversation for herself, Lady Gwen and the duke.

It ran rather like this.

"Your grace, I expect you know, Lady Gwendolen
is known for her handiwork."

Lady Gwen was pleased to show her knotted
fringe.

"What ho! Top ho!" was all his grace said. Silence
again. Stara next turned to his interests. "Your grace
has quite a collection of horses, not only at Clairidge,
but your stables here are much talked of."

"Rather."

"Did I not see you in a rather smart tilbury with a
pair of spanking grays, going round Hyde Park, just the
other day?"

He nodded at that, with no small indication of
pleasure—pretending to be catching his whip up high.

"Ah yes," she said, applauding. "You are a capital
whip. As your grays are prime goers. How I should love
to see the two showing their paces!"

That roused the duke to describe their pedigrees.
But he was immediately cut off by Lady Gwendolen's
wishing the duke to observe her latest interest—a new
game taught her by Lord Silverdale, called Patience,
that kept her amused for hours at end.

The duke, after listening to her complicated explanation, nodded and said, "Devilish fine game, that. But I ain't one for playing by meself."

Silence again. Lady Gwendolen continued to play Patience, and thus unwittingly gave Stara a chance to draw out his grace. The young companion's rule of making a conversation interesting to a gentleman was to make him the subject. So Stara began with his name. "*Marmaduke,* what a fitting moniker for a duke."

His grace condescended to smile. "Called Duke-duke, don't ya know, by me friends. Sometimes, Doubleduke."

"Oh, I really fancy Duke-duke," Stara exclaimed. "Rather like a cheer, for a winner, I feel."

His grace was pleased that this beautiful lady should so see him, and more than willing to discuss all his names and titles with her, when Lady Gwen looked up from her cards to pronounce, "Duke-duke is . . . repetitive. Marmaduke is perfectly unexceptionable."

No one wished to dispute that, and so silence triumphed again.

Lady Gwen, while not willing to put herself out to win his grace, did not wish him won by another lady and certainly not her companion. She actually hoped Stara would not receive a single offer, and thus remain as her companion, even after her marriage.

On her side Stara was somewhat losing faith in her dream of becoming a duchess. For as well as Gwen, she had to combat his grace's own consciousness of his standing. Regardless of Lady Gwen's indifference, he had continued, lemminglike, to court her, assuming it was his duty. Something daring had been needed to distract the two nobles from unenthusiastically following in the expected pattern of linking their glorious heritages together. It turned out to be not something but *someone*—a certain gentleman returning from his European travels, Mr. Marcus Justus. He strode into the ballrooms and had all the ladies fluttering. Not only was he a gentleman of superior charm and good looks, but he was known to have collected ladies as others did objets d'art. That naturally had those not collected wishing to prove they were worthy of a connoisseur's attempt. From ladies to ladybirds, from first season misses to their mothers, Mr. Justus never discriminated against a woman either for her position or age. If she was an attractive female she became his target. Small wonder the gentlemen resented Mr. Justus as a competitor both for the ladies and the tables. For Marcus, despite the adage, was lucky at both love and cards. His long nights at White's, a select club where the nobles gathered to gamble, were always rewarding. Half the lords at play emerged indebted to him. The secret of Marcus's success was his enjoyment of gaming as a sport—relishing the risking of all to gain more. There was a story that as a young lad in his first season in London, he'd once stayed all night at tables and come out ahead by ten thousand pounds, only to go directly, without stopping for even a nap, to the races in the morning and doubling his winnings. Every penny of that was spent on a necklace for Lady Pomfit, his current flirt, whose husband, Lord Pomfit had been one of the gentlemen losing to him at faro. And while Marcus gambled less compulsively now, he continued to win.

So much gossip was attached to Mr. Justus the young ladies persuaded themselves his mere gaze would capture their hearts. For Marcus had quite a memorable way of gazing at the ladies: deep long stares that always culminated at the point just below their necks, actually focusing on what jewelry hung there, be it locket or string of pearls. His concentration in that vicinity had the young misses stared out of countenance and turning bright red. Whether it was that tactic or his person, Marcus was never refused, either for a dance, and later for a kiss. His intentions were always clearly dishonorable—until he met Lady Gwendolen and began suing for her hand.

As a younger son, Marcus had had years of living by his wits here and abroad and he was tired of it. He began to think seriously of marrying Lady Gwendolen. His father, who had so long looked with disfavor on Marcus's life-style, might then reinstate his annuity. It was suspended on the eve of his departure for Europe due to a scandal of major proportions with a married lady of equal proportions.

Of late there was a new impetus to Marcus's seeking to reestablish himself, for he suspected his sharp interest in gaming was blunting, and that was one step from beginning to lose. Further, even his other pleasure, flirtations, was wearying him. Lady Gwendolen and her vast fortune and estates would give him ease and she was a lovely prize to top it all. But after that night at the ball when Stara and he had instantly recognized each other as cut from the same cloth, Marcus's concentration on Lady Gwendolen was fading and that was a certain way to fail at one's objective. It was essential therefore for Marcus temporarily to avoid the young companion. He was aided by Stara's keeping away during his visits to the marquis's town house. Although once upon entering he spotted her in the vestibule ducking into the conservatory. Unable to resist, Marcus followed her.

"Your sense of direction needs sharpening!" Stara reprimanded.

"On the contrary," Marcus said with a lazy grin, enjoying disconcerting her. "No better place for a cuddle than a conservatory."

Stara was sufficiently amused by his remark to respond, "Is that similar to a caress on the common or an ogle in the orchard?"

He threw back his head in a laugh. "All very commendable enterprises, but they all pale next to philandering in the ferns, as we are about to demonstrate." And he planted himself staunchly before her, but Stara drew back, remembering a lady would be seriously compromised if found alone in the conservatory with a gentleman. When he persisted in cornering her, she said coldly, "Mr. Justus, I wish you to respect my privacy. I've come into the conservatory to be by myself to think."

"One only wishes to be by oneself to think of another. And as I am usually the *other* ladies think about, I have simply saved you the preliminaries. You have now directly reached the subject at hand." And he swiftly reached out his hand and took her into his arms.

Pulling away, Stara said matter-of-factly, "Extraordinary thing about egotistical men. Since they cannot think of anything but themselves, they assume everyone else is similarly limited in scope."

Marcus continued smiling, pleased by their fencing. But time was passing and Lady Gwendolen was probably waiting in the morning room, so Marcus dropped his light manner and maneuvered Stara against the ferns, drenching her in them as he whispered, "Stara, Stara," and gave her the kiss both of them had been aching to repeat. Then satisfied, he strolled away to join Lady Gwendolen.

After that Stara vowed never even to be in the house when Mr. Justus was expected. And Marcus never asked for her openly. But both showed where their thoughts were by constantly including the other in their conversations, which annoyed Lady Gwendolen, leading naturally to an immediate change of topic. Stara and Mr. Justus were assuaged by the promise of being together at Hillcrest where they could play as many games as they wished, verbal and physical.

The news that Marmaduke was going to tie his horse to Lady Gwendolen's carriage and join her for the ride had Stara momentarily regretting her absence until she concluded both nobles deserved time together without the intervention of her sparkling asides and assists. Let them finally discover what her presence had shielded them from realizing, or how awkwardly silent their life together would be.

In truth, Stara had not at all wished to stay behind to help the marquis, but once asked, she could scarcely say him nay, after all her obligation. And then he sweetened the offer by mentioning her lack of a suitable riding outfit. His own tailors would whip one up for her gallops at Hillcrest. Stara always perked up at a gift. That came from her years of surviving only through the offerings of others. Every loan or gratuity meant she'd be able to carry on with her pretense of belonging a jot longer.

The marquis, she had long sensed, was taken with her, but astounded with himself for daring to want such a lovely young thing. Stara, as yet uncertain of her future, neither encouraged nor discouraged such brimming inclinations. With the duke roused to competitiveness by Marcus's attentions to Lady Gwen, Stara felt fate was directing her to stay behind and fix the marquis's interest. But that she was loath to do, for there was still sufficient time in the season to receive a respectable offer (though she'd had plenty of the other kind). Her main reason for pleasing the marquis was the arrival of a letter from the Pinkertons advising Stara they'd gone over their records and discovered quite a sum owing them for funeral expenses of her parents, and other such advances made on her principal, which through unwise investing (by that same guardian) had dwindled to nonexistence. Stara must send them something on account or they would feel obliged to approach her titled benefactors. The Pinkertons had always roused terror in Stara since her childhood by continually threatening the safe worlds she fashioned. First, it was school. Now, her London season. To prevent their annoying the marquis or in any way spoiling her plans, Stara knew she had to find some ready money. And then in the midst of her desperate devising came the marquis's fortuitous offer of a riding outfit. If he were in such a generous mood, possibly, Stara hoped, he might be willing to grant her some funds for her guardians. And so Stara determinedly remained behind to have a long conversation with his lordship. Then too without having to dance attendance on Lady Gwendolen, she would be at leisure to rearrange her outfits, for she wished to have both the duke and Marcus see her as a prime beauty. Particularly Mr. Justus. She was unable to forget the way that gentleman stared at her, as if she were everything to him. In her lifetime she had never had anyone to whom she was anything at all. Though she told herself that he was a cad, and an experienced rake, and that his stares, just like his kisses where part of his practiced maneuvers, she could not help enjoying and encouraging both.

If Stara had known that Mr. Justus was going to accompany Lady Gwendolen's carriage, riding alongside to be at a ready to help her in and out of her carriage, nothing would have prevented Stara from going along. But his joining the carriage on the road was a last minute decision on Marcus's part. The marquis had not arranged for outriders for he would have felt it an insult to his own countryside, not to mention himself, as a justice of the peace. Not only did his lordship assume the coat of arms on his coach would assure safety from attack, but he had implicit faith in their old coach driver and the experienced footmen. Further assurance came from the duke's presence. Unquestionably his darling daughter would be suitably protected.

When that topic of safety came up during their travels, the duke informed Marcus that he had a pistol in his cloak pocket.

In response Marcus laughed, assuring him that, though unarmed, merely the sight of his riding alongside would dissuade any possible attack. Nevertheless, Duke-duke chatted on about highwaymen, enjoying alarming the lady by relating their exploits. He'd heard of one fellow, not of this vicinity, but further south, called One-Jewel Jack. That name was known to both Lady Gwendolen and Marcus, but it did not have any association of terror. Actually that highwayman was rather romanticized by the ton, for it was said he never took more than one jewel from the beautiful ladies, although he lifted several from those whose countenance he found ill-favored. And so every lady was certain to spread the tale she'd been so singly honored by One-Jewel Jack.

This discussion took place during the last of the stops to change horses and to allow Lady Gwendolen the refreshment of a stretch. Actually her ladyship required more rest than the animals. The overnight stay at a wayside inn had been extended beyond a night to an extra half a day before Lady Gwendolen had deigned to awaken. Both her ladyship and her maid were somewhat restless after the duke's mention of highwaymen, but eventually the coach reached familiar neighborhood sites and all fears dissipated. As for the coachman, not privy to the duke's *on-dits*, he was not afeared, even when passing a particularly dense area of trees, until nonplussed by the sight of a highwayman riding up and boldly obstructing the road. It was a tall figure of a man, all enveloped in a dark cloak. A mask fully covered his face and a low-brimmed hat his head.

Pulling on the reins, the coachman soon had eyes only for the two large horse-pistols pointed directly at him.

There was no question it was One-Jewel Jack himself, for he had his trademark of the one jewel on the crown of his hat. And he gallantly bowed before the window out of which Lady Gwendolen was screaming. Swiftly the coachman and footmen were ordered to descend and approach. This was One-Jewel Jack's way of separating the nobility from their underlings. When the coachman was almost at the pistols' points, the highwayman issued his instructions and the coachman obligingly repeated them aloud to the others.

"This cove says you is all to . . . 'Stand and deliver!' "

Marcus, who had reined in his horse, laughed at that. "I will be delighted to deliver—a flush hit to his cowardly masked face!"

One-Jewel Jack whispered again to the coachman who was by now near incapable of speech. But he managed one more command, "He says—you is to come down off your high horse!"

"The hell I will!"

The highwayman's next request was in the form of a threat. One-Jewel Jack held up one of the horse-pistols and aimed it directly at Marcus's horse. Unpersuaded, Marcus rode forward until the pistol discharged and his horse shied. Cursing and leaping off, Marcus was coming on foot toward the highwayman, when the other pistol was raised and aimed directly at Marcus's chest. That momentarily halted Mr. Justus. He was distracted as well by his horse's whinnying, which had him rushing back to examine the injury, during which the coachman held a hat under his nose.

"You is to deliver, sir," the man said apologetically.

Muttering, Marcus tossed in all his guineas. Yet the

highwayman signaled for more, indicating the fob hanging on his waist. With suppressed rage and great reluctance, Marcus removed that favorite and disdainfully tossed it within. Satisfied, One-Jewel Jack then gave orders to the quaking footmen, who along with the coachman were so terrified they became very effective accomplices. The duke's pistol was obviously forgotten in his cloak pocket as he hurriedly dropped not only his money but his fob and even signet ring into the hat. For the lady, the footman repeated the highwayman's instructions that since she was of such beauty, only one jewel would be demanded. At that, the sobbing Lady Gwen ceased her tears. Compliments were always the way to her composure. She even began to smile, realizing she would now be able to tell all her friends that she had been so honored. But her smile froze when the one jewel demanded was her famed matched string of pearls. Nevertheless on her ladyship's signal, her maid made haste to remove the pearls from the traveling jewel casket she was guarding and dropped them into the hat. Now fully loaded, the hat was taken to the highwayman, who accepted it with a satisfied nod. In reward for their accommodating obedience, the coachman and footmen were ordered to seek their safety in the forest to the right. All were quick to do so. While everyone was observing their hasty departure, One-Jewel Jack made his exit in the other direction. It took the duke and Lady Gwendolen an additional moment to realize they were no longer under threat for their lives, but Marcus was quick to rush for the duke's horse tied to the back of the coach. In a flash he was after the culprit, pausing just long enough to call back to the duke to take care of his horse.

In outrage, the duke insisted Mr. Justus stay there and assist in hunting for the coachman to get the carriage going.

"Drive it yourself!" Marcus shouted back, and rode off.

For a moment Marcus assumed he had lost his prey. While galloping forward no trace of One-Jewel Jack was to be found. The road was clear. Anyone else but a man of Marcus's daring and determination would have given up at that point. But to Marcus this was a personal challenge for the horse was one of his favorites, making it a score to be settled. And confound it, he wanted his fob back! The only answer was that the culprit had ducked into the thicket. So Marcus doubled back examining each side, until he triumphantly noted some horse prints going into the woods, and further on several broken branches. At that point, Marcus charged in.

The duke's horse had led a pampered life, like its privileged owner, and it objected to the branches, snorting so often Marcus feared he'd give them away. But a noise in the distance covered their approach. It was a thundering of water. A waterfall by Jove. And quite a one. The pool it made below was wild with eddies. So distracted was he by that sight that Marcus almost missed the movement of a black-clad figure.

There was One-Jewel Jack before him and afoot! So certain was the scoundrel of not having been followed, he was not even glancing backward. Indeed the road had so many twists and turns, it was amazing Marcus had kept up. But one ought never underestimate Marcus's daring, especially when he was on an adventure and determined to win. Striding about in his secret lair, One-Jewel Jack approached a small cave. It could only be reached by jumping over some of the whirling water. Doing so, the highwayman was swiftly across. At the cave's entrance, he ducked inside.

Quickly Marcus dismounted, tied up his horse and crept forward. His approach was silent and unannounced as possible. At the cave's entrance, he bent down and entered. The light filtered through into the first chamber and revealed One-Jewel Jack stripping off his clothes. Scarf and cloak went first and then the heavy leather waistcoat. Once that was removed, Marcus groaned, for it revealed the gentle curves of a woman's body. Next the hat was dropped and long dark hair floated down.

"Confound it, you're a woman!"

One-Jewel Jack turned in horror. She still wore the mask. Her gender but not her identity was revealed. Rushing for her pistols on the ledge, she was stopped by Marcus's tackling her. The two were down on the stone floor, rolling together. A tall strong woman, he sensed as he clasped her. Distracted by the feel of her, Marcus allowed her to wiggle away. Cursing himself, Marcus knew his only defense was to rush for her pistols. But she was already grabbing one as he seized the other.

The two stood there, armed and face to face. Very much like a duel. But there was no person acting as a second to call, "Fire." After a few moments of this standoff, One-Jewel Jack whispered, "Yours is unloaded."

"I shall scarcely take your word for that."

"One of them is," she said calmly. "We shall see whether it is yours or mine. I'll not shoot unless shot at." And with amazing sangfroid, she turned and walked away from him.

He could have shot her in the back, but could not bring himself to harm such a beautiful body.

"Your gender saves you from a shot," he said at last. And she turned and laughed.

"But you are not scot-free!" he said, releasing some of his feelings. "You injured my horse, you jade! And I shall be recompensed for that! Your body will appease me somewhat for my loss." And with cool authority, he approached her.

But acting as if she'd not even heard him, the lady continued deeper and deeper into the cave. The shadows were thick there, and Marcus could no longer see her. Further she moved so silently he could not hear her either.

At the end without a lantern, Marcus could not discover any turnings. Cursing, he stomped back to the front of the cave, prepared to wait her out. She had to emerge sometime.

But at the entrance, as Marcus stepped out, he was dumbfounded to find her there, astride her horse, waiting for him. She'd once more donned her One-Jewel Jack hat, and was holding the pistol directly at him.

He stood entranced by her. The long black hair fell to her waist. It rippled as she reached into a bag and took something out and threw it at his feet, before turning the animal about and riding away as swiftly as a deer. Her lovely laugh came ringing back toward him. He looked down at his feet and saw his ivory carved fob.

There was something gallant about that. A certain lady had recently suggested he might lose it, he recollected. And then it all clicked.

Stara! By Jove, it had to be she. And he grabbed the fob as if it would have some of her warm life still attached to it. What a woman! he thought and wished to heavens he had unmasked her and made her pay dearly with a forfeit that would pleasure them both.

Holding the one jewel, he wondered if she meant it as a tribute to him. And felt himself immensely flattered and flushed with the chase and challenge of it all. He shot off the pistol and found it unloaded. Hers then could have killed him. That proved how much at risk he had been. And Marcus laughed at his escape and the

pleasure of the threat. Yet since neither one knew which
was the loaded pistol, she too had risked her person,
and been so composed about it all.

"Stara, my dear girl, we have many more rounds
ahead. By heavens, I've finally met a lady who plays her
games as I do—with no holds barred and . . . to the
death!" His cold, blue eyes were flashing with thoughts
of meeting her again and this time he would be the one
armed—with the weapon of the knowledge of her secret. He savored the thought of using it against her—at
will.

Ah, this gathering at Hillcrest would be more delightful than he'd ever imagined. And doubly rewarding.

Two days later Stara arrived at Hillcrest to be greeted with the exciting news. Marmaduke was first to see her and give his side of the tale. A bruising ruffian had held them up, supported by others hiding in the bushes, all with pistols aimed directly at them. His grace had kept remarkably cool ordering the fellow off. He, Marmaduke Melton, seventh duke of Clairidge, had handled it all, including calling back the cowardly coachman and footmen, supporting a fainting ladyship and her sobbing maid and bringing all to a safe arrival at Hillcrest. Mr. Marcus Justus had ridden off, not appearing until the situation was well in hand, and everyone was safely home.

Stara oohed and aahed at his bravery, wishing she had been there to witness his magnificence, but assuring him she could visualize it and left him feeling much better about the entire experience.

No sooner was she in her old room and unpacking her portmanteau, when Lady Gwen rushed in and fell into her arms. The entire experience must be heard from her ladyship's view. Marcus sought to defend her. The duke sought to defend her. But the gentleman overcame them. And then he rode up to her coach. A dark black hat with one jewel on it revealed instantly who he was. Lady Gwen had been calm and superior in her dealings with the fellow. It was obvious he was struck a'cock by her beauty. Not only did he immediately decree no more than one jewel, but he bowed before her window to show his homage for her charms. She realized he was most prodigiously fascinated with her.

"I do not doubt it, Gwen dear, but how particularly did he show his partiality for you?" Stara could not resist asking.

Lady Gwen lowered her eyes modestly and then raised them to gaze fully into Stara's twinkling ones. "I daresay I can confide in you."

Stara assured her she could. Whereupon Lady Gwen let it be known that the highwayman had actually dared approach, taken her hand and placed a fevered kiss on her palm. Stara exclaimed at that daring, and Lady Gwen assured her she still felt the warmth of it.

"But, dear friend, as wonderful as it is to strike such passion in passersby, think of the repercussions of your striking such into the heart of a callous ruffian. He might never be able to recover from the sight of you. Wish to see you again and again. Further attempt to discover who you are and follow you here—just to once more avail himself of the joy of gazing at your beauty. You are in dire jeopardy. Your beauty shall be your downfall, indeed, I always feared."

Lady Gwen was uncertain how to feel at this combination of flattery and warning. She enjoyed the thought of the highwayman being so struck that he could not forget her, but she did not relish the idea that he would come to Hillcrest seeking her out.

Stara seeing her ladyship discomfited, put a soothing hand on her small shoulders. "Have no fear, I shall be here. And while I am with you, One-Jewel Jack shall never be able to appear. I shall stand in his way!"

Reassured by that, Lady Gwen allowed herself to feel comforted at having such a loyal friend.

"But you must realize what a responsibility such beauty is and perhaps you should not allow the common people the opportunity of being struck by it. A hat with a larger brim, perhaps?" Stara could not resist suggesting.

Lady Gwen sighed at the responsibility of her unequaled charm of person. While flattered by the burden, in a short time her ladyship had concluded that next time she traveled out of their sphere, she might jolly well don a veil. That was said half in jest, but taken up with such approval by her companion that Lady Gwen ran to discuss with her maid the possibility of adding such to several of her hats.

Stara suppressed a giggle and sat down on her Grecian sofa for some time alone without having to attend any of the aristocracy. She shook her head at the wildly different stories of the actual event and wondered what Mr. Justus's version would be.

After her rest, Stara changed into a particularly demure gown. It was sprig muslin white with a high-necked frontpiece and long sleeves, which came to a point over each hand, giving the illusion of being gloved. An innocent young lady stared back at her from her glass. She'd arranged her hair in bunches of curls on each side and was delighted with the fashionable air, somewhat at variance with her schoolgirl dress. A conflict she hoped would give someone as observant as Marcus pause . . . even lead to confusion. Considering how starched up he was over his ability to peg a person, sum them up with one of his measuring glances, it was always a delight to give him a shaft of insecurity about his assessments. Actually it was pleasurable to give him a shaft on all occasions.

On her way to the tea spread, Stara was looking forward to seeing Mr. Justus again. She had yet to hear his version of the episode on the road and was eager to do so and more to feel the excitement she always did in his presence.

Thinking of him was apparently the secret to calling him forth. He too was entering the saloon, and stepped back to give her precedence. None of the nobles had yet arrived, Stara noted and could not but feel some pleasurable expectation at this privacy despite the gentleman's familiar mocking smile. She merely nodded and wandered about the room, pretending indifference. He kept his eye on her every move.

"We are ahead of the rest, I gather," she said civilly.

"You are ahead of us all, Mistress Highwayman."

Stara felt her heart flip at that bald statement.

"*Ahead?*" she repeated. "How excessively complimentary! You are referring to my new coiffure, are you not? Rather advanced I should say for the country, but I wished to rehearse its effect here. I am delighted you approve it."

"Stop trying to sound like the simpleton you are not."

"Speaking of which, Lady Gwendolen also prefers my hair simply done."

Marcus grinned, bowing at her refusal to be pinned down, and smoothly continued, "I admit when it comes to your hairstyle, Miss Carltons, I vastly prefer it simple. Loose and flowing from a dark hat with one jewel on it. Madame One-Jewel Jack."

Stara did not flinch, her face a prototype of innocence. "That style you describe does not sound suitable for me. If you have hopes of being a hairdresser, I urge you to begin with Lady Gwen—for she has just recently dismissed her stylist. I, however, always do my own designs and have no need of any assistance."

Marcus enjoyed this fencing, but he refused to continue it, making a sudden home thrust. "You do not ask about my calling you Madame One-Jewel Jack, which would be the natural, outraged reaction. Your reticence betrays you, my dear lady."

The butler's entering caused a natural interruption in the interrogation. It was time to lay out the tea settings. Turning away from Mr. Justus, Stara walked to the heavily draped window, looking out at the distant formal gardens. Outwardly composed, inwardly her mind was ringing a peal over her. She should not have allowed herself to meet Marcus alone. There was always the possibility that he might have seen through the disguise. She had at times presented that theory to herself, but confidently dismissed it. Even now on rethinking his bold statements, Stara concluded he was fishing, expecting her to respond to his lure. She would not do so.

This gentleman always caused a ripple in her smooth plans. She recollected how shocked she'd been upon riding up to the marquis's coach and seeing Marcus alongside when it was too late to abort her mad scheme. Actually Stara could not believe, even while impersonating the highwayman, that she was engaging in such an improper not to mention illegal act. The need to pay her guardians, the Pinkertons, had spurred her on and before she knew it, she'd been caught up by the dare of it all. At first she'd not expected to do it— merely to see how far along she could get before an impediment arose to stop her. But nothing did. Rather, she'd sailed through, despite Marcus's attempting to foil her. It was even a double accomplishment, if one considered her subsequently outfoxing that gentleman in the cave and departing undetected. At least that had been her assumption until his innuendos. But if he suspected her of being the highwayman, why hadn't he made that accusation to the others? Obviously he hadn't. Nor even hinted at his discovery of the culprit's true gender. Or certainly that would have added an odd twist to Lady Gwen's fantasy, Stara thought with a smile.

It was a relief to be able to smile, for directly after the escapade, Stara had found herself surprisingly blue-deviled—almost overwhelmed by an unexpected emotion of remorse. While thinking of the deed beforehand, that aspect had not occurred, and so Stara was flummoxed by her constantly reliving the terror on her ladyship's face as she leaned out of the coach window. Worse, she must always hear the accompaniment of that lady's initial scream.

To block that sound, Stara kept herself occupied with completing the principal reason for her robbery, riding posthaste to a distant village to send the fair share of the booty to the Pinkertons. She'd included a letter assuring them that was all she could raise, therefore, it would be pointless to harass her for more, as she had no intention of putting herself to the risk of asking for additional sums. If pressed, she would be forced to request the marquis's assistance in reexamining her financial situation, as he had so often offered to do. Mailing all without a frank was Stara's only pleasure—putting the Pinkertons to a minor expense to receive what had cost her so much to acquire.

There was some relief afterward in being rid of that major dread. If it were not for that annoying remorse, Stara would have been at last all easy in her heart and mind. Admittedly one thing that had instantly soothed was Lady Gwen's necklace of matchless pink pearls. They were magnificent. Lady Jersey was known to have a somewhat superior string, but Stara had not been privileged to view it. These pearls seemed glorious enough. Never having owned any kind of jewelry, Stara was unable to resist faithfully wearing the necklace during her several days hiding away in an abandoned cottage, a short distance from Hillcrest. She remained there not only to give the impression of a later arrival, but also to rest from her speedy drive up in a hired post chaise and four horses. This hideaway had been discovered during Stara's first visit to Hillcrest. In its Home Wood, at its densest area, Stara had come upon a ramshackle cottage and instantly appropriated it, naming it Haven. She'd turned it into that by bringing at intervals certain possessions of hers, a small mirror, a tapestried pillow and from the Hillcrest's attics, a painting of a lady with pale hair, reminiscent somewhat of her dear deceased mother. Wherever Stara went, she attempted to make a little nest of her own, and bring her mother into it, finding safety for them both. Haven had become that for the jewels as well.

Stara kept her highwayman's booty in a small cedar box in a hole above Haven's mantelpiece. The duke's jewels were left untouched in there. But the pink pearls continually called to Stara. She must stroke them, wear them, until during one of those moments of display she had an unbidden remembrance of the saying that pearls were frozen tears. Possibly they could be hers, if she were discovered. Or they could represent Lady Gwendolen's tears called forth by the loss of her necklace. More remorse—dash it!

The latter image was not obliterated until Stara discussed the actual robbery with Lady Gwendolen herself. Her ladyship expressed the smallest possible regret for the loss or even regard for the necklace, since Lady Jersey's pearls were always mentioned by the ton as larger and pinker! Waving away the entire topic as inconsequential, Lady Gwendolen turned to her true concern or the impression she'd made on the highwayman. In recompense Stara offered a welter of compliments which were undoubtedly on One-Jewel Jack's mind, and gave Lady Gwen such satisfaction all Stara's compunctions for taking the pearls were dismissed. The duke had also absolved her of regret for taking his fob, ring and money by demonstrating his only interest was rearranging the sorry figure he had cut.

If only she'd known the nobles' indifference to their jewels during her days closeted in Haven, Stara would have enjoyed her seclusion so much more. That left Marcus's loss to consider, but since she'd returned his fob, he'd only been deprived of less than one evening's gambling stake. Obviously his cutting up stiff had to be due to the blow to his pride that a lady had led him such a merry chase.

Marcus was not only in her thoughts while gazing out the window in the saloon, but next moment at her side. Reflexively, Stara moved away. But he followed. His attitude was of complete confidence he would unmask her. That riled Stara sufficiently to concentrate on defeating him once again. She reminded herself he had no hard proof of the identity of the highwayman. She must keep him guessing. Indeed keeping him guessing had been her delight since their first meeting.

Hard upon the staff's exit, Marcus struck. "Your very failure to react to my naming you as the highwayman is an admission. Your silence says it all."

The easiest way of defeating a direct attack was to deflect it. Stara did so by looking so confused she hoped to confuse him as well, airily commenting, "Ah yes, indeed, the escapade with One-Jewel Jack, thank you for reminding me. I meant to ask about it. Obviously my silence is due to reticence. I feared it was a most shocking experience. Further, having heard several versions, I am rather surfeited."

With an amazing amount of sangfroid, Stara advanced to the tea table and deliberately disturbed the pattern of the triangles of bread and butter by taking one and nibbling. "Altogether the stories are too much to swallow, I daresay," she concluded, coughing a bit, illustratively. Then with a chatty style of one clearly uninvolved, she carried on, "First on my arrival I was greeted with the coachman's complaints. Next on entering the hall, his grace did me the honor of his confidence. And no sooner had I reached my room, than Lady Gwen was there to express herself on the occurrence. Not one of them, I recollect, described the culprit with long hair. Your version is quite unique. Actually," she now gasped openly, "one is aghast at the lack of agreement among the witnesses. One would assume each person imagined what they wished had happened. What delightful Canterbury Tales from such an exciting pilgrimage!"

Marcus laughed aloud at her statements and performance, assuring her his version was the correct one. But Stara continued to play at a pretty confusion. The coachman, she said, had made claim of *several* ruffians seizing him by the throat, leaving him incapable of speaking for a full day. "His grace's tale, I conclude, is the most shocking. I should unquestionably have sunk into a near decline if I had had to face such a band of desperate men, led by a monstrous villain with a voice that shook through the woods. But, of them all, I prefer her ladyship's romance, although I blushed to hear One-Jewel Jack so forgot himself as to make free with her person. One shudders to think how little two gentlemen were willing to rush to her defense. But happily the villain himself was a gentleman and apparently left with a Cupid's arrow rather than a bullet piercing his heart. Oh yes, I forgot, the duke is most displeased with you, Mr. Justus, for fearfully riding off to hide, leaving him to take charge of the situation. For shame, sir!"

"What the devil! He said I did *what*?"

At that moment, fortuitously his grace himself entered. Marmaduke Melton was attired as if for the highest social gathering with a floral waistcoat, buff, tight-fitting pantaloons and several new fobs, stickpins and watches on his person, not to forget a very shiny, gilt quizzing-glass dangling from his waist. Instantly Stara appealed to him to set Mr. Justus straight on the escapade on the road, for Mr. Justus seemed to have it sadly a'cock. "Your description, your grace, agrees more with her ladyship's. I cannot imagine how Mr. Justus can have let his imagination run away with him so."

"Egad, if anyone was said to have run away, it was you, sir! Ran away and left me with two swooning females on my hands! Dashed uncomfortable situation."

"But *you* handled it to perfection, did you not?" Stara interposed. "Despite the armed cohorts that ruffian had hiding in the woods? Her ladyship says she believes it was ten, but the coachman claims closer to twelve."

"Twenty, at least!" the duke protested. "Egad, twelve I could have handled with my own pistol. But I was overwhelmed. And left alone, while the only other gentleman took my horse and rode off, I say. Rode for his life!"

That was too much for Marcus. The first expression of amused entertainment, changed to appalled exasperation. "I rode *after* the *one* culprit! And you were not in the least danger then. All that was required was to soothe the ladies."

At that point the lady in question arrived and was appealed to by both the gentlemen to back their version of the story. She was wearing a small veil in her hair that dipped over one eye, which Stara was almost unable to view without breaking into giggles. Rather she complimented her ladyship on the effect, as well as on the intelligence of seeking protective covering, and her ladyship was not loath to show how the veil could be lowered, hiding her face completely, if any ruffian dared seek her in her own home.

The duke interposed to assure her he would stand by her as he had at the highway and protect her if One-Jewel Jack dared approach.

Stara turned to the flabbergasted Marcus, and inquired, "And you, sir, what would you do if you were to find her ladyship within arm's length of that blackguard?" And she reached out her arm and put it deliberately around the quaking Gwen and stared him down.

Marcus shook his head, realizing with so many different versions of the escapade and all determined to think it had occurred that way, Stara either by chance or by manipulation had protected herself. When the marquis arrived from London in time for dinner, he was presented with quite a finished tale, so many times had it been repeated. A mild lord he found himself forced to have to rise to the occasion of protecting his guests. Stara quickly assured that obviously the situation was not as alarming as it seemed at first hearing. For she had herself arrived subsequently and was not subjected to any annoyance on the road. Nor had he himself who must have just passed over the same locale. Obviously the danger had passed. The highwaymen had ridden on.

"They certainly have disappeared," Marcus inserted mischievously, looking pointedly at Stara, "I daresay they returned to their place of origin."

The duke, between bites, added with a great deal

of braggadocio, "Sent them all packing. And as for the highwayman, no need for anyone to fret over that brigand. Shot the fellow!"

That was too much license for those present on the occasion. Her ladyship particularly denied it. So loud was the objection, his grace grumbled and retracted. "Shot . . . someone, by gad."

"Shot yourself in the foot, no doubt," Marcus commented helpfully.

"No sir!," his grace bristled.

Stara attempted to stop the gentlemen from coming to cuffs with the reminder that there were ladies present—"one particularly who has just recently endured a great ordeal."

Confused at first, her ladyship recollected herself in time to appear properly overcome.

"Indeed," Stara was continuing with concern, "and I fear we are all forgetting that her ladyship's ordeal might not yet be concluded."

Lady Gwendolen put down her forkful of mutton and for several seconds suspended her meal while Stara continued anxiously, "That lowlife must not be allowed to come close to her ladyship, for if he did, what thoughts might the sight of her inspire!"

"What thoughts?" Lady Gwen inquired, half in delight, half in dismay.

The duke did not deviate his attention from his food. Marcus choked on a laugh, but quickly coughed in concealment and added, "You perhaps would know best what the eh, highwayman was thinking."

"I do indeed," Stara exclaimed, unruffled by his dig. "For I have been close to her ladyship and seen the effect she has on every gentleman. We must all hope that the ruffian does not attempt to abduct her from Hillcrest. She must stay close and perhaps Mr. Justus would stand by as guard, while his grace would be so

kind as to ride with me in the morning and demonstrate
the entire event; I so wish I had been there."

And thus Stara had arranged all as best suited herself and yet as suited each one. Naturally, Lady Gwen
was not adverse to seeing herself as the beloved of a
well-known romantic highwayman, needing the protection of one of her swains. In fact, urged by Stara, she
intended to write several letters to her friends to describe the incident in that very way. His grace was more
than willing to ride with Stara and demonstrate his daring. But as for Marcus, he could only look at that
demmed, daring lady and shake his head, half in exasperation, half in admiration. By Jove, he would trip her
up yet. This was only the first day of their fortnight.

5

The marquis, despite reassurances, continued in a state of alarm at the presence of highwaymen in his district. Further fidgets resulted from the notion that One-Jewel Jack had formed an unquenchable passion for his daughter. Therefore he arranged to hire several additional footmen to keep guard around Hillcrest at all hours of the day and night.

Naturally this spread the tale throughout the estate and from there to the whole district. Rumors that One-Jewel Jack was threatening to abduct her ladyship delighted all. Particularly worthy of relish was the additional gossip stemming from Lady Gwendolen's own maid, Mary, who had private information such as the culprit's sending shockingly passionate letters. This sprang from Mary's overhearing her ladyship reading aloud portions of her own diary to Stara in which such a possibility was mentioned. Stara, irrepressible as ever, instantly concluded nothing was more like! "He is probably pining for you under the pines at this very moment. Writing you a note of his feelings. Something of the ilk: 'Your ladyship is the kind of vessel I hope some day to board.' "

Lady Gwen was shocked by the indelicacy of that, but assured by Stara that highwaymen were very direct in their speech and not likely to settle for smiles and kisses on the hand. "Ah yes, he is probably imagining how he could clasp you in his arms. . . ."

"And . . ." Lady Gwen asked breathlessly.

"And press his lips on your . . ."

"My?"

"Bosom!"

"Heavens!" Lady Gwen expostulated. "He would not dare to presume. Would he?"

"I expect he would. Rough and ready creatures these men of the road. Probably has hopes of taking you to his cave and keeping you prisoner there until you agree to be his."

"To his cave? Keep me locked in his cave? I shouldn't at all like that! Rather damp places those. Could he not have a lodge of some kind with a comfortable sofa?"

Stara, staring at her ladyship's breathless enjoyment of the fantasy, was obliging enough to locate the hideaway wherever the lady wished. "Yes, a comfortable lodge would be best, I collect. With a roaring fire to match the fire in his eyes as he approached you—struck by your beauty as you lie before him on a prodigiously comfortable sofa . . . with a crimson velvet pillow behind your head."

"What am I wearing?" Lady Gwen asked eagerly.

"Aha! That is the question. Are you wearing anything at all!"

But that was going too far for her ladyship's fantasy. That brought reality to tear the dream asunder. Instantly her eyes were in a flutter of panic. "He would not wish to deprive me of my raiment?" she said in a small, stunned voice.

Stara debated whether to soothe or shock. Seeing the lady's face turning red, she decided to keep to fantasy, being accustomed to making life pleasant for her friend. "Ah, now I see . . . he has removed your outer dress for the purpose of covering you with a splendid ermine robe that softly snuggles against your lovely white skin and reveals one naked shoulder to his rapacious eye."

"Ah!"

"Ah, indeed. What a vision you are for his eyes."

"Yes, yes. I am a vision. Go on. Go on!"

"He approaches hesitantly, reverently bowing before you. His eyes are almost blinded by the perfection before him as he kisses the hem of your ermine cloak and says, 'Will you be mine?'"

"Yes, oh yes!" her ladyship cried, so caught in the bliss that Stara could not help but climax it for her by concluding.

"He leans over and kisses the bare white shoulder, and then continues up to reach your lips with his. He has reached them. He kisses you. Once. Twice. You lean back your golden head on the velvet pillow and look closely into his devilish eyes. Softly he begins to part the ermine robe and, and . . ."

"And?" her ladyship whispered, eagerly, waiting.

"And," Stara teased, uncertain what to say next.

"He tumbles her, he do!" a loud breathless voice broke in.

With alarm, both ladies turned. Mary, the maid, had not only been listening, but could not resist finishing it! All this hedging around had her in a pucker. A short, fast tumble was what they was talking about and afraid to say it. She herself would not mind being tumbled by a highwayman. But he probably would not give

her an ermine robe. More than likely steal her cloth
robe offen her. At the shocked glances of the two ladies,
she realized she had broken an unspoken rule of service
and let the aristocracy know she actually heard what
was being said in her presence. Bobbing a curtsy of
apology, she attempted to busy herself with her mistress's clothes, but her ladyship would not let the matter
rest.

"I hope, Mary, that you have not been eavesdrop-
ping on private conversations!"

"Oh no, your ladyship. Just that you was speaking
so loud no more than two steps away. Me ears don't
know their place—they hears what they hears."

Stara was amused at that and Mary's impish face,
but her ladyship took every word literally. "Your ears
should be trained *not* to hear. Your mind should be
concerned with your duties. For instance, my yellow
pelisse has not been mended this sennight. And, Miss
Carltons and I would wish for a cup of tea, would you
not, Stara? Further, Mary, you are not to repeat anything you happen to hear in this room, for it is privileged information. Especially anything you happen to
hear that comes from here." And she indicated her
diary.

"Oh yes, your ladyship. I mean, no your ladyship.
Me lips is sealed as is me ears. I knows noting about
One-Jewel Jack being so besotted with you. As all gen-
tlemen are."

Appeased by this conclusion, Lady Gwen smiled.
"Whether he has hopes for me or not must not be
thought of. Certainly must not be spread about. Except
to warn the staff to be on the watch, in case he becomes
so maddened by desire he attempts to break in and
seize me."

"Oh, my lady!" the maid exclaimed, properly horrified. "I shall watch you, even while you sleep!"

Pleased by that devotion, the maid was dismissed with a smile. Rushing away Mary was quick to report to all downstairs that her ladyship had received wildly wicked notes which she read to Miss Carltons, all about One-Jewel Jack's desire to tumble Lady Gwen and snatch her to his lodge. After that, every servant was on alert. While certainly not wishing their mistress's abduction, if it was to occur, they longed to be present to see the lady wiggling in One-Jewel Jack's arms, as he rode off with her.

The rumors soon spread to Marcus through his valet, and he was quick to interrogate her ladyship. A sharp flurry of his questions assured him she had not actually received letters from One-Jewel Jack. Rather it had been all supposition between the two ladies of what that gentleman of the road would have written, if he had written. At that, Marcus quickly left to give vent to his suppressed laughter. "That minx!" he thought, awed by the way Stara was making it impossible for anyone to ever believe the highwayman was not a gentleman. He further listened with amusement when Stara, during dinner, brought out further proof along these lines. Deftly the conversation was directed to the son of the marquis's friend, Lord Lickinspure, who had had a confrontation with One-Jewel Jack in the past.

"At what year was that, my lord?" she pressed.

"Had to be four, no, five years ago, egad! And the fellow's still around. There was a period when everyone thought he'd been done for. Hadn't heard of him. And now he reemerges."

"A strong gentleman, would you say? Or rather would Lord Lockinspure's son say? I recollect you said he sparred with him and the fellow was . . . eh, handy with his fives."

The marquis was pleased that the young lady remembered his tale. Stara was always such a devoted listener. He was particularly pleased that she'd picked up his boxing cant. Tolerantly he expounded, "Gave him one in the bone box. A wisty castor to the jaw. But the fellow was no stranger to the science. Threw him a cross-buttock. . . . Reminds me of the time I watched Mendoza. . . ."

"Then you conclude," Stara interrupted to nail her point home, "that One-Jewel Jack is quite a strong, muscular man with a knowledge of boxing."

While his lordship was agreeing to this, she looked at Marcus who merely smiled, and interrupted, "I expect there have been several One-Jewel Jacks about since he became such a legend."

That was instantly denied by everyone. Especially Lady Gwen, who could not bear being adored by an impostor, and his grace, Marmaduke let it be known he had proof that theirs was the one and only One-Jewel Jack. "Wore the beastly jeweled hat. Had to be the blighter."

"More than one dark hat about, I daresay," Marcus said with just the thin veneer of tolerance. And the real highwayman," he insisted, refusing to back down, staring at Stara with a challenge, "was never known to fire his pistols. Scarcely needed to. Certainly would not injure an animal. Only a coward or a rank novice would wing or should I say flank a helpless animal, especially such a prime one as my Shadow. Had to send for another of my horses."

"I say," the duke interposed. "Seems to me if one is talking of a prime animal, my Fancy is worth double your cattle, any day of the year! He was *scratched*, my groom says. The result of your panic to be away!"

"To be *after* the culprit! I've told you. I went toward not away, as the rest of you did!"

"And did you catch him?" Stara's laughing voice,

interrupted the recurring disagreement between the gentlemen.

"Thank you!" his grace nodded to Stara. "That is the question we have all been wondering about? Did you catch the fella? No, you did not! How do we know you even followed him."

"Because he gave me this." At that moment, with a dramatic pause, Marcus surprised all by taking from his pocket and casually tossing on the table—an ivory carved fob.

Lady Gwen was shrieking. As if she was experiencing the event again. "Mr. Justus, speak! You met the ruffian. Did he speak to you about his plans for me?"

Marcus stared at her and at Stara who was grinning. He realized as did she that he could not shatter Lady Gwen's conviction in the highwayman's fascination with her.

Stara pressed home his difficulties by adding this other doubt. "And if the gentleman was so obliging as to return your fob did he also give you Lady Gwen's pearls and his grace's ring? Or was not that the agreement?"

"I say! What ho!" his grace exclaimed, aware something was being said against his opponent and wanting to understand it and join in the attack, but not certain what to say. He merely glared at Mr. Justus. The marquis, quicker of wit, demanded an explanation from Mr. Justus for not informing *him* of a meeting with the highwayman.

"Unfortunately," Marcus backed down. "I was not able to have a hand-to-hand confrontation with the *gentleman* as I wished. I saw him riding off and, and . . ."

"He tossed your fob back at you to distract you from further pursuit?" Stara said helpfully, but with amusement.

Marcus refused her assistance. "Actually, he tossed it away. Probably concluding it was not of much intrinsic worth. Callous gentleman of that stamp are not aware of sentimental attachments."

"He evaded you?" the marquis concluded, satisfied.

"Temporarily," Marcus replied, and all were set to allow the matter to rest there.

Marcus brought out the fob the next day when he spotted Stara in the garden; she was awaiting his grace to take her for a ride in his phaeton that had just arrived with his second groom. First Lady Gwen had been asked but she refused to dare the roads, fearing being ambushed by One-Jewel Jack and his band of panting, passion-struck abductors. Stara volunteered to accompany his grace and look thoroughly about to assure the place was safe, in case her ladyship should wish to go for a ride on the following day. His grace as well vowed to scour the countryside for the villain. Thus Stara was to have her wish to be alone with his grace. But since they did naught but discuss her ladyship's safety, and the passion of One-Jewel Jack for the titled lady, which had doubly affronted his grace, and added to his determination to protect one of his class, Stara, rather than winning points by the turn of events, was finding the episode of the highwayman had only served to add to her ladyship's attraction. Another setback for Stara was that it had almost put her in the hands of that fellow adventurer, Mr. Justus, until she had confused the issue. Hopefully he no longer assumed she was One-Jewel Jack, or at least was having enough second thoughts not to blare out that assumption. But still she found him looking at her with less respect than he had before. Her act had made her accessible to his basest instincts, she divined. Where before he had dared to kiss her at will, she now assumed he wanted something more to buy his silence, and she kept away from him as much as possible. But the look was there in his eyes. An unabashed desire, he no longer troubled to mask with honor. Having proven her lack of propriety in one event, he assumed she would not hesitate to dispense with it in all cases. Her face flushed at his dismissal of her as a lady. She simply could not bear to be the target of such a demeaning assumption. She closed her eyes at her remembrance of his expression that of late seemed to take more open liberties with her person. At length, when she opened her eyes, it was to discover a carved ivory fob swaying before her.

Pushing it away, she stood up and confronted Marcus. "Are you not tired of your game?"

"You warned me I should lose this. How decent of you to return it," he teased, his own lids closing, so that his eyes were giving her a narrower stare, rather like a cat fastening on a mouse hole.

"Is *that* the flimsy weight of your evidence?" Stara retorted, with a laugh, lifting her head high with aplomb. "Piffle! Might as well accuse Lord Silverdale who told you at the ball that he had a fancy to get one just like that."

But Marcus would not be deflected. His voice was cold as he pressed her for the truth. In fact he moved closer to her, so she could not find any way around him or the answers he demanded. "Tell me, Miss Carltons, why return this to me? What did you mean? Was it concern that I cared so much for it? Or did you want me to realize that One-Jewel Jack and Stara were one?"

Backing away from him and his confrontation, her voice flippant, Stara refused to be cowed. "Still continuing with this fantasy? First you claim to have found it on the road, now you claim I gave it you. Most likely the highwayman never took it from you. Or that you confused it with another of your fobs and are now fobbing this one off as the other? How do we know what the truth is?"

"Stop this gammoning. You know I recognized you upon removing your hat, my lady adventuress. I shall keep your secret if you agree to meet me tonight in my rooms."

So now the parrying was over. He gave a home thrust, but she pushed him away with both hands as if he was smothering her with his nearness. Indeed Stara had often felt a sense of suffocation from the people in her lifetime who had attempted to reduce her to the lowest level possible. But she'd fought back against all of them and maneuvered her way to the top. Nor would she allow this Marcus Justus to reduce her to a level of a common ladybird! Her face was whitening; her eyes wild as she seethed, "How dare you speak to me like that! Because I am not titled, do you assume that I am not a lady! My breeding is equal to yours. From my mother, my heritage goes back to the real aristocracy of England, before the Hanoverian newcomers. As for my father, he was a decent soldier who gave his life for this country to keep you and his grace and the marquis and all you maw-worms secure in your comforts. He received the Regent's Medal for fighting off a troop of Napoleon's men. I have my father's bravery in me to fight off not only my relatives but you and all the rest of you heartless rakes seeking to destroy me."

Marcus's voice cut in to remind her coldly, "You are the one who collects hearts, as you rob jewels. You are the heartless jade."

"I am not what you think!" Stara insisted. "I am poor of funds but not of values! Never ever approach me with this degrading assumption again. You have tread not only on my heart, but worse, on my honor!" Here, she all but collapsed on the settee, trying to suppress the tears beginning to spill down her face. "Heavens, I have sunk each day, but I never thought a friend would cast me down so low."

Taken aback, Marcus stood there, uncertain. The sobs seemed genuine. But then this was a lady who was a past mistress at altering reality. She played highwayman so skillfully, even he had been astounded at uncovering the deception. Then there was the inspired way she used the very witnesses to alter the tale, so the truth was turned upside down. No, she would no longer gammon him, not even with tears. "You might stop this charade, my dear lady, it is neither convincing nor affecting me." In truth he was now viewing her falling tears with amusement as he seated himself nonchalantly next to her. "It is rather belated—this watery defense of your honor. For dare we assume you have even a jot of it left?"

Her face contorted, as years of suppressed humiliations, were rawly touched. She gasped to get back her breath and her control, when a perfect retaliation presented itself in the form of his grace just entering. Instantly Stara began to sob louder.

"Egad, what have you done to this lady!" his grace thundered. Aghast and agape, the duke could not believe he'd found the lady he was to escort for a drive reduced to tears by a gentleman in the home of a lord and visited by a duke! Not the thing!

"Step away from her, you braggart. No lady shall be brought to tears while Marmaduke Melton is present."

Stara, never one not to seize her opportunity, ran to the duke and clutched his arm. "Oh, your grace. It is such a relief to have you here!"

"This gentleman insulted you?"

Aware that if she answered yes, the matter would escalate to proportions that might reverberate against herself, Stara drew breath and denied that, explaining

hurriedly that she was feeling a trifle out of curl due to
unease about the threat of One-Jewel Jack. But just one
look at his grace and her spirits had revived. She was
certain a ride in his carriage would set her aright. So the
matter was resolved to the pleasure of both his grace
and Stara.

What Marcus felt as he watched her being handed
into his grace's carriage was far from pleasure. He resented indeed the moment when her cry for respect almost had him believing her. He'd been on the verge of
taking her into his arms to gently comfort her. But at
the last moment that impulse had been reined in. A
timely caution he realized while watching her playing
off her tricks on the duke. She was more of a shamster
than even he had imagined, Marcus grimly concluded.
What an intriguing hoyden—who'd almost had him
gammoned and placed under her tapping, shapely foot.

For a few shillings an undermaid stood guard
while Marcus searched Miss Carltons's rooms. He
needed some proof that could convince not only the
others but himself that she was the highwayman. But he
found nothing. Certainly not her ladyship's pearls. Nor
the duke's stickpin. Her belongings were meager and
mostly confined to books. Marcus's only recourse was
to continue his close watch on her every move, which
was rather what he enjoyed doing after all.

Who was this lady? he began to wonder and questioned the marquis, discovering with no little amazement that she'd been honest about her lineage. Her
mother was an authentic lady whose family had royal
connections but so much pride they disowned her immediately upon her marrying a common soldier. He
turned out to be a national hero. Samson the Rifleman.
So renowned, even Marcus remembered his exploits.
But regrettably a medal could not rid his lineage of the
smell of the shop. Her mother's family was unrelenting

—the more publicity, the more blind they were to Mrs. Carltons and her daughter's existence. So they were left to the tradespeople on her father's side. That clearly devalued Stara, marking her forever as a mere social fringe—despite Gwen's giving her some temporary standing.

Her compulsive crusade to become a duchess was thus not only comic but showed her lack of understanding of society's values. One could not conquer a world one did not understand, he scoffed, thinking less of her for being such a single-minded social seeker.

Still despite this failing, he could not squelch his overall fascination for her—continually revived by her wit, her sparkle . . . her unerring ability to surprise. Often Stara made remarks that went right over the titled heads. He similarly had to pretend not to enjoy them, but later, alone in his room, he would quietly laugh, appreciating her fully to the point of wishing they could end their breaking straws and be joined together. The closer the better!

Unfortunately since Marcus had reduced her to tears, Stara was keeping a marked distance, acting as if they were merest acquaintances, never even having kissed. Intolerable! The only closeness occurred during her singing after dinner. One of the most tiresome obligations of a country visit was having to listen to the ladies of the house perform on the pianoforte. One had to suppress a wince at each wrong note or force one's lids open at the unending insipidity of tone. He was spared that at Hillcrest since her ladyship had spared herself lessons on any instrument. Stara, who sang and played as she did everything—with charm; in consideration for her ladyship's lack of all these, rarely performed. Although when she did, it was memorable, particularly her singing the ballad of "Robin Hood's Death." At first Marcus had been amused by Lady

Gwendolen's loud accompanying sighs, calculated to remind all of her special attachment to a more recent outlaw. But then as the song continued, the sincerity in Stara's voice made immediate the outlaw's plight. Marcus felt a twinge of compunction at the line, "I never hurt fair maid in all my time." Stara's glance had rested briefly on him then, and came back when describing Robin's travels. Recollecting his own adventuring self, Marcus recognized a fellow wanderer in Robin Hood. Indeed, in Stara herself. Outsiders all. The last verse reached him more than he'd admit as her voice broke with emotion: "Then they may sing, when I am dead, and past, Here lies Robin Hood, a grave his wandering soul's bed: home at last."

Naturally Marcus feigned nonchalance, even applauding with mock exaggeration. But into his well-shielded heart she, with Robin's help, had landed an arrow that had neatly pierced through. Like to like to like.

The ostensible purpose for the visit to Hillcrest finally arrived. It was time for the showing of the Lady Gwendolen Rose. The marquis had cancelled the invitations to the neighboring gentry for fear that amidst all their servants One-Jewel Jack would sneak in and abscond with the rose itself or his beauteous daughter. A private ceremony, everyone agreed, was more select. After the display, the marquis had the honor of comparing the rose to his daughter. Lady Gwendolen stood alongside the bush and with graceful motions pointed to the various blooms, winning approval and applause.

The rose was magnificent with pale velvety yellow petals that had the faintest but sweetest fragrance. Her ladyship signaled the gardener whereupon he neatly snipped off and dethorned the most perfect of the blooms and presented it to her. With becoming modesty, she tucked it into her bodice and curtsied to all—

to her father first, then the duke, then Marcus. As an afterthought, she inclined her head to the grower of the rose. He however received a remembrance from the marquis, which had him smiling, indeed.

The duke was maladroit enough to go to the bush to sniff the fragrance. Marcus could only view his grace with contempt, shaking his head at that sapscull while he, alive to every suit, demonstrated what a true courtier would do. He approached Lady Gwendolen herself, pretending his object was the rose on her bodice, and slowly bending over, took a shockingly close sniff directly from the lady's bosom. Having used that approach before and succeeding, he was nothing loath to attempt it again. Once more it proved effective. Lady Gwen's faltering interest was sufficiently revived to accept Marcus's request of a stroll through the garden. They had scarce taken a few steps when Stara interrupted with alarm, warning Lady Gwen had already been too open a target and suggesting the safety of her veiled hat in case One-Jewel Jack had sufficient foresight to equip himself with a telescope. Instantly Mary was sent for the hat.

Marcus would liefer deal with a chaperon than that chapeau! It was impossible to carry on even the mildest flirtation with a lady constantly raising and lowering a veil and looking about in trepidation.

On their return he found Stara had used the opportunity to bedeck herself with several pink and red roses —in her hair, on her wrists, and even one on her high neckline, suggestively close to her laughing, full mouth. She was attempting to train his grace to sniff the various scents from those personal positions. His grace was flushed a bright red by the time the second couple arrived and brought to an inconclusive end this scientific experimentation.

Blast the girl, she'd used his own device for her

benefit while having arranged to make his tête-à-tête with her ladyship a farce.

But he merely returned a begrudging grin to her look of triumph and was doubly determined henceforth to abandon all gentlemanly consideration. The gloves, Stara, were off!

6

Thereafter, Marcus fixated on the necessity of finding more evidence against Miss Carltons to hold over her head. Naturally from the very beginning he'd investigated how Stara could have arranged to be One-Jewel Jack. They'd left her back in London and she was to arrive a sennight later with the marquis. But Stara had claimed she'd concluded her tasks earlier and had come by mail coach, which traveled all night. Marcus had checked and found the mail had stopped on the very day of her return at the nearby village of Synotts-dale, from where Stara had sent word to be picked up by one of the marquis's grooms. All that was irrefutable. Except no one had seen her alight from the coach. Further it certainly was curious that Stara would put up with the inconvenience of the common mail coach when within a tolerable time she could have been elegantly escorted by the marquis? What was the rush since no one was expecting her earlier? It had to be a false trail.

More investigation revealed an unknown gentleman had arrived by post chaise on the morning of the robbery in the more distant town of Lambertville, from whence he hired a horse. That could have been Stara in disguise. The question was: could she have left later than they, yet arrived in Westwardon considerably ahead? That was jolly well possible if one took into account not only the overnight stop and the general slow pace of the marquis's coach, but the frequent rests at various wayside inns for Lady Gwendolen's ease. To nail down his theory, he himself rode to Lambertville. There he experienced the up-and-down sensations of anything to do with Miss Carltons. For while the postillions verified the earlier arrival time of the gentleman in the chaise, they would not credit the gentleman being a lady. Another prodigious disappointment: the animal hired and returned was a job-lot chestnut—certainly not anywhere near the prime animal One-Jewel Jacqueline had been riding. Of course from the beginning Marcus had checked the marquis's stables to spot the highwayman's ebony stallion. There was a black one that bore some resemblance, but it had other dissimilarities such as a white spot on its forehead. Mayhap it had been disguised, but that could not be proved. As for Stara's daily mount at Hillcrest, it was a smaller bay.

Confound her! Had she so expertly covered all traces, it could never be proven the lady in the mask was Stara? Doubt was beginning to seep into even Marcus's determined conclusion. Day by day rather than being more certain of her guilt, he felt her slipping out of his clenched grasp. Actually the entire episode on the road was rapidly losing clarity with so many daily additions. Most recently the duke's recollecting having drawn his sword.

"You were not wearing a sword!" Marcus scoffed, drawing the line.

"I had it close by," the duke countered.

"Closer than the pistol in your pocket which you conveniently forgot!?"

"Gad, sirrah. Are you questioning me bravery? If that don't beat the Dutch! Considering the blasted yellow streak you showed down your back as you ran off."

"I went *after* the . . . fellow."

"Off, I say! Stab me, you seized me horse and were off and running!"

The gentlemen were steps from coming to cuffs, when inadvertently Lady Gwendolen performed a referee's function by calling them to account for not responding to her request. Both begged pardon, requesting she repeat it. With an all-suffering sigh, her ladyship was forced to once more use her voice when she had been perfectly lucid in her first request: that they describe One-Jewel Jack.

The duke screwed up his own face. Finally he said, "Masked, you know."

"Yes, but under the mask?" her ladyship pressed, dismissing his excuse as an evasion.

"Egad, your ladyship, ain't the thing to peek under a fellow's . . . eh, covering, don't you know?"

Marcus stepped in with a grin, and said suavely, "If one must look beneath fabric, I daresay I should rather peer through your exquisite apparel, your ladyship."

That was peripherally pleasing but inevitably Lady Gwendolen, as a hunting dog following a scent, was back to her fixation. Try as they might neither gentleman could recollect the color of the highwayman's eyes. Gwendolen was left to conclude they were green, very like her own. Similarly the gentlemen were most unhelpful in determining whether Jack had glanced passionately at her or hungrily.

For those niceties she had to refer to Stara.

"Hungrily *and* passionately," Stara had exclaimed without hesitation, although supposedly she had not been present upon the occasion.

Which Marcus was quick to point out, adding with a slight twist of sarcasm, "Or perhaps you *were?*"

"No, I was not. But I merely surmise One-Jewel Jack, as a man, would look at her ladyship as all men do."

That response no one could find fault with, particularly her ladyship, and Marcus was once more successfully parried.

Not able to trap Stara by words or investigation, he hoped to do so by deeds and followed her from a distance on her morning rides. There was always the possibility she would meet an accomplice or go somewhere that would link her with the robbery. Yet on all occasions, Stara kept to Hillcrest's park. Therefore her stalker received no benefit except the pleasure of seeing Stara sit on a horse. Which she did with a decided elegance.

It is an inevitable certainty, the more one hunts a quarry, the more one becomes obsessed to capture it. Many a night before drifting off to sleep, Marcus occupied himself picturing the moment in the cave with the lady. This time he would reach across and remove the mask—gaining proof positive she and Stara were one. In the daytime however, he kept to his original objective for coming to Hillcrest of capturing Lady Gwendolen. Yet, curse Stara, for when she was present, she distracted his aim back and forth between both ladies, scattering his shot.

After one such split dalliance Stara called him to account for his duplicity. "Is it *come il faut,* Mr. Justus, to flirt with two ladies at once?"

Unabashed Marcus claimed he was not flirting

with the two of them. "Rather," and he paused to add this daunting gem, "I am courting one lady—her ladyship, while I am blatantly, unabashedly, seducing you."

Admittedly he was paying more attention to the second half of his objective as day by day Lady Gwendolen was displaying a vanity of unpalatable proportions. A small touch of vanity may be acceptable and even be regarded as inevitable in one so exalted, but when it ballooned to the egotistical conviction that every gentleman within sight of her prodigious prettiness must be instantly and fatally stricken with passion— well, all romantic inclinations went flat. Marcus found himself struggling not to laugh at that lady walking about with a net over her face. But what finally turned his indulgent view to scorn was the arrival of a commissioned portrait. It depicted Gwendolen standing in her rose garden, holding a Lady Gwendolen rose. The artist had been liberal in his exaggerations not only of the size of the roses, but of her ladyship's small eyes and finally added lock upon lock to her head, transforming her skimpy curls into a glorious, hirsute crown. Not only would Lady Gwendolen devotedly stare at her image, but insist that her admirers join in that quiet, solemn, almost sacred adulation. After one hour of that, try as he might, Marcus could not be passionate about a lady that moved him only to grins.

On the other hand, Stara moved him to despair, anger, exasperation, impatience, admiration, awe. He was in short fascinated with every one of Stara's many facets. Her walk, while not having Lady Gwendolen's slow stately grace, was filled with such quick energy, it made him wishful to see her running—with himself chasing after and catching her up into his arms. Then there was her underlying layer of laughter, which clearly showed they had in common a delight in the absurd. His was more ironic amusement while hers was still an open laughter at all vanities, pomposities, dullness and conventionalities. With approval, he noted, she could laugh at herself as well. That was revealed when the marquis as an afterthought mentioned his having similarly commissioned a portrait of her. Stara had been all enthusiasm to see it. Without much ado, his lordship handed her a tiny miniature that almost disappeared in her palm. Looking up at the portrait of Lady Gwendolen dominating half the wall, Stara could scarce help giggling, concluding ruefully, "Well, that cuts me down to my proper size, I daresay. Which is probably for the best. Lady Gwendolen is always bemoaning I have too many inches as it is."

After days of obligatory admiring of her ladyship's image, Marcus was silent upon glancing at the miniature. The artist had failed to capture the essence of Stara, giving her an expression of such insipidity as to lose all connection with the subject. At first he merely shrugged, but then unable not to comment, added softly, "You are world's more than that," indicating the miniature, and then pointing to Lady Gwendolen's massive portrait added, "Or that."

Stara was astonished. It was infamous of him to resort to sincerity. For then one was generally forced to have to accept whatever was said under its cover. Or question a gentleman's very nature. But after a mere blink Stara was more than prepared to do that.

"Flummery! You know me as little as this artist. Whether drawn in words or on canvas, an artist describes himself, while the subject remains free to exist *undefined*."

Marcus touched her lightly with an extended finger as if drawing her face. "You will ne'er be free of my defining," he whispered. "You are the subject of my most devoted study. You might say," he elaborated with a twinkle, "I am well nigh to receiving a degree as a master of you."

Which was another way of asking her to be his mistress! Insufferable man, Stara thought. On the other hand, she smiled with some secret pleasure at his having unwittingly revealed his obsession with her. Not that it was to her interest to continue so immodest a conversation. It was however to his, as with a hint of devilment in his eyes and open mockery in his voice, Marcus concluded, "All my recent scholarly dedication to the subject of Stara has taught me there's a special bond between us. One might go so far as to say, we speak the same *private* language. Think of how prodigiously delicious would be a long, private, explicit dialogue."

"Speak for yourself and to yourself," Stara snapped and stalked off.

Later, as with most of Marcus's barbs, Stara found herself stopping to examine it for the truth in the center. Her honesty had her reluctantly admitting the two did share a private language. Sometimes merely a quick glance or smile exchanged said enough for both. Very much as if they were strangers in a land of natives who must continually translate their thoughts, only of a sudden to hear another speaking his original language. Then they would chatter happily together, until Stara, always Stara, pulled back, sensing further closeness would make her more vulnerable to him. During her time not only at Miss Lavadale's, but in the ton as well, Stara had protectively become quite agile in speaking in conventionalities, knowing if she fully revealed herself she might be judged as outside the pale. At Hillcrest, she'd betimes risked speaking her mind to Marcus with just the results she'd feared. He used her openness against her, even to offering a carte blanche.

Despite her light laughing ways Stara was proud to state—to herself if no one else—that she'd never gone beyond the bonds of impropriety. Unless one counted the mere trifle of holding up her friends and divesting them of their jewels. But that had been in a moment of desperation and because, because she could not resist doing it, once the thought had entered her head. It was the dare of it.

Marcus did not understand that one act was not a person. One act did not necessarily mean she would do its like again. And she fumed at his attempting to position her permanently at an extreme. Her spirit of adventure—which at times urged her to fly up high to the sun—did not mean she would willingly toss herself away to be burned.

Yet Marcus rushed to turn her afire, assuming their minds being so closely attuned meant their bodies should be so as well. So Stara rather than acknowledging their shared qualities as bonds, turned their similarities into weapons to keep him at a distance. Her most effective buffer of all was the duke. In truth, just being in his grace's presence made her more prosaic—as if she'd caught it from him. Their conversations were intolerably maddening to Marcus. He must always interrupt. As when Marmaduke with the air of the greatest condescension invited Stara for an evening turn in the garden. Filled with disgust, especially at Stara's delighted and prompt compliance, Marcus could do no less than hoot aloud.

Alarmed, the duke looked his way.

"Owl," the large gentleman whose shoulders were shaking with laughter explained, "Look out for them. It's near dark."

"Not afeared of owls!" the duke said scornfully and addressed himself to Stara, "Might I have your arm?"

"If you were not such a cawker," Marcus put in,

incorrigibly, "you would ask for an *armful* of the lady. That's what I should do!"

"You might find me more of an armful than you can handle!"

Stara had directed that toward Marcus behind his grace and while that gentleman did not take offense, the duke did, assuming she'd been addressing him. "Never dropped a lady's arm, egad!" he exclaimed.

It would be too complicated to explain the confusion, so Stara merely apologized for her comment, claiming she'd been referring to her height which might make her altogether too much of a burden.

That was a gross mistake, for the duke at once began surveying her as if he'd never considered the length of her anatomy. Stara winced at putting such a negative suggestion into his mind.

"Lots of you to . . ." his grace responded and paused. Both Marcus and Stara waited for his conclusion. The gentleman hoping for a laugh and Stara for a reprieve. "to . . . bejewel."

Stara sighed in relief, for it was known the duke always admired a well-decked lady. But in the next second he added a second sentence she could have done without. "Tall for a lady."

"That explains her tall stories," the irrepressible Mr. Justus could not resist inserting.

Shaking her head and standing her full height, Stara took a step closer to the duke and gave him her arm defiantly, as she seductively whispered, "All the better for seeing eye to eye with a gentleman."

"Quite so," his grace admitted, won over. Casting a victorious glance at Marcus, she walked off with her noble escort. Marcus was left with a smile of admiration at her tactics but not half delighted to be the one she always turned away from. With his height, they would not be seeing eye to eye, he thought with satisfaction, rather he would be looking down at her. Faith, he should have inserted that, but the moment had passed.

Whatever moment he shared with Stara, Marcus found worthy of thought and rethought. Particularly did he relive their evening musicals, more of which had been demanded of late by the marquis. Marcus had assumed the songs were directed at him until he noted the marquis wiping his brow and the duke flushing after each of Stara's renditions. The minx was making all the gentlemen feel singled out! Yet his ego would not allow them to be the objects of her songs with himself in the room!

Another who eventually felt the evenings lacked something—or herself in a central position—was Lady Gwendolen. She showed her displeasure by announcing the music was disturbing her nerves.

Immediately the marquis was concerned. Stara, realizing the real problem, claimed nothing was as soothing as music—if her ladyship herself would join in the singing, going into detail on how the use of one's voice stretched the muscles to the head, easing them. "For our mutual health we ought do a duet!"

Her ladyship was persuaded almost immediately to attempt that remedy. But Lady Gwendolen's participation had some drawbacks. She could not play. She could not remember lyrics. And she could not carry a tune. Other than that she was an unexceptional partner. Her ladyship, holding the sheet music before her, spoke the words. Stara would play and hum along to keep Lady Gwendolen in the vicinity of the tune. The song was finished after a fashion and much applauded by a father who thought his daughter could do no wrong, by his grace who felt a lady of her breeding could do no wrong and by Marcus who knew enough to pretend she could do no wrong. Indeed he complimented her on being "extremely well versed." Thus it was concluded that henceforth Lady Gwendolen would do all the entertaining.

After that there was scarce an evening not marred by music. Both the marquis and his grace slept through, but Marcus, not so fortunate, found himself losing all affection for not only songs but romance. Her ladyship turned what should have been stirring love vows into wooden, unfeeling pronouncements betokening she would give token performances to passion in any form. He was too much of a lover to accept that, even in a wife to whom he had no intention of being faithful. Looking at Stara, he thought she might keep him faithful . . . for a season at least.

While the evenings had thus sunk into farces, Mr. Justus found the mornings similarly unsatisfactory. His shadowing Stara left much to be desired. For otherwise they could have been enjoying pleasant gallops together! He was near to abandoning his strategy, when all his efforts were at one stroke rewarded. Stara, with a quick glance to assure herself unwatched, rode out of the gates of Hillcrest park at last.

Clenching his fists and risking a loud "Yes!" in triumph, Marcus stayed well back, trusting to his tracking instincts as Stara headed toward the Home Wood. Through the trees he spotted the flash of her blue riding outfit. Shortly he found the rough, narrow path she was following and hung back a mite. His horse was well trained not to whinny at sudden checks. Then noiselessly he followed. When she reached a ramshackle cottage in a clearing, he stopped.

Her blue riding habit was the new one the marquis had bought for her, and it had a voluminous skirt, which she, assuming no one was about, lifted rather higher than modesty would allow as she dismounted. He saw her limbs above the ankle and a wide smile of delight spread over his face. Here was ample reward for his days of secret accompaniment. For, like the rest of her, her limbs were long and perfectly proportioned. But she lowered her skirt, abruptly ending the show, as she went about the business of tethering her mount.

The trap was set, ready to be sprung. The fox surrounded and the hounds ready to pounce. As at those times, Marcus felt a twinge of sympathy with the cornered. She was run to the ground. Yet Marcus did not relish kills. He preferred training his prey to jump willingly onto his lap. Therefore the gentleman hung back in distaste at what must be a cold-blooded strike.

Even the most blood-mad hunting party needed riling by a chase or the yelping of the dogs to take part in the kill and the winning of the foxtail. While tethering his horse a safe distance, Marcus attempted to rouse himself by the thought of Stara alone in the cottage.

Almost at the door, he paused. A new possibility struck. In such a remote spot could she be meeting a gentleman? Was this a rendezvous? Not the duke certainly. Not enough fire in that one. A shudder passed through Marcus's large frame at the possibility it could be a menial—one of those strapping estate workers? Or worse, could it be the marquis himself? Would she have traded her decency for a riding outfit and some gowns! Making her no more than a ladybird who had sold herself quite cheaply, after all. Possible. Possible. For dash her, hadn't she already proved herself a thief!

There was no sound of a greeting within, nor any conversation. For a while Marcus stayed hidden, expecting someone else to ride up? At last his color returned, realizing this was not an assignation. Several reviving breaths spurred him on. All windows were shuttered closed. Stealthily he approached and scanned until he spotted one casement open with smoke streaming out. Though summer, there was a bit of a chill today, and she had lit a fire. Her stay then would be of some duration. Once more there flashed the thought that she was waiting for someone who might not be arriving immediately, which explained her making their meeting place comfortable.

The glower was back on his visage. Ignoring the need for discretion, he barged directly up to the open casement and stood in full view.

There was Stara using the fire not for warmth but for sight, inspecting none other than Lady Gwen's almost pink pearls. She was holding them up to catch the light. Next moment with a sigh, she had the audacity to place the pearls around her neck and fasten the clasp.

It was time for the *coup de grace*. With a thrill of conquest, Marcus casually leaned over the sill and observed calmly. "Indeed, they look better on you, my dear. But taken at what a price!"

Stara was petrified on the spot. As helpless as the fox when the hounds were circling and snatching at its tail. Did all cornered things have the same expression of stunned terror? By gad, her face was parchment white!

Nevertheless, with a true conqueror's swagger, he stepped over the sill and walked toward her. Her hair was loose and long, as she'd worn it the day at the cave. And the shine of the pearls around her neck was less than the glow of the startled, staring eyes. After a long pause, savored by him and agony to her, Stara ended it herself abruptly by throwing a wild glance about.

"I'm alone," he said, unable not to reassure her, so clear was her terror, he could almost feel the beating of her heart.

She faced him then in more control.

"Yes, it is just me you have to fear and face," he whispered with an intent look.

She smiled at that. Her breath was near normal now as she began to assess that the danger was manageable after all. For he was just one man, and a man she had been so far been able to keep in check.

"Ah, I'm not such a minor obstacle, my dear girl," he said sensing her relief. "Recollect I've caught you with the goods. Proof you are not only a thief, but very likely have murdered several lords and ladies under your persona as One-Jewel Jack."

At that Stara's eyes began to twinkle and she laughed outright, with a saucy toss of her long silky hair. "I'm not One-Jewel Jack," she said affably.

"Nor are those Lady Gwen's pearls you are wearing round your throat? Don't dare attempt to gammon me. Nor anyone else. Those pearls alone will very likely lead to a noose around this small, white . . . neck." And Marcus leaned over and circled her throat and neck with his own fingers.

She allowed that encircling, without a quiver. Even faced him without a blink. There wasn't an ounce of fear in her now.

He stepped back, grinning.

"Not afraid of me, are you?"

She shook her head.

"Why?" he asked, with some interest.

She smiled.

"Ah, you think I am too enamored of you to wish to turn you in. How do you know I've not already notified the Bow Street Runners? Or the marquis? He's a justice, is he not? He would certainly find it of some interest that the young lady he trusted and took into his home as the companion to his dear daughter—is a highwayman? Or, pardon, highwaylady."

"You will not expose me," she said with a certainty, and walked away toward a small box. Nonchalantly she removed the pearls and placed them back within. Following, he seized the box and rummaged through. Besides the pearls there was the Duke's jeweled fob, stickpin and insignia ring. Nothing else. Which proved she had not had a history of thievery. That was a relief to him. But she had taken pounds from his purse and from the duke's.

"Where's the ready? The blunt?"

"Are we talking thieves' cant?" she whispered, in a spirit of unholy amusement, just restraining herself from going into a giggle.

"One always speaks to another in *their* language."

"I'm not a thief," she said calmly, with a shrug. And then as if having second thoughts admitted openly, "That is . . . I have never before taken anything that did not belong to me."

After consulting his own instincts, Marcus accepted that, but added with no little curiosity, "What possessed you to do it this time?"

"You would not understand. For to own it, I do not myself."

Stara's heart was now back to its normal rhythm, but her brain was racing to find a way out of her dilemma. She had to find a way to control this man without having to pay him a forfeit that would destroy every vestige of dignity she had been clinging to all her life, hanging on the edge of falling from respectability. He was staring at her with his usual maddening sense of power and yet in the depths of his blue eyes there was a twinge of concern. She must reach that, by heavens. In an inspired flash, she recollected a rather severe teacher at school prepared to order the destruction of a rodent, when a baby rodent appeared from under the trapped one. Instantly the rat became a mother, leading the teacher to instruct the servants to release both. When it was done, she'd looked into Stara's dark inquiring eyes and said, "I'm a mother myself, you know." It had been a lesson Stara never forgot. You never destroyed something or someone that reminded you of yourself.

Hence Stara at once began to seek common ground with her captor, exclaiming that surely he must understand having been so long on the outside himself. And, and, both Lady Gwendolen and the duke had so much, they would scarce miss one extra jewel.

"Aha! If *that* were excuse enough, no one would have more than the other," Marcus replied unaffected. "In your case, you have the pearls. Enough one would assume, yet you wished for more. You're keeping the stickpin. Obviously by that logic, having so much, you would not miss one little extra stickpin, I presume."

"Are you suggesting . . ." her breath caught, "that I give *you* the pin?"

"Ye gods! As if I could wear anything of his grace's! Although I shouldn't mind a return of my own money."

Stara did not reply, nor would she meet his stern glance.

"Spent it, did you? So soon? Or what?"

Her face betrayed a twinge of anguish on his having touched a sore truth. Further he was looking at her with such icy judgement, she sensed she had not reached him in any way. She was in a devil of a fix. Her breath was coming short again.

"The truth, thief!"

She winced at that tone and the name. She had not in reality ever considered herself as that. Staring at him Stara for the first time since her madcap adventure saw herself as another would—as a common felon! It was there in his eyes. She'd sunk beneath all consideration, which put her in his hold at last.

Once more Marcus brusquely insisted she tell him the full reason. "I warn you, I shall know if you are gammoning me. Remember I'm not one of these nobles you have been gulling right and left. What led you on this path? Or shall I say, who? Is it a man? Are you someone's doxy?"

She lunged at him of a sudden, like a wild, trapped animal. In shock Marcus stepped back. But all at once she sank to her knees, gasping, truly not being able to catch her breath, not able to speak to him. No more jibes and schemes, Stara was wild-eyed . . . desperate for escape.

There was concern in his eyes as he approached her carefully. And when she just moaned a bit, he sat down on the ground next to her and said calmly, "Tell me, I'll understand."

But Stara remained petrified until he slowly placed his hand on her shoulder. Then she shuddered. Yet he kept it there, allowing her to become accustomed to him and his nearness. Then smoothly Marcus put his arm round, making her rest against his chest. She felt the comfort of that and for a moment sagged there, breathing more regularly. Her mind was assuring her that he would not report her, that she had reached him, after all, as one person to another.

But holding her, Marcus forgot the question he had asked. Rather he could only think they were alone . . . that there was a warm fire and a ragged sofa nearby.

His own breathing was becoming ragged. Ah, this was his dream—having Stara in his power and in his arms. He pulled her close to him and felt the velvet of her dark riding habit conforming to her curves. He followed the outline of her figure. Stroked her as if she were a cat in his arms. She let him caress her shoulders and down to her small waist and around and up. Now his mouth was nuzzling her, murmuring comforting words to keep her willing in his arms. His next move was catching her mouth, kissing her fully. A sweep of passion filled both; it was sweet, yet sharp, wild a moment, then still—of a stillness never felt before, as if reaching the center of a storm. Gasping, he covered her lips again. The kisses were turning into spirals, revolving downward . . . so he pushed her down.

They were on the sofa. That realization hit Stara the moment her head touched the cushions. Her panic cut through the swirling fog of desire. Swiftly she rolled off. He caught her on the ground, attempting to stop her squirming away. Throughout she was saying, "No, no, no, no."

"It was yes, a moment hence."

"You caught me unawares. I will *not* give myself to you, do you understand! If you proceed at this point, you are naught but a base plunderer!"

He held her against him, unable to accept her refusal. Once more he stuck to his course and took her lips, but it was too coarse an act in the face of her anger. She squirmed away so fiercely they were soon rolling toward the fire, banging against the logs. Sparks flew from there and from themselves as they gyrated together. Mercilessly he held her down under him. Her hair spread round on the floor as he leaned closer, closer. That was when Stara's spirit came to her rescue as it had in all her previous crises. Restlessly, blindly her hand went toward the hearth, plunging in and pulling out a lit stick. He felt a hiss of a burn on his arm and simply knocked it aside, but it distracted him enough to hold back and address her.

"You want me. You can buy my silence. You might even buy more than that. If you need money so much that you would risk your life on the road, why not earn it now? Name your price, damn you! I shall not let you go! I've wanted you too long and too much! What do you want for this moment? Anything except marriage. I'll keep you in comfort. I'll keep you." His voice cracked at the nearness of her and the wild, vixen eyes as she kept shaking her head till her hair flew wildly around her.

"No," she gasped. Then took a breath and said succinctly, "Release me. I hold my honor high. I will not live a life of disrepute! I shall die first. You will have to kill me to take me now."

In one agonizing second, Marcus realized he was not going to take her. He had too much honor, actually too much pride in himself to take a woman that did not wish him. He waited for some of the passion that was streaking through him to subside, but it did not.

"Curse you, forever! You strumpet!" he groaned and forced himself to roll off.

Quickly she was up, and running toward the door. There, she stopped to bring him to reason. "You have the booty. You have won something, after all. But remember, there is no way you can prove I was the one who took it. Whomever you inform of it, I shall simply say I followed you and found *you* with it. I do not know what kind of background you have, as regards to honesty. But mine is unblemished. I can scarce assume either Lady Gwen or the duke would believe I was One-Jewel Jack. Even the marquis who has not built his own version of the event, knowing me as a poor, fragile lady, would not credit your claim. Rather they would more likely believe you had a cohort and that is why you have the jewels."

Rising slowly and sitting himself back on the sofa, Marcus said with indifference. "You may keep the jewels. I shall not expose you. But if you are on that road, one day you shall find yourself caught by a gentleman uncaring of your feelings, who shall not only take you but turn you in as well."

"I have no fear of that," Stara said. "I do not intend to continue down this road. It was an act of madness. Partly led on because I was tired of being so

humble to her ladyship and his grace. They are so superior, because they have had such an easy life. I wanted
to see how they would act when no longer under the
cover of their titles and servants—without the protection of all that, when as people they had to meet a
situation—face to face with the terror of losing all, as I
have been faced throughout my life. Further, I was
pressed for money by certain people to the point that I
was near to accepting the marquis's offer—who has already in his round about way let me know I could be
his wife. I want you to understand," she suddenly cried,
and she had to stop herself to get a breath and to see if
she were reaching him at all. "I want you to understand," she repeated again, "so that perhaps I can understand why I behaved so much against my nature and
upbringing. Actually, actually, I did it because I was so
afraid, so beastly afraid, if I did not, I would accept
him."

Marcus was standing up and staring at her. Her
eyes had an openness he'd never seen in them before.
He had too often found himself in such a ramshackle
condition not to recognize it in another. He understood
more than she could know her doing something wild,
just for the sake of the wildness. Egad, hadn't he often
performed similar acts for the same reason? As for her
doing something to assure she would not have to marry
—he himself as a young lad had been near to suc-
cumbing to the easy comfort of marrying a well-
endowed lady, only to disgrace himself purposely in her
eyes to end the involvement. Ah, he understood Stara
through and through—to the core, for there he found
himself. Grinning in his relaxed, lazy manner, he
opened both his hands wide as if to demonstrate he had
no holds on her and said, "I believe you and I shall
not expose you . . . or harass you any longer, unless . . ."

"Unless?" she asked with some dread, feeling she was almost free, when at the last moment he'd stepped on her train and detained her.

"Unless, of course, you wish me to continue . . . harassing you. That would be something we might both not wish to quite relinquish."

She looked at him without replying for a full moment. And then turned and left the cottage.

7

Marcus followed his lovely prey back to the safety of Hillcrest. Her hair bounced along ahead of him, attracting with each of its come-hither switches. At first he was gentlemanly holding back, until the lure of her had him pressing the sides of his steed.

Looking to the rear, Stara was alarmed at Marcus's closeness. She frowned, wondering if that was not indicative of the way he would be keeping watch on her hereafter. Despite his pledge, he'd obviously not quite relinquished his hold on her. That had Stara urging her horse forward. It was important to reach Hillcrest ere he did—to prove literally she was always a jump ahead. Bending over she gave her horse the nudge. In the next instant the two horses were galloping like streaks of wind. The distance closed, till they were side by side. Nearing the stables, Marcus moved ahead and was off his horse first. Then turning, he welcomed her with a bow of mocking triumph. The animals were heaving and snorting. The stable hands were rushing toward them. Stara's hair had become so entangled it was a wild swirl that then softly rested on her heaving shoulders. So much, she thought, for his promise not to continue harassing her! How more clearly could he be saying the chase was on. And now he had several advantages of her. He knew the hiding place of her jewels as well as knowing the reasons for her act. Too much knowledge for her peace and comfort. She saw the usual, mischievous smile in his eyes had hardened into scorn. The haughtiness of holding power over another was there too. A slick, cruel sheen of confidence that one could hurt another if one wished. And he she concluded, her heart shuddering, obviously wished a great deal.

Marcus's delicious triumph was tasting sweeter by the moment. The anxiety in her eyes as she silently rushed ahead spurred him to keep on with the chase. Very much as a dog would be attracted by someone's movement. Sensing Stara's almost visceral desire to be away, he gloated, "You've led me a merry chase, my dear lady, shall we continue a run toward the house? What care we what the butler, nay the world, think of our behavior?"

Reining in her need to strike at him, Stara, recalling propriety, slowed her steps. But she refused to respond. So he carried on his own interchange, altering his voice when replying for her.

" 'And how did you enjoy your morning romp, Miss Carltons?' . . . 'Most exhilarating. One always enjoys romps when with such an exceptionable partner!' . . . 'Thank you, I could say the same for yourself, but I never praise ladies who are such consummate shams.' "

Stara stopped walking. "By all means continue your delightful dialogue with yourself. You have finally found your equal in brass. Do carry on. The butler or even Lady Gwen should have the opportunity to hear those alternate voices. Then I shall not be the only one aware there are windmills in your head—whirling at an indecent pace! Be off!"

Chuckling, Mr. Justus merely waited tolerantly, eyeing her with appreciation while she took time to get her breath.

"You are a joy to spar with—always a smashing return blow. But even between rounds, in intermission, so to say, one can joy in simply observing you. Are you aware your eyes have stars in them? Is that the reason for your name? Did your mother realize heaven had dropped two shiny lights into this perfect setting." He leaned forward and gently touched her cheek with his fingertip; but she stepped back instinctively, warning him off with a fiery glance. That had him sighing and grinning as he concluded, "Filled with rage your eyes sparkle with martial light. Ah, but when they are consumed with passion, the light dims into a warm, silver moonlight glow that positively sears one through!"

"Silence!" Stara looked about. No one was overhearing them. Yet she could not bear his tormenting. "You are to be silent henceforth. I shall not accept your jabs. If you feel my secret gives you power over me, you are mistaken. No one can have a hold on another unless it is granted by one's own fear."

Much struck by her remark, Marcus agreed indeed there was much to her observation. "But you see, I've had a permanent hold over you from the moment we first met. And it is not based on fear. I admit you are fearless. My hold over you was made clear the moment I held you in my arms. We are a pair. We want the same things. What a beastly pity I am not the duke. Think of the joy of chasing me rather than that stock."

"I am no more chasing the duke than you are Lady Gwendolen," she replied, beginning to walk on.

"But you see how honest I am," he claimed, both

conversationally and constitutionally keeping pace. "I admit I am seeking her ladyship for her dowry and to reestablish my position. I thought you had been equally honest with me from the first. Why are you suddenly playing social games?"

Stara turned and stared at him. "I long ago offered that we would help each other in our aims, but you have been, admit it, attempting to achieve yours while thwarting me in mine."

"A hit, a very palpable hit, I do admit it," Marcus exclaimed. "I have a twin purpose. To win her ladyship to wife and you to my bed. But you know that."

"I shall own myself extremely astonished if either of those events occur. I have made two unbreakable vows. One, to bed only my husband. Two, that my husband shall be a gentleman. If the first did not eliminate you forthwith, the second certainly does. For you are beyond a rake to a loose-screw—even a ramshackle libertine. In short, you are not a gentleman!"

"And you are not a lady!" he said, his lips curling into a sneer. "Unless well-born and well-behaved women are suddenly diverting themselves by dressing as highwaymen and relieving their friends of their jewels. True, I have been abroad for some time, but I can scarce believe there has been such a remarkable change in the standards. Lady One-Jewel Jack."

"I thought we'd agreed you would not taunt me with that!"

"When did we agree?" he asked astonished, his eyes dancing with twin devils in their blue depths. "Rather, you assumed it. I said I would not expose you, but I cannot but take it into account in my treatment of you. For that act while showing you as courageous and having some sort of flair, also shows you are beneath my touch. (Although touching you is a titillating thought.) I will continue to fence with you, my outlaw, my dear adventuress, until I have brought you down and taken you *willingly* into my bed—where I shall teach you that not being a lady can have many advantages!"

They were at the entrance of Hillcrest and Stara was prevented from giving him an answer to that by the presence of the butler. But she attempted to give him her full displeasure by a killing look.

He pretended to have been hit, clutching his heart and laughing aloud as she whirled away from him and went up the tall, marble stairs.

He stood below watching her lightly running. At the last moment she looked back, feeling the warmth of his eyes on her. He was no longer smiling. The depth of his feelings for her were so clearly in his eyes that it was Stara who smiled as she continued on to her chamber.

On his way for a second breakfast, Marcus was stopped in his tracks by the sound of a small voice crying out.

The keeper was holding a dirty urchin of no more than ten years of age. The culprit was dragged into the side saloon where the marquis was dividing snuff into several jars, and prodigiously annoyed at the interruption.

"Wilson, I am occupied. Why is this child allowed into this part of the house?"

"I brung him, my lord, to show you who the culprit be. You recalls we was conversing of all the loose sticks missing from the Home Wood. I set me spies and we spied out it was this here boy, Jack Stalks, one of your own cottagers. He been takin' wood regular and selling it in the village. Made himself quite a tidy sum. Offen your lordship's property."

In a pucker at this distraction that had him forgetting whether he had added the needed ingredient into both snuff jars, the marquis looked up. This sniveling lad was the cause of his having made a mull out of the mixing. It was an unforgivable intrusion! "Put the blighter into the gaol, if you will, but do not *ever* bring such a specimen before *me*."

Wilson was pleased. "Yes, m'lord. I'll put this scrubby thatchgallows away till he learns never to tamper with what ain't hissen."

"Yes, yes," the marquis muttered. "Just leave!"

Eyeing the crying child, Marcus could not help but interfere. "I say, your lordship, would not a reprimand be sufficient? That boy is a mere halfling! How old are you, son?"

Sensing some support in his moment of terror, the boy began to spill out his story. He had not been taking the wood regular. Only when it was scattered on the road, and so much of it were there, he thought a little extra might help the old ladies in the village.

The boy began to wail as Wilson cuffed him again and yelled. "Don't gi' me that! Fer the old ladies! What was you charging them fer, eh?"

"They gi' me a few farthings. I niver ask fer 'em."

"Really," Marcus exclaimed. "He has been cuffed several times, I gather. Surely, we can let the matter rest with that."

At that moment the duke entered and heard the tale afresh from Wilson. His grace always supported his staff. It was the chain of command one never broke. Indeed, Marmaduke was claiming excusing the urchin would set a grievous example of authority for the rest of the cottagers and village folk. That once it was established others could be free with their betters' property, the orchards would be plundered next, even the gardens. "Oddsblood, I expect the village baker will loll about in your rose garden! Her ladyship's Lady Gwendolen Rose shan't be safe. Picked for some ostler's daughter! Egad!"

At this point the marquis gave up on his mixtures, pushing the jars away, giving his ear to the duke. One must always give one's ear to a duke, and disagreement with a duke was not the usual thing, especially not one who might become his son-in-law.

Nodding in agreement, the marquis quickly repeated his previous harsh sentence, which had the child protesting and squirming. One last twitch and he was out of Wilson's hands. "What ho!" the duke called, and joined the race. But a muscularly built gentleman interfered. It was Marcus pretending to have inadvertently bumped into both the duke and Wilson. That gave the lad sufficient time to escape out the window. Leaning out, Wilson saw him running into the bushes.

"I'll set the staff on him!" he cried.

"Almost like a fox hunt," the duke said with a "Tally-ho!"

At that moment Lady Gwendolen arrived and everyone recollected they were gentlemen. Except the keeper who was immediately dismissed.

At her signal they all adjourned to breakfast. But the duke could not quite forget the incident. He had to relate it to her ladyship. His telling was so garbled, she was led to conclude that the boy had stolen the Lady Gwendolen Rose. Her alarm was great. She was ready to swoon. The marquis was quick to frown at his grace and all three gentlemen were speaking at once assuring her that event had not taken place.

"It was wood he stole," her father said.

She stared at him and then at the duke. "Then why was the topic brought to my attention?"

They all apologized. She accepted it and wished them all to state their opinions rather on her new hairdo that Stara had helped her devise. Her father was gauche enough to say, "Looks like your usual style, m'dear. You always look just fine."

She frowned at that and turned to the duke who also did not perceive a difference and so remained silent, turning his attention to his morning vittles. Marcus concentrating on the curls, finally was able to hazard a guess. "You have two ringlets on this side, where before you had one?"

She nodded, and everyone immediately perceived the vast difference.

"Stunning!" Marcus inserted.

"By Jove, yes!" his grace agreed not looking up from his food.

The marquis repeated that she always looked splendid.

When Stara arrived she was assured by Lady Gwen that the change of coiffure had been instantly remarked on by all, and Stara said the necessary things that the gentlemen had not been able to discern, how the two ringlets brought immediate attention to the perfection of Lady Gwen's profile. Lady Gwen smiling at that, turned both profiles for all to observe. There was almost applause for that and then everyone was free to eat.

But the duke could not forget the episode with the urchin. He had to bring up the event one more time; now to accuse Marcus of having deliberately crashed into himself and Wilson or they would have had the culprit.

"When he is caught, I expect the fright he has gone through not to mention the blows from Wilson should be sufficient punishment," Marcus could not help but add. "I hope the child will then be let free."

Staring at him, Stara was pleased there was some heart in the gentleman who certainly had not treated her with the slightest bit of consideration. Hearing the entire story from the marquis, she responded, "Heavens! A child has stolen a stick of wood. How shall Hillcrest continue without it! Is the entire forest denuded! Shall you have any wood left for your fires, my lord?"

"It is not that much," his lordship admitted, beginning to see how the episode could be considered another way.

"Indeed," Stara continued. "A child of ten cannot have much of a hold. I expect one should not destroy his entire life for seeking to keep warm!"

"Egad," the duke interrupted, offended. "That ain't what we are saying. He *sold* the wood, by Jove!

"Enterprising," Marcus put in with a gleam of sardonic amusement.

But the duke ignored that, continuing with his tale. "Made himself a tidy sum, by Jove. Several shillings."

"Farthings," Marcus inserted, inexorably.

At that the duke turned in annoyance. Unable to accept the gnat of Marcus's remarks whizzing about his head, he responded, "A farthing a day, me father used to say, is seven shillings a year. Oddsblood—he could steal his way to a guinea before he is old enough to pouch!"

"Oddsblood, indeed!" Marcus echoed and unable to resist added with a mocking gleam. "Before long he might some day graduate to taking your stickpin! Unless that is only a lady's choice." He shot a swift teasing glance at Stara.

The duke was flummoxed and Stara, frowning, stepped in to squelch one gentleman and soothe the other. "But your grace, you have so large a heart, as does his lordship." Turning, she pinned the hesitant marquis with her eager glance, "I do not suppose that either of you would wish a small child to be ruined by this one act. One must forgive if one ever hopes to achieve forgiveness oneself."

"You speak very well for thieves," Marcus could not help inserting.

"Egad, Mr. Justus, is correct. A thief is a thief, whatever the age," the duke insisted.

"But what did you do when you were ten year's old, your grace. Did you ever steal an apple from a tree that was not on your property?"

"Everything was my property. And why should I climb for an apple when there were always plenty in the bowls."

"Ah yes, you were very fortunate. Not all of us are as perfect or propertied as you, your grace. Perhaps you, your lordship," she turned to him with her large, dark eyes pleading. "Did you never want something out of your reach and feel you *had* to have it."

Looking at the beauty before him, the marquis admitted he had a great desire for something out of his reach.

"I knew you had a soft heart! And think on it. The boy must have a mother. What would a mother do without her child? You love Lady Gwen so much— think of your life without her."

At that view of things and concluding that he never really meant to incarcerate the boy, the situation seemed to be concluded, when Lady Gwen inserted, "But what about his stealing my prize rose? I cannot have that. No, father, the child must be made an example."

The duke was quick to agree, and what had first been agreed to was immediately disagreed to. Marcus stepped in at Stara's groan.

"But your ladyship, recollect." He was about to remind her that the child had not stolen her flower, but staring at her mulish face, he thought better, and taking a cue from the way Stara handled her, added, "The flower was scattered, but who has said where it was scattered? I expect it was scattered under your window —as a tribute to your beauty. Even a young lad is not immune to the perfection of both your profiles. All men, whatever our age, are swept up by beauty of such exquisite nature."

He bowed to her, and Lady Gwen smiled, allowing she had not thought of it in that light. With a sigh she concluded herself in agreement with Stara, after all—the child should not be punished.

The marquis who had switched sides to the point of the last speaker, was now once more assuring everyone that the child should be reprimanded but let free to return to his mother. And Stara gave him such a smile, he ate his kipper with added relish.

Stara and Marcus shared a relieved glance. Not said, but felt was the realization the two were on one side against the others. Not mentioned but realized, how effective a coalition they would make working as a team. A warm glow of unity flowed between them until Stara suddenly snapped it, remembering his remarks equating her with the young thief. She did not wish linkage with a knave who threatened exposure. The next minute she gave Marcus such a distant, glacial stare, he had to turn up his collar and pretend to shiver.

There was no pretense about the chills Stara felt up her own spine the following afternoon when the butler announced the name of two unexpected visitors.

The duke was discussing hunting with the marquis, Lady Gwendolen was in her room resting, Stara and Marcus had been pretending to read while keeping one eye on the other—covert glance by covert glance, when Stara turned round in dismay.

Rising immediately, if not to the occasion at least to the butler, Stara informed him to put the visitors in the yellow saloon and that she would be arriving directly to handle the matter.

"Shall they be offered refreshments?" the old retainer inquired.

"No! I mean, yes, of course. Some tea, but no spread."

"I understand, miss."

Smithers did not need more of a hint than this. The small saloon and 'just tea' established them as people the butler could afford to snub as much as he wished. To the duke it clearly meant they were people beneath his notice, and so he did not even ask about them. He continued his conversation.

Only Marcus was alert, sensing Stara's alarm, despite the unhurried way she walked out, airily excusing herself.

In a few moments however, Marcus followed. Recollecting Stara had said something about debts, he frowned and was concerned. Why didn't ladies know how to handle these dunners? She should have had the butler simply deny her, as he had trained his menials to do. Not that anyone dared approach *him*. Even at moments when finding himself without a feather to fly with Marcus still had an attitude that defied approach. Many a gentleman received in the best salons could live well on simply appearances. The correct invitations on the hall table, faultless attire and well-to-do acquaintances generally held any amount of creditors at bay. Marcus had all that plus such an air of aplomb, clearly announcing he was awash in expectations that kept the most tenacious creditor biding his time. Other gentlemen with more resources and not sufficient sangfroid would oft find themselves called to account for the most trifling accounts and wondered how Marcus Justus got away with it all. Some had the audacity to ask. Style, he would answer with a self-satisfied twinkle in his eye.

Approaching the small saloon, Marcus was frowning at the way Stara was lately making a botch of her affairs. Was she showing herself as a poor sportswoman who did not check the height of her fences before making the jump? Dash her! Would he have to ride to her rescue? But then perhaps that would not be unamusing, after all. For might not that be another way of getting her further under his obligation?

Voices were raised to a most shocking level, Marcus noted as he approached the closed door. It was near to a harangue as could be or should be in a gentleman's seat and with other gentlemen present to protect a lady guest.

Bristles up, Marcus immediately swaggered into the room.

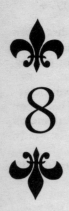

8

The sight that greeted him left him flummoxed.
His brave, daring, laughing Stara was sitting humbly on
the sofa being berated by a man and woman. He would
not honor these mushrooms to give them the appella-
tive of gentleman and lady, Marcus concluded, his air
of consequence rising as one's gorge did at the sight of
an accident.

The paunchy man was waving pound notes directly under Stara's nose. "What, miss, do you think we
could do with this sum! This don't settle half what we
put out for your papa's grave! And where's the money
for your schooling, miss? We are out of pocket for that,
as we've shown you before. That I 'spect is to be forgot.
Our care is to be forgot. We is just staff—is what your
unfeeling letter says. Even an old retainer would 'spect
more consideration than us got in those few lines! Gad,
such little feeling! Such little money!"

"I told you it was all I had!" Stara exclaimed, gasping as she caught sight of Marcus and instantly rising.

The Pinkertons' tirade momentarily abated at her inattention.

Marcus moved closer and lifting his quizzing-glass gave the two Pinkertons a look only equalled by the duke himself when spotting encroaching peasants.

The Pinkertons exchanged glances. The very haughtiness of the raised eyebrows of the gentleman assured the couple this was quality.

"Miss Carltons," Marcus said with disapproval. The high-pitched tones of the duke clued Stara instantly to his scheme. "I expect in the long, long, long years of my ancestors, duke after duke of Clairidges—me being the seventh—we have never found ourselves in the position of having to wait for a lady. Egad, did you not agree to meet me for a stroll?"

Several contrary thoughts vied in Stara's brain. Should she play along with his pretense? Or expose him as an impostor? It depended on Marcus's reason for the impersonation. Quickly Stara looked at the awed expressions on the Pinkertons' faces as they realized they were in the presence of an actual duke. Next she stared at Marcus's simpering idiotic grin, closely emulating the duke's when he was the most self-satisfied. Whatever the purpose, her sense of adventure was up. She could not but let the game continue. In fact, hiding her giggle she aided the pose by exclaiming, "Ah, your grace, I apologize. But my guardians, Mr. and Mrs. Pinkerton have paid me a surprise visit. They were just leaving, however."

"The sooner the better," the faux duke said, with an obvious yawn.

But the Pinkertons having had years of feeding on Stara, had become addicted and not likely to be so easily swept away. In fact, seeing her in such close relationship with quality, they doubled the amount they had come there to demand.

"Your grace, ahem, ahem," Mr. Pinkerton began, coughing a bit, to put his thoughts together. "As this lady's guardian," he patted himself on his plaid, expansive waistcoat, "I respectfully wish to remind you of her value. That is, ahem, she is of prodigious respectable birth. 'Spect her history goes back to the Conqueror. Demmed fine lineage." He paused to point at the lady with both of his thumbs. "Ahem, ahem . . . well brought up. Best schools."

Staring the man silent, Marcus's eyebrows rose higher if possible. "You ain't, by Jove, trying to *sell* this young lady to me, is you? Oddsblood, to be speaking in such a way about a friend of me intended! I shudder to think what her ladyship would say. We'd hoped to offer her a post as governess to our children some day. But if you're implying her morals are not what one would hope for that position, I shall urge Lady Gwendolen and the marquis to cast her off. As low as her position is in this establishment, still one would not wish for any *taint*."

In a flash Mrs. Pinkerton thought it best to intervene here. "Forgive my husband, your grace. He be speaking without thinking. He often brags about her background. We are so proud of the chit. Her teachers at that real fine finishing school—Miss Lanadale's, no less—always writ us how smart, how fine she plays the pianoforte. She is prodigious fit to be your intended's companion, I vow."

The duke waved them silent. "I don't wish to discuss such trivialities. You are all . . . trivial. I rather hoped you'd made yourself scarce. Not one to bother chatting with me inferiors, don't ya know. Have honored this lady with an occasional word, just so she could keep puffing me up to her ladyship, you know. From time to time one must deal with menials."

"You honor me, your grace," Stara said, understanding his drift now. He was set on presenting her as so lowly, her relatives would feel there was no use to further gouge her.

Indeed, this new image of Stara's position was not to the Pinkertons' liking. Nor was Mr. Pinkerton so easily ready to give up his hopes.

Quick glances darted between the couple. The husband however would not desist. The very panic in his wife's eyes reminded him she always collapsed at first charge, and he had to take on the battle. "I begs to say, your grace," he persisted, "Stara be much beloved by your beloved—or Lady Gwendolen. Her value to her ladyship and her pa, the marquis, makes her valued, I warrant, to yourself."

The duke who had gone to stand before the fire and was gazing into its depths turned at that. "Someone is still speaking!" he said, in shock. He'd made an exaggeratedly slow turn, reacting with affront at spotting the Pinkertons still there. "You were leaving, I thought."

"I was saying," Mr. Pinkerton said with a great deal of peeve, and he repeated his summation of Stara's value to the marquis and his daughter.

"Ah, yes. Ain't far wrong there. Valued a valet once meself. Fellow had the impudence to ask for a raise. Told him—you is fortunate just to be in me presence. Still, known for me liberality. Didn't turn the fellow off. But I couldn't have a gouger in me presence. The marquis was shocked I didn't boot the fellow out. Kept him on as a footman—in deference to his years of service. Soft heart, you know. Me one fault. The marquis is made of sterner stuff. Arrested a lad today for taking extra sticks from the Home Wood to warm his dying mother. Sad, sad case. Miss Carltons had the effrontery to speak for the child. Came nip close to losing her place here. We don't want gougers around us. Do we, Miss Carltons? I trust her ladyship made it clear you were never to overstep again or ask for more than is occasionally tossed your way."

"But she has such elegant clothes," Mrs. Pinkerton insisted, seeing all hopes of money for her daughters' dowries evaporating, and readjusting her wants down, to perhaps a gown or two.

Stara stepped in at that. "Yes, her ladyship is kind enough to give me some of the dresses she no longer wears. But I am obliged to pass them on to her dresser who has first call and has been with her longer. She would not have given me this dress, except that my other *one* she claimed offended her."

"Good heavens, yes! Positive scandal. Never thought to find myself in the presence of a lady with torn sleeves. There was a fire mark on the hem. (Marcus made a show of shuddering in disgust.) Quite overcame me. I mentioned it to her ladyship. One can't have such tawdriness in one's view. I said, 'Either give her a dress or banish her from me sight.' Poverty offends me, you know. Can't bear to see beggars coming near me with outstretched hands for handouts. *Chop 'em off!* I say!"

The Pinkertons jumped at that. Mrs. Pinkerton even put her own hands behind her back. They had indeed come for a handout. Stara who had been looking down at the ground humbly, looked up and saw the Pinkertons losing fight, edging toward the door. Indeed, Mrs. Pinkerton was even turning the doorknob, but her husband would not go without one last stab.

"I wish to see the marquis," he insisted, mulishly. "Surely he would treat your guardians, Stara, with accommodation?"

"Vain hope!" his grace replied. "More likely order you to take your charge home with you. He's been tallying up the charges he feels she owes. Saw the list meself. Board and food. I said to him. 'Let the chit work it off.' Her ladyship likes to have her hair dressed, and indeed, did she not give you that added assignment?"

"Yes," Stara breathed. "I am working off my indebtness to them by such tasks, but I was questioned by the marquis recently if I had any relatives who might be willing to supply some ready money, instead."

"Indeed," the duke said with a laugh. "Never saw a fellow so anxious for ready money. Loses so much of it at White's, don't ya know?" Without a qualm, Marcus destroyed the good, sedate marquis's reputation. Then as if struck by a thought, he said enthusiastically, "Got a notion he'd like to see you both! Miss Carltons always plays 'poor mouse' about her relatives. Says you ain't in position to help her financially. But you seem prosperous enough to me."

He paused to lift his quizzing-glass and give them a penetratingly one-eyed assessment. "Clothes without taste, but not frayed. Cheeks filled out. You ain't starvin', I presume. Bound to be able to clear some of this lady's indebtness. What say? Shall we call Old Sewed-Pockets himself. Probably owns the first shilling his father ever gave him—except for those he gambles away. Another notion! Egad, I'm filled with 'em! Did you come by your own coach? His lordship has a very knacky fella that can sell them off for a fair profit. No saying his lordship might even let you keep part of the leftover. Might not—though. Told you, dashed scaly fellow. Close as wax!"

"The carriage is not our own, your grace," Mr. Pinkerton inserted in dismay, panicking that rather than getting more money from Stara, he would have to pay some of her debts. His face was red with the terror of that. He too had reached the door, when the make-believe duke stopped them.

"Egad," he exclaimed. "Come all this way to see

your ward and not going to leave her a guinea or so to pay her *own gambling debts*! She owes me a couple of yellow boys for last weeks whist!"

That was beyond all. Pinkerton was coughing and mumbling about his debts as he bowed and backed out of the room, pulled out quickly and firmly by his red-faced wife. The door slammed behind them.

There was a momentary silence. Next second that was broken by the sound of Marcus Justus dropping his ducal persona and roaring with laughter. Quickly Stara rushed to the window. The Pinkertons were all but running to their own carriage, springing the horses. Gone.

Only then did Stara allow herself to join Marcus's laughter. So much glee did both feel at having given the couple the boot, they were unable to refrain from running into each other's arms. Marcus welcomed her with a mighty hug which had her recollecting her position and pulling away.

Next moment Stara was shaking her head at her own laughter and relief. These two had intimidated her for years—how was it possible that a mere performance would remove them? It was rather as if she'd had a lifetime of being haunted by two fearsome ghosts and Marcus had simply waved his hand and they'd disappeared. Her eyes were still hopeful but not completely euphoric. A pucker of a frown appeared on her forehead as Stara sat down on the settee and considered—was it possible she was now in a worse predicament? For Marcus's helping her meant she was further in debt to him. Nor did she relish his knowing her secrets. Then too, she was experienced with the Pinkertons.

"They are not usually so easily turned off!" she said, with a sigh of realism. "I must compliment you on your performance and your ability to send them away. But knowing them, they will reconnoiter and return.

They have always come at me for more. They are . . .
unremitting."

The voice was so unlike the spirited Stara he knew,
Marcus was aghast. The situation was not as amusing
as a moment before. "They've been bleeding you?" he
asked gruffly.

"Dry," she replied.

"And that's why you needed to play highwayman?"

"That was the incentive. They are my incentive for
everything I do. They took money my mother had arranged for my education. I had to teach and other
things to equal what they refused to pay at the end. But
when I called them to account, they presented me figures I could not disprove. Yet—blast them—for the
amounts they charged for the little stone on my
mother's grave, one would think it was a national mon-
ument! And other such charges of that ilk. Every piece
of bread I ever ate in their home was tallied up against
me. I have to be free of them," she suddenly exploded.
"At whatever cost! Yet I probably shall never be.
Rather they shall contact the marquis and he will be
kind enough to pay them. Whereupon once finding a
new source, they will never cry enough! They will become his pensioners, and I shall be under an intolerable
obligation to him. Eventually he will tire of paying
them for they are voracious in their demands. And I
shall be sent away."

Stara's eyes narrowed for an instant, in order more
easily to have her mind's eye receive the image of
Haven, her cottage in the wood. That would be lost to
her. As would her room in Hillcrest and the small one
in the London town house. The panic she'd felt at
school upon being told her tuition had not been met
and she must be dismissed—came back. Flooded her.
Stara faced the blue eyes above her that were show-

ing more and more astonishment. Obviously Marcus wasn't comprehending. She had to make herself clear to him. "I need to be *safe* someplace! Have a home. I would steal again if needs be for that . . . or marry an old man. Whatever the cost, I must have a *home*!"

That desire did not strike a sympathetic chord in Marcus. "What's a home?" he scoffed, with a bark of laughter, nonchalantly concluding, "Where'er I am, I'm at home. I'm a traveller. Thought you were a fellow spirit. Are you not an adventuress at soul? I had concluded you had enough daring to put to shame all the insipid ladies I've met round the world. Loathsome to see you reduced to groveling before those two naughts. The fire in you I swore could never be quenched was wiped out! By Jove, listen to yourself! You are even now thinking like them. Concluding money is all. Those money-grubbing underfoot Pinkertons are just base crumb takers off the tables of their betters! Is that what you wish for yourself—sniffing about the gentry for handouts! For shame!"

Ruffled at that, Stara slowly lifted her head, expanding from her cowered state. "And you! Are you not sniffing around Lady Gwendolen with the same objective of security!"

"Not a bit of comparison," he said unfazed. "I am a gentleman willing to allow a lady of means to have the immense pleasure of having *me* in her life. It is an even proposition. Just as when two gentlemen engage in a sporting proposition—one wins, one loses, but both understand the rules and both have the pleasure of the contest. Lady Gwendolen is aware of the rules of society. I shall either win her or another. It actually shall not be of great moment to me either way. Regardless, I shall be what I am. And whatever I do, it shall be done with style and for the proper purpose of my own amusement. It's all a game, is it not?"

"To you, perhaps," Stara replied, attempting to walk away, but he held her. "Where's my gamester girl —pluck to the backbone, risking all in her bouts with the lords and ladies, laughing all the while?"

Stara allowed she had enjoyed a laugh or two with the ton and at the ton, but basically she wished most earnestly to belong to the ton. Which she planned to do by enticing a lord to share his position with her. "Everything is an exchange, as you so wisely stated. The difference is that other ladies have parents to make these arrangements for them. Since I was a halfling, I've been my own mother and father in charge of my own future. I earned my own education, made my own connections into society. Marriage is basically used by a lady for advancement. Unless she is a Lady Gwen who has had everything given her all her life and thus finds it exciting to imagine being the concubine of One-Jewel Jack. Mere flummery! She'd swoon in shock after one day! Although I saw him once and he had a tolerable charm, possibly due to the mask. Yet as adventurous as one feels—marriage is the only honorable path for a penniless lady. So please do not stand in my way. If you think to use your knowledge of the Pinkertons against me, I warn you to think again. I play in earnest, because I want in earnest. If needs be I'll marry the marquis or even Lord Withers, who has been kind enough to send me a letter with an offer of marriage."

"Are you that mad for security, you would throw away all that makes life worth living!" Marcus exclaimed, truly aghast. "Is there nothing you would not shirk from in this mad dash to establish yourself! Lord Withers is ancient and corrupt. Thunderation! He is known for his severity to his wives. Used up two to the present. Do you have a desire to join them in the graveyard?"

Abruptly he paused to eye her silently, concluding

in amazement, "Are you after all another of these walking ice ladies experiencing all—once removed? Content to read about pleasure in the purple passages rhymed by our society's pet, the notorious Lord Byron?" He did not wait for her reply, rather answered himself "I think not. For *you* need not read about love nor adventure. You have both. And you can continue to experience both . . . with me."

"What a self-serving conclusion," Stara replied, laughing scornfully and then matter-of-factly, as if reminding herself of something of more pressing nature. "Speaking of serving oneself—it is near dinnertime and I must change." Then neatly evading his outstretched hand, she exited the room.

That left Marcus striding around the room until he was struck with a developing resolution that had him well pleased with himself. Obviously since the lady had her priorities out of balance, it was incumbent on himself to straighten her out. For it was infamous to allow such a woman to become one of old Withers's leavings! No, by heavens! Since it had come to that, he must use more than persuasion to take her away. He must act.

Three days after the Pinkertons' dismissal, Stara was beginning to think that Marcus had performed the impossibility of actually dislodging them from her back. In the midst of that miraculous hope another such loomed. The duke was becoming more attentive. Their private walks on the grounds were now everyday occurrences, during which she kept him interested by discussing himself, especially his estates. One spoke with the pride of present ownership and the other listened with the hope of future ownership.

"A pond, did you say? Directly before your castle?"

"Righto. Filled with feathers. Whole courtyard's amuck with peacock feathers. From peacocks. Beastly birds spread their tails and, plop! a feather! Snout-teasers! Oddsblood! Can't target the blighters. Fore-fathers liked 'em. Musta. Stocked up on 'em!" he ended gloomily.

That was similarly a gloomy conclusion for Stara. For it showed how massive were the obstacles in her path to becoming a duchess. If his grace kept birds he disliked just to oblige tradition and his ancestors, would he not more likely marry for that reason as well? Had she been allowing her hopes to fly too high—as Marcus's sardonic glances indicated every time he spotted her with his grace. But yet she had some indications his grace was veering past friendship. He'd gripped her hand with unnecessary force when helping her over a rock fence the other day. Then too there was the moment when he leaned shockingly close to peer into her eyes. "Fiery orbs, what?" he had said. "Could light a man's lamp at night, I daresay."

She thanked him with a bashful curtsy, and he bowed to her. Then they walked about, both rather pleased with his grace.

Later on, Stara advanced on that advance by mentioning she had recorded his remark in her copybook for its poetic beauty.

There was a slight setback when the duke had to be reminded which remark she meant, and she was forced to shyly show him the couplet on the page, which she'd improved. "Your eyes are like fiery orbs, I say That could light a man's night into day."

He was pleased to see it there. "Said that, did I? By Jove!"

She did herself no disservice by claiming the lines would fair equal Byron's. (May that poet forgive her, she thought with a qualm, but recollected that he was suffering a great many worse jabs of late.)

The effectiveness of Stara's comparing him to that poet became evident the next day when his grace appeared with a volume of Byron's short poems in hand! He wished her to mark two or three phrases that were comparable to his own?

Blinking at that audacity, Stara was quick to comply. His grace explained he did not wish to put himself to the fatigue of reading *inferior* poems. The bubble of laughter within her had to be firmly squelched while she circled the lines he might honor with his attention.

"Maid of Athens, ere we part, Give, oh, give me back my heart!" was one, which his grace however found objectionable since he had no acquaintance with ladies from Athens and would not bestow his heart on a mere maid, regardless of her country of origin. "Not the thing," he reminded her gently, "for a duke." However he was well satisfied with "She walks in beauty, like the night of cloudless climes and starry skies."

"Like clear weather meself," he said to that. Afterward he surprised Stara by committing it to memory and quoting it to her during their walks, again and again, until she, like the matrons of the ton, was near to banishing Lord Byron forever!

Without doubt, his grace's interest in her was becoming more marked. Oh, Stara exclaimed with a qualm of anguish how easily she would have won him if she'd had even minimal standing! Or if only Lady Gwen were out of the picture. To make this happen, Stara found herself daydreaming about the real One-Jewel Jack abducting her ladyship. But Stara cut through those fantasies with a vigorous shake of her head. Heavens, she was beginning to believe her own stories. One-Jewel Jack was not in love with Lady Gwendolen! But as long as her ladyship believed otherwise, no other gentleman—duke or rake—was able to win her total attention, which left maneuvering room for Stara.

Then into this happy time came a sudden shock. Just when she'd persuaded herself to forget the Pinkertons, she heard from them. It was with true dismay she opened their letter. The contents threw her into a confusion and then upon understanding the gist into a full-fledged flutter. The redoubtable Pinkertons had concluded that since Stara was no longer in position to redeem her obligation to them, she must *earn* her debt! They would be kind enough to find her a position as governess and arrange to attach half her wages. They preferred a speedier return but were showing consideration. If she did not posthaste agree to this most equitable arrangement, they would be forced to send notice of her delinquency to the bailiff.

After the obligatory quaking at any mention of that happy pair, anger predominated. How dare they continue to harass her? There was no debt owing! Never had been! She would no longer be tormented by such an imaginary claim. Insufferable clodpoles! she exclaimed, shrugging her shoulders as if she could shake them off. Encouraged by his grace's recent attentions, Stara took heart and wrote to refuse both the position as governess and all further claims on her. This was signed with a flourish of three lines that communicated her contempt.

With the letter on its way, Stara steadfastly continued assuring herself she'd acted correctly. Undoubtedly she'd been too accommodating to these people all her life. Time they were shown the door in no uncertain terms!

Stara's firm resolve lasted for several days until the butler brought a salver with another letter—this one from the Pinkertons' solicitor, Mr. Lantern. Obviously they had been expecting her response and had prepared a checkmate. Mr. Lantern went to some lengths to prove the legality of the Pinkerton claim, fully documenting the entire history of the debt, based on several signatures of her mother's. If Miss Carltons further disputed the matter, she was informed, it could be brought to magistrate's court. In the interim, however, they would be forced to have her placed in bailiff's jail, until the matter was adjudicated.

Stara turned white. Her eyes fiery orbs indeed! "Oh tenacious!" she groaned.

If the Pinkertons had gone to the expense of a solicitor, they must be confident of their case. Her mother undoubtedly could have been persuaded to sign anything they wished. Reviewing all options, Stara could find no escape. For her thoughts led only to the realization of how firmly she was held! She had been in society enough to recollect tales of several lords themselves who had been placed in bailiff's house for debts. The tales of conditions in there were not what a lady could countenance. As well as being barred and locked, the places were known for filth and for people of the lowest breeding. Imprisonment in a sponging house would henceforth have her regarded as having lost all shreds of decency. Further, money was needed just to survive there—bribes continually demanded for the most basic necessities. Normally relatives or friends quickly arrived with the sums to effect the speediest liberation. But it was relations who would be putting her in! Stara closed her eyes. More than likely there was worse ahead. Lacking money for solicitors, she had scant hope of winning upon the case's advancing to magistrate's court. Indeed it was whispered once the courts had one in control, even if the decision was in one's favor, fourfold as much money was required in court fees as was owed in the first place! Thus the general solution was to make some agreement with creditors before the Point Non Plus was reached. Most dire of all would be losing her case. For if being under bailiff's arrest was difficult, Newgate prison was a monstrous agony. None but the most hardened could survive it. That explained why gentry in her position, without accommodating friends, concluded it was preferable to flee the country rather than trusting themselves to the tender mercies of this proud English penal purgatory.

For several days Stara was pale—castigating herself for replying in so cavalier a manner, which had precipitated her present position. She was in the deuce of a fix. Yet eventually, as was her nature, Stara caught herself up by the scruff of her neck and stood up to her problem. She'd always had a most dependable recourse throughout her life and that was to her own wits. Now she concluded the main object was to gain time to decide which way lay her future. Reluctantly Stara sat down and wrote a conciliatory epistle to the Pinkertons. Having gone down on her knees to Lady Gwendolen, she claimed, her ladyship finally gave her an amount which, though less than that of a governess's salary, would at least lessen her debt, forthwith. They had to see the benefit of so immediate a recompense especially since there was no assurance she would be suitable governess material. Of late she'd sunk in health, she confided, which made it most unlikely she would give any satisfaction. Undoubtedly she would be quickly dismissed. What avail would that be to the Pinkertons? Or even her being under bailiff's arrest? For she could scarce *ever* get a job afterward. Yet a little patience would reward them well, as eventually Stara hoped to persuade her ladyship to more liberal an offering.

Grimly, her face and eyes devoid of all their usual sparkle, Stara went to her hoard of money from the

One-Jewel Jack expedition and emptied it of all but a few guineas. Her nest egg was gone. Gone the buffer against the possibility that none of her matrimonial plans would come to fruition, against even Lady Gwendolen's marrying and no longer having need of her. Yet one security remained. She still had the pearls and the duke's stickpin. When the Pinkertons came again for another slice of her, those would protect against final imprisonment. The insignia ring, Stara concluded bitterly, could not be sold without fear of discovery, so it was of little aid. How earnestly did she wish now that she'd taken more from her ladyship's jewel box.

A letter from the Pinkertons arrived, agreeing to a reprieve, begrudgingly consenting to accept the money but urging her to strive for the balance. Incidentally that very balance had strangely increased rather than decreased despite Stara's payment, since they were forced to add the cost of their solicitor to the amount of her debt. Stara almost shrieked. Every attempt to extricate herself from their hold only revealed added strings!

Ill fate always attacked in groups, she'd believed, and was proven correct when Marcus, observing her growing closeness with the duke, acted. It began after she'd make an unwise remark alerting Marcus to the very sizeable inroads she was making in the duke's regard.

"What think!" Stara said with a proud twinkle in her eyes. "His grace is attempting to write me a sonnet!"

So aghast was Marcus at the very image of the duke stomping through the poetic fields that he could not even smile. Rather his face took on a very set and determined expression that should have forewarned Stara. But he gave her a bow of respect and said, "It appears I have been remiss," which she took as a compliment. Later she realized it was a warning, not obvi-

ous till the morning when he returned from his ride and
called all the breakfasters to attend him and his discovery.

Lady Gwen rose languidly from the table and the
marquis approached with some interest. The duke
sauntered in, with quizzing-glass in place. Only Stara
stood stock-still, feeling she would shortly find herself
at a stand. It was there in Marcus's tone and the sudden
glance her way. At length she could not but join the
company, especially when Marcus said with a devilish
delight, "We await your pleasure, Miss Carltons." And
there he stood, blond hair in some disorder from his
gallop, eyes mocking—turning amethyst with anticipation of his pleasure to come—as he tossed a sack on the
drawing-room table.

"What is in that bag?" Lady Gwen inquired, politely.

"A discovery that proves your ladyship is correct
about One-Jewel Jack," Marcus began, after a dramatic
pause.

Instantly both ladies cried out.

"Yes, that devil of a highwayman has been lurking
round here. I saw him myself, and gave chase. Upon his
hearing me approach, the ruffian took off, dropping
something in his rush. I gave further chase, but his cohorts were close by, gathering round to protect him,
and then all together the band of thieves rode off."

Many exclamations were punctuating Marcus's re-
cital and one noticeable deadly silence from Stara. Marcus carried on in an exaggerated tone, his deep, blue
eyes filled with the devilry of his decision. Indeed while
noting the absolute numbness of Stara's face, he became
even more exuberant, "Thunder and turf!" he continued, "I was without a pistol, having just gone for a
morning jaunt, so he escaped my clutches, unwinged.
But I did not return empty-handed. No indeed! I recol-

lected the object he had dropped and made a dash back
to retrieve it. And brought it posthaste . . . here . . .
to you . . . all."

With a grin of total triumph, Marcus pointed to
the sack.

"What ho!" the duke said rushing forward.

"You frightened my admirer away?" Lady Gwen
whispered in disapproval.

"Good show," the marquis said.

Stara just continued to stare a hole in Marcus's
forehead. He was smiling back at her, content she was
not carrying her pistols. Otherwise he was certain there
would be one shot already through his head and another through his heart. But Marcus was unintimidated,
rather he returned an unfazed, unrepentant, irrepressible gleam of mischief.

In the next moment with a flourishing gesture, he
opened the bag and revealed the duke's insignia ring
and stickpin. Laid them flat on the boulle table before
everyone.

His grace uttered an oath, apologized to the ladies
for it and quickly snatched up his lost property. He was
particularly pleased with the return of the insignia ring.
Not that he cared for the value of it, but there'd been a
gnawing thought that some other fellow would be
wearing the Clairidge crest. "Confusing, what?" he
said. And now, all would be clear again, he grinned
happily.

"I doubt anyone would have imagined that One-
Jewel Jack was your grace," the marquis said, but was
pleased nevertheless that his honored guest had re-
claimed his lost property. No one even mentioned the
lost guineas. They meant so little to them. Rather Lady
Gwen was still grumbling about Marcus having chased
off her admirer, concluding with a plaintive hope, "He
might have been planning to send me a note."

"But, your ladyship," Marcus exclaimed. "Would you not have preferred the return of this!" And he held up the pearls.

Languidly Lady Gwen reached for them. They had not been missed. Actually she preferred to think that One-Jewel Jack was holding them in his hands and thinking of her beautiful neck, as Stara had so poignantly visualized for her.

The return of the jewels was a mere day's wonder. After that forgotten. Only Stara would never forget Marcus's act. That ramshackle, rackety knave had beggared her. She had risked her life, after all, for naught! Even after emptying her purse for the Pinkertons, she felt some ease knowing she still had the security of the pearls. Now her pockets were clearly to let. And what was the benefit of the return of the jewels, she thought in justification for her act. Lady Gwen was gloomy rather than glad at her pearls return. But most vexing was Marcus's behavior. Hadn't he all but promised not to expose her? Yet though he hadn't exposed her, he'd undone her. Confound him! What a very devil of an opponent!

When that very blackguard stopped her in the garden, he had the audacity to grin and say, "I've freed your conscience of that deed . . . and its possible consequences. Are you not grateful?"

"You have beggared me. I no longer have a whit of security. That makes it essential I choose a husband the moment we return to London. And what did the gesture avail you? Do you so enjoy combat, you make a finishing blow even when your opponent is disarmed and trusted you to hold to some level of fairness? Well, so be it! I know you now for the black-hearted, unfeeling wretch you are! Henceforth I resolve ne'er to be in your company again. I am finished with you."

"I think not, Miss Carltons. All this fury over a

few trinkets! I thought you had wits enough to realize the reason for my act. Actually I have just made certain that you do not have any other option but the one I am offering. You wish a house? Very well, I shall buy you one. You wish pearls? I shall give them to you. But they shall be yours. Not stolen."

Stara's eyes glowed with fury. "If you think you can push me into being your mistress, you mistake me and my character. And further, further, you underestimate my allure. His grace is day by day showing signs of definite desire for me. Your removing the security of the jewels only makes it essential I take more risks, which as you know, I am not loath to do. Have no fear I shall come about. I have done so all my life. I shall win what I wish yet. While you have lost all. Not only me but Lady Gwendolen."

With a sigh of pleasure at this retaliation, Stara continued informing Marcus that her ladyship had confessed to her that her heart was at long last taken—by One-Jewel Jack.

"You stupid bacon brain. What a great opportunity you allowed to slip by. Your way was one of monstrous simplicity. I was distracting the duke. With the slightest effort you might have returned to London engaged to her ladyship. But rather you spent your time destroying my chances. And have just lost yours."

"Perhaps," he said, with an unusually deceptive gentle voice. "Quite possibly I've discovered a preference to have you in my arms than any kind of security?" He moved toward her slowly, step by step.

"Stay!" Stara cried in alarm, moving back. "I . . . I will not allow you to touch me again. We are finished. You . . ."

He smothered her words under his lips. And both of them kissed for several moments. He threw back his head and laughed. "You might as well stop the sun from rising than stop this feeling between us. Stop denying it," he was whispering now, but still the need was there, in the breathless linking of his words, in the firm, unswerving glare, holding her eyes with his uncompromising ones. "You *do* know. I see it in your eyes. This feeling shall devour both of us, unless we give it its head. Come to me tonight. Come and let us seal our future together in a blaze of . . . joy."

In response Stara stomped hard on the toes of his boots with her heel and walked away with satisfaction. "A heel for a heel," she said with a laugh. "Now go spend the night with the devil and may he or she take you for his own!"

She could hear cursing as she ran up to her room. Enfevered, she began packing for her journey back to London.

The devil take him indeed, Stara vowed. For, if not, Marcus would have her, ere she could protect herself from the disgrace he and her heart was pushing her rapidly, unremittingly, toward.

9

London *was all delight to have its two ac-*knowledged beauties back in the midst of its social whirl. Lady Gwendolen was looking more languid than usual, and the *on-dit* was that she was feeling a *tendre* for a gentleman. Since both Mr. Justus and the duke had been with her, the bets were about even as to which had won her favor.

The second beauty was of course, Stara. She looked even more glorious than before; her spirits higher, her flirting more daring. The gentlemen were entranced while the ladies primly justified at her finally showing her true spots. She was near, the ladies assured each other, to tying her garter in public; they would keep a wary eye to see if all this flirting and smiling, which was up to the line would not cross over. Then, they would have the pleasure of announcing her ostracism. But Stara, though in a frenzy of flaunting her wares, to be gross about it, stopped before she looked shopworn. This determination to attract came from the hysteria that the Pinkertons would strike, that Marcus would win her over to a life of disrepute and worse, worse, that this was her last opportunity to make a respectable connection before she would very likely be locked away either in a prison for debts, the prison of a life as a governess or at best, the more elegant prison of being a companion to her ladyship. Now or never she kept saying to herself. Her dark eyes that had always seemed like velvet, capturing in their softness and smoothness all her admirers, were of late roguishly dancing. They'd become like flint and a gentleman who looked deeply into them did so at his peril, for sparks would fly out and sting him, burn him, even set him completely afire.

Marcus was grimly aware of this newly unleashed Stara and kept a wary watch. Flitting about, he longed to pin back her wings and sweep her away from all. Yet he could just follow her about. There was always the moment when he could take no more of her being surrounded by some of the most disreputable rakes and younger sons and a few eligible lords, and then he would drop his cool composure and frankly take her away from them all.

"You are making a spectacle of yourself. Even Lady Gwen has mentioned that she cannot understand why you have become so wild. What are you attempting?"

"I am displaying myself," she said with a small laugh.

"I gathered that. But to what purpose? Every gentleman here would bed you in a blink, if that is your aim. But I believe I was first there."

Stara gave him a glance of such fury that left him deliciously awash in her emotion as she whispered, "Why do you speak like that! Do you enjoy insulting me? I have explained I am not interested in disreputable proposals, *from anyone.* Nor am I likely to succumb to

one no matter how offensively phrased. Although one
wonders how you assume that being coarse shall so
enrapture me that I shall throw away all scruples just
for the privilege of continuing to be so offended. The
mind boggles. Have you ever achieved success with a
female by that vulgar route?"

He threw back his head and laughed. "You are
always so refreshingly frank. 'Tis true I would never use
such tactics on a lady I was attempting to woo, but I
have already won you. Your heart is mine, it is simply a
matter of reducing your high expectations, so you
might accept my lower position."

Stara shook her glowing dark hair that had flowers
wound through the curls and made her look like the
queen of summer. She had chosen fragrant vines of
honeysuckle and hung them alongside her thick, dangling curls to contrast the darkness of her hair while
bringing attention to the flowerlike softness of her
shoulders. The rest of the ladies were positively erupting with jewels. Every kind of stone was blazingly present as well as gold and silver and simple strands of
pearls for the younger maidens. None equalled Lady
Gwendolen's famous pink pearls, which she wore now
with matching pearl combs bought by her father to recompense for the trauma of the pearls temporary loss.
Ladies usually wore one comb at the crown or even two
on each side, but Lady Gwen wore five altogether—the
three in the usual positions mentioned and the other
two stuck over her brow—giving the illusion of a
pearled fringe. Altogether regal, she decided, befitting a
queen of society. Lady Gwendolen further promoted
that impression with her gown of gold net over a silk
petticoat, outdoing the rest of the ladies merely in lavish
lace and silks, and possibly overwhelming Stara in her
simple white muslin.

Still, inexplicably, Stara shone.

It was a topic of discussion amongst several rakes as to the cause of the glow. Without a jewel, a silk, whence came the sheen? It was agreed it came from within. Radiating a light, as if she were inner candle-lit, Stara moved among her admirers. Here a smile, there a sparkling glance, here a toss of her long black curls, there a touch of her hand. She centered their attention. Stara, well named, all the gentlemen concluded, but none had leave to so address her. Stara—a shiny, pure star of white surrounded by the dark sky of her hair.

"You are so prodigiously beautiful," Marcus said, momentarily forgetting his stratagem and giving her an all-encompassing, warm smile she felt with pleasure and returned with delight.

"Beware, Mr. Justus, you are flattering me. That is not your aim, surely. Heavens, I might think you have a heart, after all."

He laughed at that. "We have already established that I have not. As you have not. But *I* make no pretense that I do. I am honest enough to admit my lack."

"Ah, that is better. Back to insults. I am dishonest? Yet it is my honesty that has overset you. I said I am here to find myself a lord for a husband. Why do you keep *not* believing me. Indeed, I shall be further frank. I have, I am pleased to announce already won the heart of Lord Stockley. He is not above two and thirty, but regrettably he is hunting-mad, which is the principal reason I have not succumbed and thrown my heart over his fences. To continue with my remarkable honesty, Marmaduke is being less particular in his addresses here than at Hillcrest. High-ho! If it is not to be he, it shall be someone else. One must lower one's sights. But never, *ever* sink them to the depth of depravity you have set for me."

He whirled her around silently, not replying. In perplexity Stara stared at his fixed visage, adding another jab to awaken him to their jousting. "Can I have been more honest with you, Mr. Justus, more clear about my answers and my purposes?"

That roused him to respond, but he did so with a tight voice and his eyes flaying out at her for her very honesty. "You pretend honesty. But you are false—as long as you speak only from your will and not your heart. Look inward and you will know, as I do, that you are mine and have been mine from the first moment we met. And that is why I have dropped my pursuit of Lady Gwen and am waiting for you to be honest for both of us. I have accepted you as you are—a money-mad, position-climbing adventuress in society. Why cannot you admit what is between us? With every beat of your heart, you must hear the truth that you are being false through and through, not only to me but to your own self."

His blue eyes bore into hers and for the first time that night she was forced to feel some shame. She danced in silence with him for a step or two, and then cried out, "I will not care for you! You cannot shame me into that! You best leave me and my purposes and my false heart . . . to beat to its own rhythm."

He held her closer then, until the rhythm of both their hearts pounded in both their ears and senses. She closed her eyes to her thoughts and he to her purposes, and they just felt their way through the dance. When it was over, he bowed to her. Stara stared sadly and then reached over and gently touched his cheek, as if in good-bye. Marcus felt that fluttery stroke through his body. Upon her walking away, he observed her being instantly snatched up by the waiting Lord Stockley, and Marcus closed his eyes to it, awash in the sickening sense she might be an unattainable challenge, after all.

Abruptly Marcus left the ballroom. Rather he joined the gentlemen in the card room and relieved his

failure with Stara by winning several thousand pounds
from the best gambler around, Lord Finmore.

Looking about, Stara felt his departure and neglect
with a physical unease. Regardless of Stara's wishes, it
was nigh unto impossible for her to forget Marcus. If in
the same room, she was always sensing where he was. If
he were not yet there, she was anticipating his arrival or
chagrined at his departure. What centered her so completely was the way Marcus's eyes always reverted to
her, even while conversing with the other beauties of
the ton. Stara belittled that possessive glance by equating it to a hungry man who while supping on more
substantial fare, checked to see if the sweet tart he'd
reserved for himself was still there, in case he had need
of a snack in the middle of the night. By heavens if a
gentleman wanted her, it would have to be for the main
course.

Her constant comparing his attitude with hunger
was really most apropos. For indeed Marcus's devour-
ing stare relayed the sensation that if he were not eating
her with his eyes, at least, he was stripping her with
them. From the beginning even matrons had whispered
that Mr. Justus gave them the sense he could see them
all in their petticoats. Stara, having overheard that, conveyed it to Mr. Justus leaving him in a roar. "Egad,
what a picture! All the ladies in their underclothes before me. Even I could not have dreamed that one up.
Tell them I am much obliged for the thought."

One could not reach Marcus with insults. Whatever chastising term—vulgar, ungentlemanly, even a
scapegrace, left him merely amused, taking it as a mark
of credit. Once, upon Stara's using almost ten such epi-
thets in a row, he was in such delight he asked her to
slow up and say them singly, that he might relish each
one of her endearments. And his eyes would twinkle.
Unabashed.

At every ball or rout other women continued to throw lures his way. In Stara's presence, Marcus would often respond to them, just to show she was not completely in charge of his heart. In fact he would on certain evenings pretend to have forgotten her totally, concentrating on ladies of title and wealth. So blatant were his attentions that Stara, against her will, felt a flush of jealousy she would struggle all evening to suppress.

What particularly galled was that Marcus never bothered to offer her a single gallantry. Unlike the others. Lord Stockley constantly asked for her glove to hold or the privilege of leading her to the marquis's carriage. So determined was Marcus not to be a husband, he husbanded even the most minimum courtesy of sending her flowers while first time acquaintances filled her room with blooms!

So Stara, if she did not cut him, at least maintained an attitude of deliberate nonobservance. Until the moment when unexpectedly one spotted the other. Then there would occur a lift, a blending, even a new energy that instantly sank when the other departed. Both felt it. The lady squelched it. The gentleman savored it. His certainty of eventually winning her increasing. But the waiting rankled.

One morning having returned from Manton's Shooting Gallery in which he had won much applause for hitting six wafers in a row (imagining each one was Stara's beau), Marcus entered his apartments to be handed a letter delivered two hours previous. From the frank or the signature on the outside, he knew at once it came from his father, Lord Windsor. Not having seen the earl since returning to England, Marcus opened the letter with some foreboding. The last communication between father and son was when his lordship had cut off his allowance, being vastly displeased at his mode of living. One wondered what more the old man could do to him, after having set him adrift.

A quick scanning through the note had Marcus letting out a mighty laugh!

Dash it all, his lordship be praised, he was *reinstated*! Who could have expected this? Throughout his life he'd trained himself to expect the least from Lord Windsor. But this! With no forewarning, no quibbling, no negotiations. Just capitulation! It was not to be believed! Nor could he recognize the style, which had actual edges of kindness. That left Marcus knocked acock. Once more he read the letter to understand the specifics. His annuity was reestablished, on the basis of reports reaching the earl that his offspring was living a more conventional, even honorable life. He hoped, indeed, to have the pleasure of someday soon welcoming Lady Gwendolen into their family. A further mark of favor was the earl's willingness to grant his son an audience.

While delighted at the income, Marcus did not feel this was the moment to be away from Stara. Not only was Lord Stockley becoming marked in his attentions, but other gentlemen as well were attracted by her fire. The chit would be wed before he returned from his father's estate.

Reason told him it was of first necessity that Marcus seek the earl and mend fences before his father heard Lady Gwen was no longer his object. Still, still, blast her, he could not be away from Stara. She lured him with her smile. She kept him fluttering round her with her sparkle. He'd rather risk an annuity than risk losing her. Actually his heart was buried deep within her eyes and he could not leave it for any span of time.

That sudden realization had Marcus opening his own eyes. Obviously this was more than desire, more than a *tendre*. Egad, he loved her. Finally Marcus Justus had fallen headlong into the dashed pit of love.

After all the ladies he had flirted with and dallied with to find himself getting the same treatment! Just punishment at last. And yet, it was delicious to feel this love. It took away the ennui of each day. It gave hope of future. Desire to the present. And joy to each hour knowing he would see her again.

For all his years in Europe and previously while well earning the title of the rake of London society, Marcus had laughed at people controlled by their emotions. Proudly he'd kept his firmly in hand. No lady, no friend could quite reach past his armor of amusement and mocking self-preservation. At one point, he'd even almost forgotten his love of England while basking in the variety of new lands. But there had come the day in all his travels when he'd heard an English voice and had jumped up from his table at the café and accosted the gentleman, just to hear how things were at home. In typical British style, the gentleman was offended at the intrusion and Marcus had to beg pardon and sulk away, laughing at himself for wanting something so obviously not worth the effort. Yet, it had reminded him of home, of his youth on the earl's estate, of the portrait gallery, which held the last memory of his mother. Relegated to an unimposing position in the rear was the picture of the second countess. He'd heard some poet had called her the beautiful Lenore. The portrait verified that, showing a fragile lady of guinea gold hair and blue eyes, like his own, holding on to a young boy that was himself. Someday, when his brother took over the earldom, he would ask for that painting.

There were several of the viscount's mother—a hearty, dark-haired lady depicted in a riding outfit with her favorite hound. She had fallen over a fence and died, shortly after giving birth to the heir. And then the

earl had married again some ten years later. He'd
proved unfortunate in the health of his wives, for the
second one died when Marcus was five. The earl had
not chanced a third. He'd settled for two sons and concentrated on his horses and the pride in his lineage to
take up his days. His lordship was a cold, unfeeling
man who just about tolerated both sons, although he
had some pride in his heir. Thus Marcus, never having
been taught love, except for the dim memory of his
mother, assumed he as well could do without that cum-
bersome commodity. Rather he'd determined to laugh
through life. When that paled, he took chances to dis-
place the boredom and gained his reputation as a wild
boy, earning the displeasure of his brother and father.
Yet admittedly wild starts were the only way of ever
winning their attention. So he continued on till he became a past master of daring. As a youth in London
that reputation of hell-bent won him a score of ladies
which oft resulted in secret duels on morning hilltops.
More respectable were his victories in racing. Driving
his curricle he'd beaten even the regent's record, although that was never officially acknowledged. In all
games of chance he excelled, priding himself on never
exhibiting emotion—whether winning or losing. That
attitude hardened on the day his father disowned him.
Not only did Marcus keep his composure, but he cyni-
cally concluded that abandonment proved love did not
exist in the best of families. Henceforth his mask of
nonchalance grew thicker, seeing him through exile and
times of poverty and loneliness. Indeed the Honorable
Marcus Justus actually taunted fate to present him with
any event or person that would affect him in the least.
And it was fate that had finally to admit defeat. Marcus
lived untouched. In his most dire circumstances,
through all his exile and return, he trusted to his luck in
gaming to see him through. Inevitably the right card

turned up as well as the right lady to share in his winnings.

Then, quietly, perversely fate dealt him a card that left him dumbfounded. Marcus was presented with a lady adventuress who forced him to reexamine his facade. It was small wonder he was reluctant to admit how deeply she'd reached him. To do so would mean having to dismiss his image of the unaffected, sought-after blade of a gentleman. Eventually Stara made such inroads in his life he found himself altering his prior life-style. Hadn't she already stopped him seeking Lady Gwen? Even her strict refusal to be his dishonorably had him finally, grudgingly coming round to considering the possibility of offering her marriage. The very thought of that had him in shock. But he'd said it to himself and soon began to accept the word if not the actual deed. He was prepared to think of it but not quite prepared to propose. Many opportunities presented themselves but Marcus could not quite bring himself to his knees.

In a sennight there would be an unexceptionable occasion for that grand gesture—at a ball of greatest magnificence given by none other than Lady Jersey. That lady was one of the most respected women of the ton who had earned her status through the most unimpeachable and unenvied manner as the prince regent's mistress. Although long succeeded by other ladies, that royal touch apparently had lasting qualities. She'd become a patroness of Almack's, the most august of all the clubs, and thus could signify who was or was not socially acceptable. To gain entry to Almack's one needed a voucher by any of the several select patronesses. There was no way around these ladies—hardly a problem for Marcus whose main talent apparently was getting around ladies of all ages. Lady Jersey, although in her forties, still assumed she had sufficient charm to be admired by a most attractive young man. Marcus needed just one of his lazy smiles followed by his deep, concentrated gaze to have her forcing a voucher on him, unasked.

Without question, Lady Gwen had a voucher for herself, but nothing could persuade Lady Jersey, nor the other patroness, to give one to Stara. So while invited to the lesser affairs, Stara ached in her heart to scale the hallowed walls of Almack's. Lady Gwendolen might have exerted herself to request one for her companion, but her ladyship had purposely not done so. Indeed, when a kinder patroness, Lady Sefton, asked if she wished a voucher for Miss Carltons, Lady Gwen had concluded complacently, "Stara does well enough at other balls."

Consequently Almack's affairs were always rather dull for Marcus. Naturally he supposed since Lady Jersey's grand ball was to go beyond the usual Almack's dimensions, she might ease the rules for a wider attendance, admitting Miss Carltons. He hinted as much to Lady Jersey only to be rebuffed. After which Marcus was uncertain whether he would attend; it was more than likely going to be as deadly boring as were the rest of Almack's affairs without Stara. Yet it was to his interest at least to make an appearance to secure his position, which was at best unsettled and to flaunt his better entry before Stara's envious eyes.

He took occasion to twit Stara with his Almack's triumph during their morning rides at Hyde Park. Despite their continuous sparring, it seemed essential to have some private moments together of a week. The ostensible excuse they used was enjoying each other's horsemanship. Instead of the sedate style of most lords and ladies, they rode together at a matching pace.

"Anybody who is anybody will be at Lady Jersey's ball and those excluded shall be marked, indeed," Marcus could not resist mentioning with the twinkle in his eyes, yet keeping his voice at its most consoling. As usual Stara surprised him by her honesty, confessing how far from pleased she was. "The marquis if not Lady Gwen, I am persuaded, could have gained me entry." While she was expressing her outrage, the gentleman fell into a reverie on her many points of beauty —her seat on the animal, her fine, light handling of the reins and her plumed riding hat over a new hair arrangement of one long heavily coiled braid drifting down her back. He centered in on her eyes now, since they were shooting fire at being excluded. Always such a dashed pleasure to see her riled. It was but a step to imagine her awash in some other emotion such as sensuality . . . and himself the cause. To stoke her fire Marcus suavely mentioned *en passant* that he'd heard from an unimpeachable source (Lady Sefton, herself) that Lady Gwendolen had purposely turned down a voucher for Stara when one *was* offered.

His ploy at first succeeded beyond his hopes as Stara's face turned red. But next minute she'd regained her color and composure, answering matter-of-factly that was "obvious twaddle." Her friend might not have put herself to the trouble of securing a voucher, but she wouldn't *purposely* exclude her. The only response to that was a sly smile so steady that Stara began to have more doubts than if he'd used a dozen arguments. He goaded her further by asking suddenly if she'd heard about the unusual decoration planned for the ball. It was whispered that crimson, being her ladyship's favorite color, was going to bedeck the ballroom. Awnings of it were to be positioned on the balconies holding the orchestra, from whence the elegant sounds would come wafting down upon the select, blessing the crème de la crème. Stara attempted to turn the conversation into other paths, as she turned her horse toward the gardens. But Marcus, shoulders beginning to shake with quiet laughter, was continuing on. He understood Lady Jersey was to wear a crimson gown.

"She shall then match the drapes to perfection. And put all taste to the blush," Stara could not resist countering.

Yet Marcus would not be stilled. Was it not true that the Duke of Clairidge, no less, was escorting Lady Gwendolen to this affair? What had happened to *her* attraction? A passing fancy? A sign that she was being passed over by all—as shown by her exclusion from the most social events? And so on. Marcus pinked her here and darted her there, until Stara was maddened by her exclusion. At last she blew, showing herself the madcap hellion he always suspected was at the core. "I shall not be overlooked like this! By heavens, I'll do something to shake them all! Break into the affair, if needs be. You are correct, this affront rankles and I must do something to ease it! Oh if only it were a masquerade I could come masked and watch you all! But I shall be nearby, I vow. If not actually," she said, spotting her groom and tipping her riding crop to Mr. Justus in adieu, "then at least in spirit. Dance one waltz with an unknown lady, and pretend it is me!" she cried back, with an exuberant laugh he could hear floating back to him as she galloped away, shocking several riders and disappearing in a cloud of dust.

Marcus stopped smiling, stopped teasing indeed and frowned. She so reminded him of himself, especially at such moments when his will was crossed. His only relief was in a wild escapade that often had culminated in challenging someone to a duel! Thankfully ladies had to find other ways to vent these feelings. He wondered if he had not lost an opportunity by attempting to take advantage of that wildness? If she were to play the wanton he certainly intended she should do it with himself! Therefore, he rode to where Stara and her groom were just leaving the park and cantered alongside. His phaeton was there being held by his groom and although he knew Stara preferred riding back to the town house, he attempted to persuade her to join him in the carriage for a spin. She was not in the mood for a light flirtation she said baldly, her black eyes still pools of dark fury. To which he matter-of-factly stated, "If you must expose yourself thus to society by galloping and scowling, you are merely proving how correct is your social exclusion."

Stara stared him down at that. But unaffected, he said airily, "You've just cut Lady Blendinham." To show her the correct manners, he turned and made a full bow to her ladyship. Recalled to propriety Stara nodded and smiled. Both were rewarded by the pleasure of Lady Blendinham stopping to chat for above a quarter of an hour. By the time they'd heard the full details of all her recent illnesses and her grandchildren's virulent measles, Stara had been pacified to somnambulance. "A timely opiate," Stara said as her ladyship drove off. He laughed with her and they were in charity with each other again, especially when he admitted Lady Jersey gave beastly dull parties. So much so he was not adverse to chucking it if she would agree to meet him for an evening at Vauxhall Gardens. There would be fireworks and dark walks, he urged. They could even go *masked.*

Stara's eyes glittered at the possibility. But when he grasped her hand, she pulled it away. "It would not be an outing for us," she said, softly. "It would be a commitment, which I have told you I will not make." And she shook her head decisively, "I am not sunk so deeply into the dismals that I would trust myself to your mercies."

"You could do a great deal worse," he said, gruffly, but she merely laughed, assuming he had been jesting, but he was not.

10

Marcus's prediction about the entertainment of the Almack's ball was proven correct within a half-hour of his attendance. It was a totally vapid affair. Lady Gwendolen did not find it so. Rather without her recent rival present, her ladyship was the main star, which justified her refusing Stara a voucher and had her realizing of late Stara was become less companionable. At the season's beginning, Miss Carltons had been a soothing second to her ladyship. But since their return to London, Stara had not only neglected her but advanced too close to the center of attention for countenancing—although naturally still beneath her.

Another suspicion that occasionally arose in her ladyship's mind was that Stara might be competing with her for Marcus Justus's attentions. But immediately Lady Gwen dismissed as an improbability Stara's cutting her out. How could anyone with her in view seek a lesser sight? Actually Gwen did not devote more than a passing thought to either Stara or Marcus or her many admirers. For she was still preoccupied by her

torrid romance with One-Jewel Jack. His hold over her
she herself increased each time she confided to a new
person that gentleman of the road's obsessive attachment. The London entertainments occasionally distracted her ladyship from her culprit. But at night, ere
positioning herself for sleep, she did not count sheep,
but different compliments from One-Jewel Jack, all of
which she was obliging enough to repeat the next day
to Stara and with her assistance and alterations record
each one in her copybook.

On the night of the ball however, her ladyship was
more concerned with her third admirer—the duke of
Clairidge, who was to be her escort and was ungallant
enough not to be present. That dereliction Lady Gwendolen was quick to point out to Marcus on his approach.

Lifting a chicken-skin fan, Lady Gwendolen
pointed with it toward the door.

"Why is his grace not coming through that portal
of admission, I ask you?" she asked him. Marcus
merely lifted his eyebrows as she continued in cold
peeve. "He was to escort me here. I requested he not
come to our home, for he has a disquieting predilection
to chat with Stara, which on other occasions has delayed our setting out. So we made an arrangement to
meet at this spot, precisely at ten o'clock. But is he
here? He is not. The only excuse is that he might have
misunderstood me. He often does. It is the one thing
about his grace one can rely on. So I have concluded
that he misunderstood again and appeared at my town
house after I had departed. In which case it is possible
he has been *waylaid*."

She shook her fan with some vigor.

Marcus was amused. Apparently things were very
far from amicable between the two ladies. "You suggest

perhaps that Miss Carltons waylaid your escort and persuaded him to . . . eh, give you the slip?"

Lady Gwendolen did not wish it put so explicitly and gave him a look of reproach. But the thought rankled, and she said with some ire, "I do not know the cause of his delay, but delayed he is. I shall have to assume he does not wish to be my escort tonight. Therefore I shall give that opportunity to one of the many gentlemen here who would have wished for it. Perhaps . . ." she gave him her widest smile, ". . . yourself?"

Marcus bowed. As a gentleman, there could be but one answer to so blatant an appeal. "It is an honor I had not hoped for."

"Hope for it. It is yours," Lady Gwendolen said sternly. He just bowed to her, accepting his assignment with some amusement. Actually it would be pleasant to inform Stara on their ride tomorrow that he had stepped in for the duke, whatever the cause of his grace's delay. But when Lady Gwen was off dancing the quadrille with Lord Beaufort, Marcus took the opportunity to question the gnawing sensation he had of ill fate approaching. Since Stara's suppressed discontent on their morning ride, he had been alert for some form of her retaliation. The rake in him looked forward to some wild escapade that might very well make her an outcast and available for his proposition. Hence he was no little disappointed to think her only action was a delaying of the duke.

Yet on further consideration that seemed too anemic a response to all her fury. The heart in him was concerned. A lady who had not caviled to impersonate One-Jewel Jack might break into the ball, might do all matter of wild starts—such as dressing as a gentleman and joining the orchestra. He grinned at his conjecture and lifted his quizzing glass to examine the musicians

carefully. His smile turned to a frown thinking of another possibility—of Stara donning her highway garb
once more. Instantly he dismissed that. It was not very
likely a highway robbery would be attempted in the
heart of town, for then it would become common thievery, robbed of all romance. No, no, Marcus assured
himself, banishing those fears; she obviously had gotten
herself in control and was merely, as Lady Gwendolen
feared, waylaying the duke.

Several dances later, almost time for the supper
and just before the twelve midnight curfew, the duke
walked in. Another duke, the heroic Wellington himself
had been refused admittance upon appearing seconds
after the midnight hour. But the duke of Clairidge had
been before the last gong. That timeliness did not explain the crowd surrounding him. Marmaduke very sel-
dom was flocked about. Clearly not a crowd pleaser,
yet tonight he was evidently doing so. Approaching his
grace with foreboding, Marcus eyed him intently.
Something clearly was amiss. Marmaduke had an exultant expression. The fear that Stara was somehow the
cause, had Marcus quickening his step. But he was
stopped by Lady Gwendolen. He languidly pointed out
the duke's arrival. His grace's very sight offended her,
she said with a snap and turned her back. After an
entire evening's disregard, the duke would have much
to do to win himself back in favor. Marcus's curiosity
was fast being fanned into concern. Never had he seen
such alertness in Duke-duke's manner. Here a chat,
there a chat, everywhere a chat-chat. Another crowd
about him now. Good grief what could the fellow be
saying!

Marcus could scarce recollect himself ever being so
anxious to be relieved of a beautiful lady. He almost
embraced Lord Silverdale approaching and suing for
Lady Gwendolen's company on the dance floor. But in

that interval, he lost Marmaduke in a crowd. Sir Wilken waved him close. "Marmaduke, egad!" he said with a laugh between each word. "Who would believe it of him!"

"One finds it difficult to believe there is such a fellow at all," Marcus said with one brow lifted and keeping fast his mask of unconcern. "But what particularly astounds you, Willie?"

"Brace yourself, old boy, Marmaduke did in a highwayman!"

"You jest!"

"No, by this hand. He was on his way here and was stopped by a highwayman and took the blighter on!"

So unbelievable was that announcement it turned Marcus icy with disdain. "Not dashed likely. You forget, Willie, I've seen his grace in just such a situation. He cowered and complained throughout and since. Not he!"

"I would not have laid odds on it meself! But he is exclaiming to all that he was attacked outside Almack's by a highwayman. What's more, he shot him."

Marcus's face went white while Sir Wilken chatted on. His words floated back to Marcus—something about Sir Percy arriving behind his grace and spotting the body of the highwayman sprawled across the road. "Egad! Marmaduke is taking credit for a direct hit! Claims the blackguard is cocking up his toes. What say? Who would have believed it of that fribble!"

Marcus moved away, unable to hear more. Yet he was attacked by the same versions of that story from two or three other amused noblemen. He spotted Marmaduke bowing before Lady Gwendolen and made his way there in time to hear his grace himself explaining the excellent cause for his delay.

With a deep sigh, her ladyship ruled against that

excuse. There should have been nothing to delay an appointment with *her*. But a second thought had Lady Gwendolen's eyes wide with concern as she demanded who the highwayman was!

An exultant smile wreathed his grace's face. "It was One-Jewel Jack, himself," he pronounced with a decided preen. "I told you I would get the blighter!"

"Damn you to hell!" Marcus cried out. "You killed h . . . him! No, by heaven, you could not have!"

"I did, i'faith," the duke cried out, his chest puffing out. "With my own pistol. I whisked it out of me pocket and aimed right at the fella, and shot him through the heart."

"You have shot me through the heart," Lady Gwendolen said with more animation than anyone had ever seen on her visage. "Who asked you to end his life! He was perhaps only interested in following you to find *me*? Did you give him time to speak to you?"

Aghast at her ladyship's reprimand rather than the commendation he expected, Marmaduke bewailed her attitude. "Oddsblood, the fellow had a pistol aimed at me chest!"

Although an unimpeachable excuse to his grace, it made no dent in her ladyship's displeasure. "So did he once before," she snapped. "And you are still alive, I observe. He wanted a mere trifle—a stickpin or so. You would not have missed it. For *that,* you ended the life of a gentleman with great perception of feeling and under-standing! Fie upon you, your grace. Fie!"

"Egad, that I should be treated thusly! And by a lady who has had the honor of knowing me for several years. And by one of me own class!" He mumbled some more, and then continued still on the same point. "A lady defending a lowlife hedgebird against a *duke*. Not done, egad!"

Lady Gwen ignored him. Her handkerchief was

out and she was dabbing her eyes. She looked to Marcus to comfort her and was astounded at the whiteness of his face.

"What did you do with the body, you pudding-hearted turnip-sucker!"

"How dare you speak to me in that tone. I'm the duke of Clairidge! Forget what is due me!" He was off on that tangent when Marcus captured his grace's attention by thrusting out his strong hand and grabbing hold of the duke's white extruding cravat—all the while demanding the location of the corpse!

"Who knows where the body is? Not me concern. Unhand me! Egad! Egad, gad!"

Marcus did not. Rather he twisted the starched monstrosity until his grace felt a definite pinch in his throat, and between coughs, cried out, "Nothing to do with me, sirrah! Left it to me outriders."

At that Marcus released his grace and was off, while Marmaduke rasped after him. "Gave the ruffian an easy death. Should have been hanged!" And he massaged his own mauled throat.

Spotting Sir Percy, Marcus pulled him aside for a quick questioning and then immediately was seen to be running like a deranged man out of the ballroom.

Lady Gwendolen was pouting. She had been abandoned twice tonight by two different escorts. And just when she should have been treated with extra consideration for the loss she had suffered. Her heart felt heavy —so much so, she felt the need of a composer and rushed to a turbaned lady on the sidelines and begged use of her vinaigrette. The lady was nothing loath and all concern. His grace, after being practically assaulted by his inferior, and ignored by her ladyship, was similarly in need of some relief. He found it in the sudden attentions of a group of ladies, giving him the lavish praise he felt he deserved. So appeased was he under the ministrations of these young misses and their mothers, his grace ignored Lady Gwen for the remainder of the ball.

The ball was far behind Marcus as he drove his carriage down the road, springing his horses to their full bent. His thoughts as well galloped ahead to Stara. Was *this* the wild thing he sensed she would do tonight! No, he had more confidence in her good sense. Wild, she was to a fault, but not a peagoose. Her wits would have stopped her. Must have stopped her. Had to have stopped her. And yet.

If she acted thusly, she had truly gone her length! Marcus's only hope was that the duke was as inaccurate in his description of his second holdup as he was about the first! That lifeline-conclusion held strong for a moment. He tossed himself another: the duke was a notoriously poor shot. Another: Sir Percy had not himself examined the body. "Not bloody likely I should touch a bloody corpse and smear my outfit before appearing at Almack's. Not done, old boy," Sir Percy had protested. "Also ain't likely to care if a highwayman were dead or not! Not our sort of chap!"

That encouraged Marcus to believe Stara was alive. He would chase her down and find her, alive and laughing . . . grateful for his rescue. By heavens, even if she was injured, it might not have proved fatal. There were so many possibilities that went beyond the worst one. Let one of the others be true. Let her, in the name of God, not be wiped out of existence!

Curse Marmaduke, that cork-brained, rackety maw-worm! But thinking of the duke gave Marcus confidence. So contemptible a specimen could not possibly have ended such a glorious life! Yet if one were to curse someone, he himself deserved more than a tongue lashing for pushing her to the edge! Why hadn't he left her the pearls—just for security? He was the knave. He, the

shuffling rogue that had tormented such a wondrous
being. He, blast his soul, was the one who had pushed
her, indeed wished her to go beyond the edge of propriety, to turn her into a hurly-burly creature of wild
starts! And just recently during their morning ride
hadn't his sarcasm about Almack's been the final goad?
Yes, his mocking had been the very thing that sent her
back on the road to meet that limp-wristed, walrus-
faced ass! And be blasted away by him!

Marcus revolted against that picture, groaning,
crying out that if that was so, then he himself should be
blasted to blazes, forthwith! There were tears running
down his face as Marcus drove on. His horses snorted
as they gasped for breath to keep the pace he set for
them. Galloping on, stride by stride! He used his whip
to turn the corners in a whirl, holding the horses tightly
to move them in unity forward, onward. All this had to
be a nightmare he could drive down and dispel. And he
drove on. Speeding. Seeking. Her name a desperate
echo, leading him on—like a distant, dimming star.

11

Reaching the scene of One-Jewel Jack's death,
Marcus did not find a corpse. Yet he would not allow
relief to weaken him, knowing the search was not over.
Grimly he went from Sir Percy's servants to the duke's
outriders checking out every rumor as to the disposition
of the highwayman's body. Each claimed the other
household had disposed of it—which meant, thank
God, none had. Even possibly that there was no body.
Just as this hope was solidifying, one outrider recollected spotting a trail of blood to a ditch where something like a body was lying.

"Dead as a doornail," the outrider insisted. "Seen
enough corpsies with these peepers to spot un. Jem
filched the hat with the one jewel, thinkin' it were real."

Jem protested that accusation. There was a violent
dispute during which Marcus walked away in disgust.
Doggedly he still clung to the hope that a wounding did
not mean the death of the highwayman. Rather that the
injured victim had possibly struggled to safety . . . or
home.

If it were Stara, she had only one home.

By that time it was dawn and a haggard but hopeful gentleman presented himself at the marquis's residence. The shocked expression of the usually unflappable butler had Marcus remembering himself, realizing it was too early to be calling at a gentleman's establishment. Indeed, he was promptly denied entrance. In despair, Marcus returned to his lodgings and his valet's ministrations which shortly had him transformed into a more presentable caller in correct morning attire. Unable to wait any longer, Marcus set off, walking the five blocks to extend time. But it was still early when he rapped with the knocker. This time Marcus made an effort to assume his accustomed air of sangfroid, knowing he would scarce receive information from anyone by continuing to act as he felt—as if a hole had been blasted out of him.

It succeeded. He was shown into the morning room and left there to wait. Thoughts of doom barked at his pacing heels. How long was this uncertainty to continue! When would he know if he had lost all!

The room itself recalled memories of meeting Stara. Before this marble fireplace and ormolu clock, he had looked at the invitations and gibed her for being excluded from the most select ones. On that satin settee, he had taken her hand and read her future in the palm—always it contained him. The memories had Marcus's face growing grimmer. Why in God's name had he played games with the lady? By heavens, he should have assured her that he would provide for her forever, so she need never, ever again risk her life in her foolhardy, adventurous ways! He should have . . . ought to have kept her in his arms safe from harm for the rest of her life!

He rang for the butler and was informed in the loftiest tones possible the marquis had not yet arisen.

He wanted to ask for Miss Carltons, but could not receive the news of his lifetime from a menial. Rather he waited some more. Thought some more. Agonized some more. And then unable to withstand a second more, he opened the door to haunt the hall. In not above half an hour he came bang up against Lady Gwendolen. She stared at him coldly, as if he were an intruder. He did not immediately sense the cause of her displeasure. A further offense was his not humbly requesting *how* he had offended. So she was obliging enough to tell him.

"I expect you found something of major interest to draw you away from escorting me home," she said, in her languid, measured tones.

"Ah yes, of course, your ladyship. I was rushing to . . . complete a task I fancied might win your approval." He said the words automatically, despising himself for *still* continuing to pander to this idiotic woman when there was the possibility the woman he loved was lying dead. Yet the Honorable Mr. Justus Marcus had been too well brought up to say what he really thought. He gave her an impeccable bow and Lady Gwendolen brightened a bit.

"Explain yourself," she said, wanting more than a hint. Indeed, Lady Gwendolen always insisted on everything being spelled out for her.

Marcus did so. Claiming that since she showed herself so much concerned over the fate of One-Jewel Jack, and knowing the special relationship she had with the eh, fellow, he had rushed off to determine if the duke's words were true or not, assuming Lady Gwendolen would not be able to rest until he had the final answer for her.

"Ah," she said, and her small, blue eyes darted about as she rethought the entire situation. Nodding, she smiled, concluding he had been acting to please her and so she could hardly chastise him for that. "Truly, Mr. Justus, I scarcely slept a wink thinking about the demise of that . . . gentleman. I would have wished to have seen him face to face, that is without his mask, one time before he met his end, so that when I thought of him, there would not be this blank space where the face should be. But, one cannot have everything. The memory of the devotion of his heart is sufficient for me. As Stara said."

Marcus jolted up. His breath caught. "When did she tell you that?" he said with such fierceness her ladyship gave him a look of reproof. He apologized for his vehemence, and just holding himself in check, he repeated his request in a lower tone, adding, "When did you see Stara last?"

Her ladyship gave him one of her long stares that always drove him into a fit of impatience. Doubly so at that moment. His heart was leaping while he waited for her thought processes to move along. Indeed another pause had him just barely holding back from shaking her into a response. But he must wait. Wait.

At last Lady Gwendolen contributed some words, but no clarification. "Why, what mean you . . . last?"

Marcus almost bit his lips in his speed to reply. "I mean, your ladyship, when did Miss Carltons say that to you about the highwayman?"

"From the moment we first discussed him. I am uncertain what you are asking? I can scarcely recollect the exact time. Nor can I imagine its relevance? The point I was making was about my feelings . . . my memory of the . . . eh, gentleman."

There was a Sèvres vase in the alcove in the hall to his right and Marcus had all he could do not to smash it on the floor and tell the woman to go to the devil. But he remained standing like a stock, sunk in a drowning wave of disappointment. After a moment, he gained

control of himself and grimly attempted to put into
words his worst fears. Had Lady Gwendolen or any
maid seen Stara this morning?

If she said no, then all hopes of Stara not being the
one impersonating One-Jewel Jack last night would be
dashed. Still, still, he could not get himself to ask it. For
while he did not, Stara was still alive to him.

Lady Gwendolen was comfortable with silences.
She herself was prone to them and understood one had
to reshuffle one's thoughts occasionally, and further,
she assumed, as always, that the gentleman was thinking of her. So she always took pauses as compliments.
Actually she took just about anything a gentleman did
in her presence as a sign of his devotion. Except turn his
back on her. Which Mr. Justus was rude enough to do
now and almost blindly walk toward the door.

"Mr. Justus!" she called sharply. "Are you leaving? Without biding me adieu?"

Marcus turned back, recollecting himself, and
bowed.

Not sufficiently appeased, Lady Gwen said, "Stara
is perhaps correct. You are overset that it was Marmaduke and not you who ended the eh, gentleman's ca-
reer?"

His heart beat quickly. Yet Marcus feared falling
again into that trap of asking *when* she had said that.
Actually his own brain was moving slowly under his
grief. But at length it concluded with a click of relief
Stara could only have said that *after* One-Jewel Jack's
death. Hope surged and his blue eyes turned brilliant
sapphire. "Dash it, when did Stara say that! This morning? Say it! Say you've seen her *this* morning?"

Lady Gwendolen stepped back as he approached
her with such vehemence. "There is no need, sir, to be
in such a piffle over a simple remark. I defended you,
actually. I said you were concerned only for my sake."

"Ah God, will you never come to it! When, blast you, did this conversation take place? Just tell me directly—is Stara alive?"

A laugh came from the stairs. Marcus turned and gasped. His eyes were barely able to focus on Stara standing on the landing. But getting her at last in his sights, he could just fiercely stare. Gradually the whiteness of his face and the terror in his eyes were replaced by stunned relief and pure joy.

"Are you well! Not hurt!"

Instantly Stara understood what he had been supposing. She grinned back at him, making a pirouette to show her unmarked person.

At that Marcus surged toward her, forgetting the presence of Lady Gwendolen. But Stara held up her hands in a stopping motion, lightly continuing down the stairs, exclaiming warningly as she neared. "Really, Mr. Justus, you should not allow your concern for Lady Gwendolen's feelings to lead you into such a whirl."

Stara passed directly by him, putting her arms around Lady Gwendolen who realized she was supposed to be mourning and allowed the comfort. After a few more pats, Stara turned to Marcus, hoping she'd given him enough cues to watch his words. He was still staring at her with his heart in his eyes and Stara attempted to tease him to his usual aplomb. "I cannot imagine else why a mere footpad's demise should so disturb you? For certain you did not think highly of him, if I recollect. Was it not you who found his cache and reduced the highwayman to penury again? After that, what did you expect but that he would strike again?"

Uncharacteristically, he would not rise to that bait.

He just continued fixing her ferociously with his eyes and she could sense to her toes his desperate need to take her in his arms. When he stumbled too close, she had to keep her hand on his chest to keep him at a distance. Obviously he was too overwrought to long remember the proprieties. Sensing his need to take her in his arms, she was nothing loath to let him. They must be alone and Stara had to contrive a way, for she was concerned for him. His eyes which normally looked at her as if she was a prey and he a blink from pouncing, continued stunned and staring so fixedly she began to feel some of his anguish. Next, she felt the waves of relief following hard upon, and a need for closeness so acute it seared through both. Stara was an instant from forgetting Lady Gwendolen's presence, from forgetting all but pushing this closeness to its ultimate, when fate came to her aid. The outer door knocker imperiously sounded. It caused Stara to snap to herself. The taut connection between the two sagged and both Stara and Marcus momentarily reeled.

During their straining attempt to take themselves in hand, the butler walked by, answered the door and introduced the visitor without being observed by either one. Only when the visitor spoke did they turn and register the sight of the resplendent duke of Clairidge.

Lady Gwendolen totally unaware of all that had taken place directly before her could only wonder why they were all standing in the hall, and as lady of the house led the visitors into the small dining room where breakfast was being served. The butler was quick to lay the additional settings. Before Marcus had a chance to do more than whisper an agonized "Are you well?" and receive an amused, "Of course," from Stara, they were being served sirloin steaks and eggs. The duke and Lady Gwen fell to. Stara waved the steak away and contented herself with tea and biscuits. She had been brought up to eat sparingly and her constitution had never been able to accept her altered circumstances, especially when she was so often at a dread of soon having to content himself with pauper's meals again. Marcus was becoming more himself. Better, by Jove, than he'd felt for hours. He realized he was hungry, thirsty . . . wanting to laugh, to live. Stara was alive and close enough to touch, and for the moment that was sufficient. He too was living again. Felt something like this after a duel—always ravenously hungry. And he fed himself. The conversation was general until the duke, chomping to bring the topic to his act of heroism, between bites, addressed Marcus.

"Me servants say you wished to see the body of the highwayman I dispatched. Oddsblood, if you've a fancy for such gore! Fellow was a bloody mess."

Lady Gwendolen silenced him with a look, for his words were disturbing her enjoyment of her rare steak. Her glare as well reminded him of her special relationship with the highwayman. Fumbling, mumbling, his grace fell back to his food. Everyone munched on. Marmaduke's thoughts however could not long stay off his proof of valor. While chomping on his food, he was chomping at the bit to show off. More than ever he wished to preen a bit, especially before that smug, smiling, suave Marcus Justus. So strong was his desire to show that gentleman he was not only ahead of him in daring but knowledge, he risked her ladyship's displeasure and said with some insouciance, "Fellow was deposited at Bow Street. Seek him there—if you've such a passion for the blighter."

Marcus's eyes narrowed at that, looking at Stara. So she had not been involved at all. Not a miraculous escape, but rather, as with anything that involved the duke, a colossal muddle. And yet it had nearly torn him asunder! But Marcus was in charge of himself by now. Shrugging his shoulders he responded with all the disinterest he could put in his voice, "I was merely performing a duty for her ladyship. I assumed she would wish to know he was properly buried."

"I am pleased at your assistance," Lady Gwendolen said with a gracious smile, "but I have no concern with the . . . eh, remains. There was no need for you to so bestir yourself. I must, as Stara says, forget the fellow and remember only that he had the saving . . . eh, what did you say exactly, Stara?"

Stara was quick to elucidate. "He had the saving grace of being able to appreciate beauty. I expect he carried that picture of your beauty with him to his grave, wherever that might be."

"Ah, yes. Let us hope so," Lady Gwen agreed and continued her hearty meal.

Marcus had several cups of tea and did more than justice to the victuals presented.

Stara's thoughts floated back to the moment she'd heard last night of the death of the highwayman. She'd been excessively blue-deviled over the news—more so than all of Lady Gwendolen's dry-eyed sighs. For Stara had met the actual highwayman. Indeed their meeting had been the incentive for her emulating him. It had occurred when the legend of the roads had held up the coach of Miss Lavadale's students on their way to London. Those less affluent had been traveling together in that establishment's carriage, superintended by a young teacher, when the boredom of the journey was delightfully interrupted. Just past a turnstile, a tall man astride a splendid dark mount appeared. He came riding alongside, a sparkling gem on his hat, calling for the coachman to halt. The coachman had promptly hid by flattening himself on his seat. Upon seeing such poor sport and realizing the coach was filled with a handful of schoolgirls, One-Jewel Jack was aghast. He even was lowering his horse pistol and prepared to ride away, when one of the young ladies stuck her head out of the

window and called him to account for his actions. It
was of course Stara.

One-Jewel Jack had swept off his jeweled hat and
bowed his apologies. But spotting the beauty of his ad-
monisher, the highwayman suggested a compromise.
He would allow all to pass, if she would pay the forfeit.
Stara had instantly agreed, but her bravery wavered as
he escorted her out of the coach. Even more so when
she was picked up and placed before the highwayman
on his horse, riding off a pace. There under the bright
moonlight he claimed his price of a kiss. Primly Stara
turned her cheek but he refused so paltry a fare and
leaned down, stroking her lips with his, and gave her a
deep, toe-tingling kiss that had her in a shock. So swept
up by the romance of the moment was she that Stara
kissed him back. The highwayman gallantly stopped at
one, declaring in delight she'd given him the greatest
jewel he'd ever collected. Then with all deference he
brought her back to the coach. Stara watched him ride
off into the moonlight, hearing echoes of his laugh
floating back to her. Surrounded by the crying girls and
the outraged schoolmistress, Stara had to contend with
the fear that her reputation was lost ere she was old
enough to have one. Even as a young miss, Stara knew
how to arrange matters. "Surely a lady of your responsibility would not have allowed me out of your sight,
Miss Melliven. You saw he was only asking me for di-
rections and that he did not touch me." Remembering
her position and that Stara's being disgraced would
have meant the disgrace of the school and thus herself,
the schoolmistress stonily assured all she had kept an
eye out . . . and thus Stara had been myopically
chaperoned throughout.

Subsequently at school Stara had often recalled her
moment with One-Jewel Jack. When in despair, she'd
taken to calling out to him to ride to her rescue. Those

cries doubled whenever receiving a note from the Pinkertons. Then she'd retire to her room and imagine he
was riding up, sweeping her onto his horse and taking
her away, where the two would live a happy, carefree
life on the road.

As the years passed and no more was heard of that
legend, Stara had assumed with a sadness that he'd
been killed and her dreams of him slowly faded. And
yet, yet, she remembered the kiss. And himself. Subsequently she used that memory at her moment of need.
Paradoxically, impersonating him had fulfilled her
dream, for she'd been rescued by One-Jewel Jack, after
all, only it was herself. Thus when Lady Gwendolen
returned from Lady Jersey's ball and announced her
highwayman had surfaced only to meet his death, Stara
was cast into the greatest affliction. Not that she was
idiotic enough to expect that One-Jewel Jack had any
remembrance of her, as Lady Gwendolen would have
been quick to assume. But it had been pleasant to think
of him alive and happy somewhere, riding off on his
fast horse. His finish had wrung tears from her as she
said good-bye to that laughing, daring highwayman
who had kissed so well. By this morning however, appalled at her excess of sensibility, Stara had stopped her
romanticized mooning, declaring herself as idiotic as
Gwen. An occasional regret would still slip by, as now
at table when he was the recent topic. Once more she
squelched her feelings only to discover Lady Gwendolen was either picking up her thoughts or having her
own in that direction, for she put down her fork and
sighed deeply. "I cannot believe he is not out there
thinking of me. I've become accustomed to thinking of
him thinking of me!" Another sigh as she stared at the
person who had ended her fantasy, and she began chastising his grace afresh. "If combat was necessary, Mar-

maduke, why choose as your opponent one with such a romantic heart?"

The duke would not accept that as an exoneration, insisting a criminal was a criminal, regardless of his amorous inclinations. In a few sentences the nobles had all but come to cuffs over whether a romantic heart exempted one from judgement. Appealed to, Stara came down squarely on both sides. Only to be rudely interrupted by his grace who said in an aggrieved tone, "Ain't romantic to hold up people! Dashed inconvenient. Downright beastly, I say. And *uncivil*. Interrupts one's journey. Puts one out of pocket. Wakes one from a snooze." Becoming more and more agitated as he enumerated the inconveniences, Marmaduke concluded, "Nasty fellows, highwaymen! Clean out the lot! By Jupiter! Hang 'em all!"

A silence greeted that. Only Stara was eventually able to rise above that moment of reality and continue pitching her gammon—as she made some effort to come about by exclaiming over his grace's bravery. To that his grace could not but agree. As a reward, he gallantly offered to take her up in his phaeton and show her the exact spot of the highwayman's demise—which Stara claimed would be a high treat. She shot a glance of amusement at the exasperated Marcus. Yet due to the shock he'd recently sustained, he was holding back from his usual reproofs of her larking about with other gentlemen. This time he appeased himself with the thought she would shortly not have to toady up to any of the nobles anymore. He had not gone through all his agony of losing her to let her leave him again. She was his. And he would claim her. In his heart and in hers was the firm knowledge, exchanged silently when they first saw each other that morning, that they belonged to the other. He needed only to make her admit it.

And then, with an irrepressible gleam in his eye, he

lifted his teacup and said almost under his breath, "To my lady adventuress."

Attuned as she was to his every expression, every breath, she heard him, and over the heads of the others preoccupied with their meal, Stara gave him her most wicked grin in pleasure at that tribute.

It took several days before Marcus could maneuver a meeting alone with Stara. For almost daily she was occupied with his grace.

Through the judicious use of a tip to her maid, Marcus learned that she was attending the auction of Beau Brummel's personal and household items. He contrived to be waiting at the door as she and her maid were about to step into the marquis's carriage. Pretending to be calling to invite her to that very occasion, and having his groom with him in his carriage which sufficed for propriety, the maid was dismissed. They were off. Together at last. For a pleasant moment Stara enjoyed watching this sportsman turn the corners with a flick of his whip. But before long, she was aware that he was turning off into the park.

"It is not the hour for driving in the park!"

" 'Tis the correct hour for a private discussion here amongst the flowers." he announced glibly, alighting from the carriage, holding out his hand to help her out as well.

"I am not descending," Stara said with some peeve. "I wished to see the auction."

"And so we shall. But it is bad ton to appear too early. The city merchants and creditors will be flocking there. One must always arrive when the more valuable items are to be auctioned off."

"I cannot afford those," she said bluntly. "Nor

frankly anything. You have arranged for me to be totally flat in the pocket."

"We shall discuss your financial circumstances and all details of your future—*amidst the flowers!*" he insisted, and he almost forcibly helped her down off the carriage, leading her toward the flower walks. Roses in all shades were gloriously growing about.

"Keep in sight of your groom," she insisted, hoping for some decency.

His eyes twinkling, Marcus exclaimed, "My groom is known for being shortsighted when I wish him to be."

With a flourish, he sat her on a stone bench and seated himself close to.

"If you are going to make another improper proposal," she began with annoyance.

"Never again shall I treat you with anything but propriety," he said and took her into his arms.

This was the moment he'd been anguishing for since first fearing she'd been dispatched as the highwayman. Understanding that, Stara allowed the impropriety for a moment. Even permitted his arms to tighten around her own quivering body. A kiss would appease both of them and so Stara acceded to that as well. But on the third one, she pulled away.

"So much for your pledge of propriety!" she gasped.

"All our kisses shall henceforth be sanctioned by propriety, for I intend to make you my lawful wife."

Decisively Stara moved away at that—her bristles up as she stood and faced the smiling gentleman.

"Indeed! I don't recollect agreeing to that state? Perhaps I have been asleep and something occurred, a proposal or such, when I was not aware . . ."

Laughing at her dudgeon, Marcus dramatically threw himself at her feet. "My dear Miss Carltons. I do not wish to alarm you. But my feelings have reached the point of boiling over, egad!" he began with full-blown mockery. "Thus, lest I splatter you with my fervor, I must beg you to turn down my fire by accepting my offer of matrimony."

"No," Stara snapped, and turned to walk back to the carriage.

He stumbled getting up and grabbed her back. "*No?*"

"Yes, *no.*"

"Forgive me for pitching it too rum," he said, getting serious. "But you have not understood. I am not in jest! I am asking you, with all respect, to honor me by consenting to be my wife."

"No," Stara repeated.

"You say what? But, confound it, I'm offering you *marriage!*"

"So has Lord Stockley. I told you. And frankly, recently, I am beginning to reconsider the possibility that I might even be her grace. Marmaduke has sent me a most exquisite gift and a note written in his own hand, rather than having his secretary do so—as was his way with all missives he's sent to Lady Gwendolen. I cannot but believe so much effort denotes a great deal of feeling."

"He shall never forget his dignities," Marcus scoffed. "He shall marry Lady Gwendolen. We both know it. As for marrying Lord Stockley, the gods pity you, it would be a life of unrelieved tedium of hunting talk and hunting days. And worse, the nights will turn you into a prey he'll coarsely plunder. For neither Stockley nor his grace can appreciate your beauty . . . your spirit. And, blast it, neither will ever *love* you one iota as much as I do."

"Love? You hadn't mentioned that."

"You know I love you. Have always done so. And

you love me, say it, admit it, confess it . . . let your
heart speak, damn you."

He was holding her tightly in his arms, back on the
bench and she was beginning to tremble from the feelings his touch always worked through her body. She
was forced by her own emotions to allow another deep
kiss, and one more followed hard upon.

To get her breath she pushed him off at last.
Her voice was wobbly but determined, "My heart is
yours . . . but not my hand. I cannot continue living
on the edge as I've done so many years. I need security . . . honor. I need a home of my own. I cannot
allow my emotions to control my future. You are a delightful challenge. *But,* I have done with adventuring."

Realizing she wished to make those her last words
on his proposal, he held her from leaving. "If it is a
question of security, as it seems all your life is, I have
been reinstated in the good graces by my father, the
earl. You shall not find yourself living a pauper's existence."

"I had heard you'd been financially reestablished.
That was last week's *on-dit*. But further, it was whispered that the earl relented under the assumption you
were to wed Lady Gwendolen and bring the honor of
her title and wealth to his family. I expect if he heard
rather you were wedding her companion, the situation
would radically change. And more than probably then,
your proposal would alter as well. Before long, undoubtedly I would find myself living with you, having
succumbed to my feelings. At worse I would be your
ladybird. At best I would be responsible for your having
lost your security as well as mine. No. No!" she insisted, attempting with all her might to keep herself in
check. "We must both rein in our feelings to secure
sensible futures."

So aghast was Marcus at her not instantly rejoicing

after he'd made, what was for him, a major concession of actually proposing . . . that she was the one judging him not worthy of her, he was left in a stupefaction of silence as they walked all the way back to the carriage. There the groom recovered his eyesight to jump down and help her into the carriage. Marcus could only follow. Anger, despair, rejection fought within his breast as he silently drove her out of the park.

She assumed he was taking her home. But rather his carriage was positioning itself amidst several crested carriages before another establishment. He'd taken her to the Beau Brummel auction—her original destination.

"This is not necessary," she said consolingly. "I'll understand if you wish to return me to the marquis's town house. Most gentlemen need a day or so to recover from rejections."

A laugh greeted that, and Stara was aghast to discover that Marcus was no longer in despair. Rather he was his old irrepressible self again. He more than proved it with his next remark, "I never recover from rejection, because I simply never accept it. Nor do I accept yours. Apparently you need a bit more persuading. But however long it takes for you to acknowledge what I realized in that one blinding moment when I thought I'd lost you to death, we shall be together. However, I am content to let you find that out on your own. I shall of course be of assistance in showing you how inevitable we are."

Reaching up to hand her down, he held on to her hand a little longer than necessary or than proper. In their moment of closeness as she descended, she cast a quick glance at him and felt his gaze reaching into her eyes and settling there.

"Don't torment me!" she whispered in a huff. "I've made up my mind."

"Then it is up to me to unmake it, I expect," he said, blithely, and escorted her into the mob of gentry—there to pick mementos from the fallen erstwhile leader of their ton.

12

Stara was gazing in awe at the many precious things being auctioned off. Ahead, on a platform was the much mentioned cheval glass. There, it was whispered, Beau Brummel had spent up to three hours of a morning, perfecting his attire—from the precise fit of his coat to the intricate creation of his cravats. She held in her hand the catalogue that read, SALE—THE GENUINE PROPERTY OF A MAN OF FASHION, GONE TO THE CONTINENT. It listed all this dandy's pride and joys left behind in his nighttime escape from his creditors. For now it was revealed that on his last evening in England, elegantly attired in his familiar blue coat and white waistcoat, black pantaloons and striped stockings, Mr. Brummel had attended an opera. It was imperative the creditors not get wind of his escape to France lest they pounce and place him in prison. So he walked about, casually exchanging quips with friends. At intermission the Beau had lazily risen and walked not to the refreshment area, but to a back door where a nobleman friend had positioned his chaise. Exchanging that subsequently for his

own waiting carriage, Beau drove all night to Dover
where he and his carriage boarded a hired vessel and
were deposited safely in Calais. In permanent exile.

It was the end of an era. An amazing story of rise
and fall—of a former valet's son who through his wit
and knowledge of dressing and just plain audacity had
ruled society, until his gambling at White's Club destroyed him. Debt, Stara thought with a shudder. Heavens, if the moneylenders could bring down the Beau
with all his social connections, have him actually fleeing
for his safety lest he spend the remainder of his life in
Newgate, how much easier it would be for the Pinkertons, claiming debt, to dispose of *her*!

Stara also shared with the Beau the precarious position of being a hanger on in society—fringes to that
exalted world. The slightest shifting out of favor set
them atremble. Debt or dishonor could dash them
away. The only safety was a title and plenty of blunt to
back it.

Stara dropped the catalogue in panic at her
thoughts; only quickly to pick it up, pretending her
emotions had been aroused by overwhelming interest in
the offerings. Many things listed had already been ac-
quired by the Beau's friends as a remembrance. The
duke of York himself had bought Beau's green Sèvres
vases with flower and fruit mouldings for nineteen
guineas. Lord Bessborough was there looking at the
double-barrelled Fowling Pieces. And Lord Yarmouth
was especially interested in the wine stock—laying out
five guineas for the claret.

Marcus was sharing a laugh with Lord Yarmouth
while Stara was examining the sheets and huckaback
towels. She would have not been adverse to having one
of those towels as a memento of the gentleman who had
once dubbed her as too intelligent for society. "One has
to perfect a vacant stare to fit in with the vacant aristoc-

racy, and you, Miss Carltons, unfortunately, and very inappropriately, twinkle!" She had laughed and begged pardon, promising to do better subsequently. At their next meeting, she had given him her blankest stare. He had bowed and applauded her effort. "However," he added, in a gentle admonitory tone, "I detect a stray sparkling ray at the core of those eyes—as well as a glimmer of a smile. One is never amused when one's life is unchallenged. Lady Harwick there personifies the aristo look. I daresay it takes years of inbreeding to produce a vacancy so profound one assumes she has long vacated her body."

Glancing at that lady Stara had had to admit the truth of the observation. Indeed, even Lady Gwen had a fair amount of that admired air of absence. Although Stara had been valiantly striving to fill in that lady's blankness with her own ideas. Admittedly, at times, she'd had to hold back from open laughter upon hearing her own thoughts repeated by that elegant high voice as if her own. She had enjoyed it, feeling rather like a puppeteer for a time, but lately, Lady Gwendolen had cut the strings between them, and was sinking back into her own silence, punctuated by dogmatic announcements.

Stara's attention was caught by a phrase between Mr. Justus and Lord Yarmouth—something about "she has the propensity to please but too much density to know when to leave off pleasing." They were exchanging a quiet snigger, as men do when discussing a woman of ill repute. It was with some astonishment that Stara noted Lord Yarmouth directing his quizzing-glass at *her*! That gesture had her overcome by the thought she was the subject of the gentlemen's sneering allusions. But when Marcus turned round and spotted her, he did not look guilty, but rather pleased to find her so close, and so she relaxed. It was some other lady thus being skewered. While relieved, Stara could still not countenance their attitude. It was her experience that gentlemen who spoke lightly of one woman would eventually do so of another. With the exception of their mothers. Although often even giving life was scarce sufficient to escape their sarcasm.

Oblivious to having displeased her, Marcus directed her attention to Brummel's library. "Odd collection, would you not say? From Shakespeare to shelf after shelf of elegantly bound light novels. Tomes of substance overrun by those of surface value. Rather like our society," he said, looking to win her amusement.

Stara, accustomed to bandying with him, struggled to rise from the depression of spirits with which the auction had cloaked her, but her response did not have the lightness of tone required. Rather a touch of scorn sounded through her reply, "You are always the first, as was the Beau, to sneer at society, and yet both of you spend all your time attempting to belong to it."

"Acquit me of that!" Marcus exclaimed, genuinely surprised by her assessment. "I am the son of an earl. Second son, it is true, but born and bred as an honorable and always one of this group. Unlike the Beau and yourself. Also I have constantly made the ton dance to *my* tune. I tell you, as I told the Beau, do not imagine amusing them will gain you permanent entry. Everything is bloodlines! Although you have respectable lineage through your mother, your father and other relatives are far from acceptability. Moreover you are tolerated as a companion to nobility—that ordinarily assures entry only during the time you fill that function. Of yourself you would not only not been received but deemed not worthy of a nod. Make the most therefore of your time. You will have a season. Then they will find another plaything. Taking on their style, values— even outdoing them in those—will leave you with

naught of your own worth when you are deserted. As
happened to poor Brummel. He fell into the nobles'
spendthrift ways without the lineage to protect him.
You too might very likely fall into the same basket."

Stara's face went white. "What do you mean?"

"What did you think I meant? Why are you so
frightened?" He stared at her with concern. "Dash it,
once more I sense a desperation that will lead you to
foolhardy, wild starts such as turning highwayman. Felt
it for some time, actually. That's why I was certain it
was you that was dispatched by Marmaduke. What has
you in such high fidgets? You seem doubly dished here
at the auction." His glance dug deep, as he continued
probing, "Aha, my reference to your being in the same
position as the Beau is what rankled! You haven't been
gambling? No, that is not your passion." He paused,
frowning, as he pierced through her determindedly
blank expression. "By Jove, I've guessed it! You're being dunned!"

Stara turned away, rapidly enough to denote assent. Marcus was awash with a lowering presentiment
—recollecting her guardians. It was them.

Pretending disinterest in his conclusion, Stara occupied herself by staring into the Beau's famed cheval
glass in its mahogany frame with the brass lamps on
each side. Her image looked pale, and she felt drained
indeed. Next moment her breath caught as she glimpsed
Marcus's reflection joining hers and then felt herself being turned round.

"It's the *Pinkertons*! They're still hounding you,"
he said, not as a question, but as an explanation to his
puzzlement.

She could do naught but nod. "They have a writ—
legally drawn up for my debts. If I do not meet their
sum, I am to work it out as a governess with several of
their friends, with the salary to be given to them, until

perhaps I become too old to serve. I face the same fear that drove Mr. Brummel to France. The creditors can just as easily clasp me into Newgate, or I understand from the official paper, that I would be placed in a bailiff's house, under guard, until I agreed to the terms of indenture."

"Ye gods!" Marcus exclaimed. "Had I known that I would have been certain you had taken to the roads again. Blast, I'd have taken to the road for you myself to set you free from that. In short, my dear Miss Carltons, compose your fears. Rather give me the paper. I shall have you released from all debt within the hour!"

Stara broke away. "And be in debt to you? Not likely! I'm not a ladybird to be a gentleman's plaything! Rather give myself to the bailiff, than that!"

Marcus was no little astonished to see her degree of contempt and fury and he insisted on an explanation. Backed into it, Stara revealed she'd heard his conversation with Lord Yarmouth discussing a lady . . .

"Not a lady," Marcus interposed. "We were chatting about Harriette Wilson, who is about here somewhere. What is that to the purpose? We were merely recalling that lady's fascination for Lord Byron. Another member of society cast out this year. He shares the distinction with me of being one of the few who have spurned Miss Wilson's determined advances. Having entertained almost all nobility, she is currently threatening to write about it in her memoirs."

"Yes, I've heard of her. I'm delighted she is giving you all back some of your own. Even our exalted duke of Wellington himself, I understand, stood outside of her house in the rain, banging for hours for admittance. She whom you gentlemen wished to hold in your arms is like all other ladies of her group—kept at arms length away during the day. In the light, you all find Miss

Wilson's very existence so lowly it merits only a laugh.
You hold her cheap."

"She is cheap," Marcus said with a shrug.

"And so you would make me," Stara said, her eyes
blazing.

"Good grief, I've offered you marriage."

"At first you did not. Only when I held myself
aloof and showed you others were thinking of marriage, did you relent. And these ladies too I understand
have occasionally been married to nobles and then discarded. Both the regent and the royal duke of Clarence
had women considered as their wives only to be
dropped for others. In Mrs. Jordan's case after giving
him many children, she was sent away to poverty and
exile in Paris. Poor soul."

In confusion, Marcus inserted almost reflexively,
"Her children are provided for!" But he could not understand how he had become the defender of libertines.

"How gracious," Stara could only exclaim with
full scorn.

At that moment Harriette Wilson, herself, walked
by. She fluttered her fingers at Marcus, and he bowed to
her. Lord Yarmouth approached that famed courtesan
to exchange a few words. So opulently attired was she,
Stara could merely gape at her pelisse prodigiously
braided on the shoulders and the bonnet of all ostrich
feathers.

"You are her acquaintance, I collect," Stara could
not resist asking, a sharp cut of jealousy hitting her.

Marcus shrugged, as if he would not discuss that,
which assured Stara he was more than that. This gentleman who had touched her so intimately, had probably touched many a lady in the same manner. Why had
she assumed their passion was so extraordinary between them? When apparently these men had made a
wide distribution of that private emotion. Here a kiss,

there a kiss, everywhere a kiss, kiss, kiss. Her eyes were afire with fury at him and all men.

More than ever her resolve hardened to attain a respectable position. Gracious, so overwhelmed was she, if Lord Stockley were here she would have accepted his several times repeated offer on the spot! Anything to assure she would not succumb to Mr. Justus and find herself, as dreaded, some day abandoned, passed around from lord to lord, like this Harriette person.

As if aware she was in the lady's thought, Miss Wilson turned and stared back at Stara. Her face, which Stara was certain was blushing with rouge rather than shame, came closer. After a moment's examination, she honored Stara with a grin of recognition, although they had never met, which inspired a terror of precognition in Stara. Quickly, she turned away. But rebuff never deterred Miss Wilson who in the next moment was by her side. Marcus had gone to inquire the cost of a small figurine that had caught Stara's fancy, which Stara still held in her hands. She nearly dropped it upon being touched on the shoulder by a known ladybird, as if they were of a level.

Amused at Stara's discomfort, that lady purposely pressed closer, whispering, "You are with my Marc? Fortunate." Then with a knowing grin, she added, "Once one has known Marc, *once* is never enough. A lusty man that sharpens one's appetite . . . is that not so?"

In a prodigious dilemma Stara's face was white. On one hand she recollected her defense of that woman. But to be seen talking to Miss Wilson would immediately stamp her, in all probability sink her already tottering position. So Stara just remained quiet, pretending not to understand.

Undeterred, Harriette Wilson continued matter-of-factly, "Lord Yarmouth tells me you have been leading

the gentleman a merry dance. Keep'em dancing, me girl.
You have only a few years to be what they think they
wants, and then they drops you and don't care where
you is left lying. In the gutter, even. They will step o'er
the very body they adored. Hmmm, yes, I know. Even
wild man Marc! He give Violet, me friend, a carriage,
no less, because she pleased him in bed. But what happened when that gent spotted Lady Gwendolen? He run
sly on Violet, he did. Not that he left her purse-pinched,
but I ask you again, where be the *nags*?"

Harriette's eyes almost rolled to emphasize the se-
riousness of that oversight. "Where be the nags that
oughta went with the carriage? He refused her 'em,
that's what. I put it to you—as a lady of some sense,
what use be a carriage that don't have naught to pull it?
Not a gentlemanly thing to do, I say! As his new lady,
you oughta remind him of his dooty to the ones he done
with."

Bobbing her ostrich feathers, Harriette Wilson
walked away, having signaled to the auctioneer that she
would take the jade cupid figurine. When Marcus returned, he had bought the small nymph of alabaster
that Stara was holding and taking it from her hands, he
presented it to her again with a look of suppressed anticipation at her delight.

Stonily, she just stared at it and back at him. The
fury at the talk she'd had with that woman and the new
view of Marcus rose up in her to the point Stara could
only push it and him away. In all his motions Marcus
was quick. No less now when he caught the figurine—
inches from the floor. Then straightening up and holding the statuette ostentatiously in his protective cus-
tody, Marcus gave Stara a most reproachful glance and
pocketed the nymph himself.

"She shall always remind me of you. White and
perfect and yet liable to go off half-cocked and fall to

harm, only to be rescued by me and put safely away," he said with a grin. "I'll keep you in my pocket, Stara."

Stara was awash in emotions: outrage, confusion, wanting to run away from him and society and yet, yet, seeking the safety of both as well.

James Christie, the auctioneer, called all to attention. It was the moment for displaying the Beau's famous snuffboxes that the dandy had used with such dash. Doggedly Marcus bid for one he particularly favored and was pleased to get it. The last offered was an overly ornate snuffbox which evoked much response. When Mr. Christie opened it—out popped a piece of paper which was read aloud. It was Beau Brummel having the last word on them all, thumbing his nose at the top of the society that had allowed him to be cast out. It stated: "This snuffbox was intended for the prince regent, if he had conducted himself with more propriety toward me."

Marcus went into whoops at that. The rest of the lords were afraid to be so open, but the smiles were hard to suppress.

During the return carriage ride, Stara was cold, refusing to respond to Marcus's gibes, his gallantry, even his concern.

However, before stepping out, she turned to him with a martial gleam in her eyes and exclaimed, "I've been told you owe Violet some horses. The carriage was not enough. I expect when a lady has lost her newness, you gentlemen no longer feel old promises valid. It is a point, I shall not forget."

"What the devil!" Marcus exclaimed, running after her up the stairs. "Did that Wilson woman dare to . . ."

The butler was holding open the door, and Stara refused to carry on a conversation before him. She merely nodded and entered the house, leaving the humiliated gentleman on her doorstep, without inviting him for tea.

From behind, as the door was closed, she heard him blasting all women. Stara grinned. Precisely her sentiments for all gentlemen, she thought, somewhat appeased.

That evening in her bed, Stara wondered how it was possible that a woman could have hopes of a man being true to her when he was well-known for being untrue to all ladies? How could she have ignored his reputation with women of the Harriette Wilson and Violet stamp for one, but also of the ton? She ought to have kept in mind that Marcus was known for abandoning his flirts. Recollecting now his cavalier treatment of Lady Warfield, she winced. In the beginning Stara had merely reacted to that lady's anguished looks with secret triumph. Now with her own heart raked by the rake, she understood and regretted her indifference. How many ladies were in that group with her—and what a medley it must make. From Lady Warfield to the original married woman who had been responsible for his exile, to all the Violets in all the countries he traveled! Had that swashbuckling, arrogant gentleman left a trail of damaged debutantes and affected incognitas? Making Stara just one of many to him? While to her he was the only gentleman she had ever cared for? Hardly a compatible match! How could she imagine the two of them permanently fused as one?

Clenching her teeth, Stara forced herself to reconsider Lord Stockley. Once again she could not quite steel herself to accept an intimate relationship with him. His kiss on her hand always left a trace of spittle. Ridiculous, yet that was the main reason she continued to refuse him. Her skin bunched whenever he came close. One could not live in proximity with a gentleman who made one's skin crawl. Heavens, how could the Violets of this world give themselves to gentleman after gentleman—unless the variety of it made it less imprisoning. There was always the hope one would find a gentleman who would please, instead of the certainty of being shackled to one who did not, for one's lifetime.

Catching the drift of her thoughts, Stara blushed. Was she concluding that being a mistress to many would be better than wed to one? For shame. Yet, yet, what gentleman would she be searching for, if not one who would please her as Marcus did—an expert in pleasing women. If she married him she would have the best of both worlds.

No sooner had she thought that then Stara was swept over again by doubt. Marcus's mocking devaluing of society very likely meant he would not value her as his wife. All the nobles had mistresses, while pretending they did not. Too honest to pretend with her, Marcus would be quite open about his light-skirts or even matrons, scoffing at her indignant requests he remain faithful. Then where would she be? Being married to a rake meant a life of insecurity—both of affection and finances. Contrarily, marrying a gentleman who honored her position as wife meant the rewards of security and respectability. Further her heart not being engaged, she would hardly be adverse to his running off to the Violets. *Especially* if he were Lord Stockley. Nor was she convinced that Marcus had sufficient income to not only satisfy the Pinkertons but assure she'd never again find herself in fear of creditors. His life-style, his careless ease, his father's tendency to disown made that security unlikely. Nay, logic if not inclination said she must accept the wealthy, willing Lord Stockley.

Thus resolved, Stara ruined all by dreaming of Marcus. They were both at another auction only this time Mr. Christie was auctioning her. She was nude, pale and shiny as the alabaster figurine, while the auc-

tioneer pointed out the beauty of her body. Gentlemen
bid for her. Even the prince regent was there, smacking
his lips. She was told to turn and display all her attri-
butes, which she did with some modesty and yet pleasure at the waves of warm desire floating out from all
the embracing eyes. She attempted to censor her dream
while it went on, but it continued shamefully. Several
men, Lord Yarmouth being one, wished to come close
and touch the merchandise. Her alarm was great when
this was allowed. Lord Yarmouth approached with his
snaky eyes and his tongue licking his lips. That same
tongue touched her. She cried out. Several other gentlemen were gathering. In fear, Stara looked about for
protection. Marcus was there on the side observing it
all with amusement, shaking his head at her pleas. "You
wished for this . . . best enjoy it!" he said curtly, and
stormed away, leaving her to be encircled by men eagerly approaching.

When she awoke, shattered, Stara could scarce tolerate the indecency of that dream. Almost immediately
she attempted to forget most of it. All she could acknowledge was her feeling of anger at Marcus's desertion. She had regrettably awakened too soon to know
which one of the gentlemen had won her in the end. In
the clean dawn of day, she shuddered at the thought of
belonging to any one of them. Even Marcus!

13

Lady Gwendolen was viewing Marmaduke's heroics askance for having rid the world of one of her great admirers, yes, but more than that for altering his own image. She preferred his grace as a gentleman so high in the instep he would never lower himself to any action with lesser lights. He was, she concluded, showing marked evidences of plebeian behavior. Not only was he running around, apparently, dueling with footpads, but he was bragging about it incessantly. A duke of his order had no need to puff himself up. Everyone automatically accepted his high position and kowtowed. Further, she had accepted him as her follower, he following at a proper distance, of course. To suddenly see him step forward and become surrounded by the ladies of the ton, basking in their praises and shameless flirting had her losing all respect for him. Lowered him, in faith!

"Her ladyship's nose is out of joint," Marmaduke pronounced to Stara, when he'd taken her out for a drive in his phaeton. "She don't wish me to stop in. So I must take you *out*."

Stara eyed him carefully, wondering what he wanted from her. Was she to be his intermediary and ease him back into her ladyship's good graces? If that was his aim, she lost all hope. His constant attentions of late would then be explained in a disappointing light, indeed. Best to know the answer without any flummery.

So Stara put it to him. "You wish me to soothe her ladyship and win you back her favor?"

Marmaduke considered the matter for a full minute. It was a surprise to both when he concluded he did not wish that. "She don't appreciate me as you do. Like to be appreciated. Beastly tired of apologizing."

"You have nothing to apologize for, your grace. Quite the reverse," Stara said with emphasis.

"Obliged," he said, reddening with pleasure.

She smiled widely, feeling delighted that he had lost his fixation with Lady Gwendolen.

"Face I like," he said confidentially.

"Your grace?" she asked confused.

"You do. Have a friendly face. Smile at me. Never give me freezing set-downs. Beastly tiring being dropped like an old glove. Then spotted on the floor. Put on. Only to be dropped again."

"Indeed! Most fatiguing," Stara exclaimed. "But you are not an old glove, your grace. Definitely a gauntlet. If you were dropped before me, I should feel it a challenge. Why look you how you challenged that highwayman and promptly, efficiently dispatched him!"

His grace's face was red again. He signaled his groom to take over the reins and in a short time had led Stara to the pond. They stood around there. Stara had a golden parasol of many ruffles and she opened it to the strong sun. The rays seemed to be caught in its diaphanous material and surrounded Stara with a glow. She felt she looked her best today in a pale, saffron over-dress with a white petticoat. There were ruffles at the hem and the neckline. Her hat was leghorn straw with an upturned wide brim. Ere leaving, Stara had caught Lady Gwendolen casting her such a look of blatant jealousy that would please any competing lady. Yet it was unclear whether her ladyship was annoyed with her for her escort or for being in exceptional looks. Either way, Stara was set up for the day. Earlier, notions of fairness had her requesting if her ladyship would lief she refuse his grace's invitation for a drive in the park. That much she owed Lady Gwendolen, but her ladyship had haughtily claimed *she* had not the slightest objection nor interest whom Marmaduke was taking up in his carriage. And so that searing, last look had to be for her appearance.

At that moment Marmaduke was noticing the glow of the sun in the lady's face. Rather than using the moment to equate her to the sun, his grace moved the lady into the shade saying prosaically, "Makes you squint."

Definitely deflated, Stara put down her parasol and closed it. Obviously this was not going to be a romantic moment, after all. He led her to an iron bench and both sat for a significant time.

"Cold," he said with a grimace.

"Your grace?"

"The seat's cold."

Embarrassed that he should make reference to that part of their anatomies, Stara merely looked down in a blush. His grace moved uncomfortably on the seat and then stood up.

Stara was uncertain whether she was to rise and walk with him or not. She looked at him expectantly.

"Took a notion we might suit," he said after a long pause.

Stara was not generally slow to get the slightest nuance, but that statement admitted so many interpretations, she could do no more than stare in alarm.

He waited.

Realizing she was expected to say something she risked, "Indeed!"

That reassured his grace sufficiently to bow and continue bending until he was positioned before her on one knee. "Proposing," he explained helpfully.

So taken aback was Miss Carltons, she just opened her mouth. No sound came out.

"Knee's throbbin'," he said after a while.

She apologized.

"Thought you wished to be my wife, my duchess?" he said in an aggrieved tone.

"Heavens, yes!"

He rose with relief and brushed his knee. "Valet don't like me to soil me clothes. But thought the moment called for me to go all out."

"Indeed," Stara persisted faintly, uncertain what had happened.

His grace sat down next to her again and made no further reference to the coldness of the seat, feeling pleased with himself for having done what he wished.

"Meet my mother shortly. The dowager duchess. Always has something to say. We'll listen till she's through. Then go away and forget it. As I always do. Do the pretty and tell her first, what?"

"Indeed, your grace," Stara could just manage to whisper.

"Not obliged to call me that anymore. Give you leave to use my given name . . . that's the ticket between affianced persons. Marmaduke, or, I recollect, you liked, Duke-duke."

"Duke-duke," Stara managed faintly, staring in awed fixation at her fiancé.

"Stara, m'dear," he said, taking her hand and planting a quick, swift, perfunctory kiss on it before leading the speechless lady back to the waiting phaeton.

"No need, I daresay, to bother about formalities. Leave all that to me. Know how to do the correct thing. Bred to it, don't you know? Me secretary reminds me. Mr. Walt, long-headed, needle-witted chap." His grace's usually placid face had an expression of pleasure in a job well done and in himself. That assurance was conveyed in his voice as he concluded, "Break the news to the marquis and Lady Gwendolen meself."

Far from objecting to that, Stara actually was prodigiously relieved.

Not till she'd reached the privacy of her chamber did the shock of what had occurred begin easing sufficiently for the realization to hit. She was engaged to the duke of Clairidge.

Never really believing that a possibility, Stara was shaking. With all her heart Stara wished her mother were here or that she had someone who would obligingly assure her what had happened—had actually happened! As always she made do with herself. "I'm going to be a duchess," she said softly.

Unable to stop herself, Stara ran across the room to her bed and jumped onto it, falling back and hugging her pillow. All her life she'd wanted one house. Now she'd have *houses!* Dozens of them. There were four just here in London. And of course there was his grace's principal seat as well as six or seven castles. Where these were, she could not recollect but wherever they were—they were hers. "Oh dear mother," she whispered, "if only you were here! No more lodging with your inferiors. Now you could have your own estate. Rather, I'd give 'em all to you. More than your family ever had. So many properties. All mine!"

In a rush, she was up. Her mind was roaming over

England attempting to spot the duke's holdings. Then
in a stroke of delight, she recollected a mansion on a
beach surrounded by white cliffs on the Isle of Wight.
She had seen a portrait of it in a local gallery and his
grace confessing it was his, claimed he'd visited there
once and found it too warm for his taste. The cliffs
sheltered the winds from the English Channel and kept
it warmish even in the midst of winter. Roses all year
round he had said, as a point of interest to Lady Gwendolen, but she had found it against nature to have roses
out of season. Her ladyship always wished things to suit
their time and their class. But Stara had been entranced
by the magic of that place, called Cliffview. She coveted
it. Imagined herself walking on that beach, walking into
that house. Now she could do both. She would have
Cliffview!

Pacing about, Stara tried to stop herself from
counting her coming wealth—lest she discover Duke-
duke had been joshing. That possibility had Stara in a
dread. Could he have meant to propose to Lady Gwendolen and was merely rehearsing on her? No! Preposterous assumption! He'd been excessively clear. He'd
proposed to *her*! It was miraculous but true. And then
another wondrous conclusion hit—never again would
she ever have to fear the Pinkertons and their debtor's
prison. After all her panic at being placed in a lowly
gaol, she was rather to rise above everyone's touch.
Raised higher than she'd ever believed. Her starry eyes
were radiating while stray giggles kept erupting to bring
her down to earth.

Rather remarkable the way she'd managed to bring
it about, Stara thought, "Score one for shameless toadying," she concluded in self-congratulation, but with a
mischievous twinkle.

As the hours passed, the daze clung to her. Everything reminded, bringing fresh pleasure. Her hairbrush

had several bristles missing, always a dashed nuisance when brushing her long, thick hair, now that as well had her smiling. Stara had been putting off purchasing a new one, spotted at the Emporium and reluctantly refused since the price was too dear. She could purchase it now. Heavens, she could afford a whole chestful of other accessories for her hair—combs, bows, ferronières that Lady Gwendolen was so partial to, even a tiara.

But the most wonderful moment of all was composing a letter to the Pinkertons, informing them that henceforth they must address her as her grace, but that actually they were never to address her again at all! She tore it up and decided to wait until she was wed and allow the estimable Mr. Walt to write all her letters for her.

Next morning Stara awoke and was proceeding as usual, when the thought of her new eminence hit. Once more she was knocked off her feet by a rush of excessive delight. She was to be a duchess.

Her morning dress was distinguished only by the lady within it—not one trim, not one appliqué, no wadded hem or ruffles. Stara's style of simplicity would probably not do for a duchess, and she began to visualize the future wardrobes awaiting. Indeed, observing in the mirror that she was still herself, Stara kindly informed that awed, reflective lady of the prospective delights ahead. Of leading balls. Of being invited to *all* the balls! Coming closer, she whispered to her image, "You, my dear Stara, have reached the pinnacle of society. Short of winning the regent or a royal duke, you can have landed no higher. You are or shall shortly be the top of the ton. The ultimate. The *ne plus ultra*! Stara Melton, the seventh duchess of Clairidge. Stara, her grace. Her noble grace!"

Several curtsies. Then Stara must needs twirl about

for a few moments to contain her exuberance sufficiently to descend to breakfast. There was a momentary
check of her joy when Duke-duke arrived and took her
aside. Naturally she assumed he was come to shab off.
Bracing herself, she lent a wary ear while he came to the
reason for his visit. With a resolute step forward, his
grace gave Stara a kiss on the lips.

"Forgot," he explained. "Obligatory for engaged
couples, I daresay. Mr. Walt gave me the hint. Made a
dash to put it right."

"Quite right," Stara nodded, exhaling in relief. He
was pleased she'd not been insulted by his having been
remiss. Both relaxed. Stara was particularly at ease that
his kiss had not revolted her as had Lord Stockley's.
Bound to make the marriage less of a trial. There had
not been a tinge of passion either—not so much as
when Marcus just met her eyes from across the room.
But that thought was quickly squelched as well as all
romantic memories.

Any stray regrets were swiftly swept aside by the
developing benefits of her position. The first one was
the marquis offering his congratulations with more
than a little awe. Although that was accompanied by a
sad, lost expression she pretended not to observe.
Rather Stara concentrated on profusely thanking him
for his care and fatherly concern. He was quick to assure her he felt gratified that a young lady under his
care had been so honored. While regretting the duke's
not becoming his son-in-law, since, as the duke had
explained to him, her ladyship was not that way inclined, he could only be pleased that someone so close
had won his grace.

Very prettily said and with the politeness natural to
the lord. Yet it disturbed Stara's triumph. Something
altered her smiles to pursed concentration as she sifted
through his lordship's words . . . that phrase about

Lady Gwendolen's preference. Did the marquis mean the duke had proposed first to Lady Gwendolen, and she had refused him and that's why she was chosen—as second choice? A tolerable portion of her ebullience went flat. But immediately, Stara reminded herself—however it had come about—she was still going to be a duchess. So Stara's spirits inflated again.

Although she would have preferred this point settled, one could not question the duke. His attention span was of the shortest. So she let it pass. Duke-duke was occupied by fulfilling the instructions of his secretary. Actually he had a sheet of paper which he loyally referred to. "First-ho, the engagement gift."

Stara had been expecting a ring, but now her peeve at being a substitute for his grace's first choice made her push to immediately get what she wanted.

"I may choose *whatever* I wish?" she asked shyly. Eagerly, his grace assured her if it was in his possession, it should be hers.

"Then I wish to have, in my own name, and for all time, Cliffview, on the Isle of Wight."

The duke took a moment to recollect that property. Her not responding as expected left him confused, or actually more confused than his usual state. Stara realized she must end his perplexity and make her request sound conventional. She did so by speaking about the matter in a matter-of-fact way. Calmly she reminded him of the portrait in the gallery which he had claimed was of his own estate.

"The sea place," the duke recalled of a sudden. "Paltry place. Want a trumpery estate?"

She nodded eagerly, holding her breath. Whereupon he airily agreed, even to having the papers drawn up. Stara felt a wave of triumph as Marmaduke returned to his list. But then he frowned, having spotted he'd gone amiss. "Not what's on here," he said, and

Stara's heart jumped. "Gift has to be something one can show the ton. Can't parade a house about, what? Something personal. Jewels. A ring. The Dunstan Diamonds are a parure—tiara, necklace, brooch, earrings, don't you know? You were supposed to ask for that. Got my answer all right and tight for *that*." And he looked at her reproachfully.

Stara was quick to make amends. "I'll ask for the Dunstan Diamonds, if you prefer, but I did rather wish for Cliffview . . ."

"Have that," he said as if the estate was of small importance. "Meant besides." He paused to look at his paper and launched into his prepared remarks. "The Dunstan Diamonds are given the new duchess by the dowager. Not likely to happen. Mother don't want to give 'em up. Bit of a pickle, what? Must have a chat with her. Claims possession makes 'em hers. Hubble-bubble. No way out."

"I shall of course not take anything you would rather your mother have," Stara said quickly.

"Good gel. Like to think you'll be accommodating to her feelings. It was Lady Gwendolen who wanted the Dunstan Diamond Collection. Explained mother's feelings. Promised her own collection worth more. She wanted the Dunstans." He frowned at the memory.

"I shall be pleased to accept a collection of my own, along with the estate of course."

The duke was all smiles at that. "Devil of a pickle if you had been as adamant as her ladyship. Said I was fortunate to have you. You ain't one to start trouble. You make things happy around you. I'll make things happy for you. Get you a diamond collection that will make *present day* history, what? No need to have the weight of the past!"

"No, indeed," Stara said. "I trust you completely to know what is best. And as long as I have the Wight estate where I can perhaps retire when I am fatigued, I shall be most pleased."

The duke was exuberant and ready to rush away to his personal designer for the new diamond collection and to inform his solicitor to proceed with the change of Cliffview's papers, and to order his social secretary to send the notice to the *Gazette*. He had already written to his mother asking for her congratulations and now could send her a second letter assuring her that his new wife-to-be would be delighted to allow her ownership of the Dunstan Diamonds for her lifetime. "Curious how some women set such store on those diamonds. Gothic things. Trumpery settings, what? Mean a lot to me mother. And to Lady Gwendolen. You're a sensible chit." He reached over and gave her another peck. She gave him a delighted smile. He was half out the door when he returned.

"Forgot," he said, and reached into his pocket. He brought out a huge ruby ring and placed it on her finger. "A mere token till we've got the Stara Collection completed." He paused. Stared a bit. Then spoke. "Oh, I say, have you talked to Lady Gwendolen since we became affianced?"

Stara said she had not, that her ladyship had taken to her bed with a megrim.

"Thought not. Best tell you. Proposed to her ladyship a fortnight ago. Felt we were meant to be wed, don't you know? Lineage and all that. Oddsblood, what could I do? Waited for her answer. 'Stead got a tongue-lashing for actions I call correct with that Jack fella."

"Correct? Say, rather courageous," Stara inserted, unable to stop her habit of gammoning him.

He nodded at that, and squeezed her jeweled hand. "Obliged," he said with his eyes glowing and giving her another longer kiss. She responded. Obviously a mistake. The duke looked confused again, almost surprised by any demonstration. Sensing it, Stara pulled away and attempted to look offended.

"Your grace!" she admonished, to cover her fall from grace. Her blushing appeased him. It gave visual proof that she was the shy miss he'd thought. Quickly he made his apologies, and she gave him her forgiveness. They held hands respectably.

Fresh reminder to Stara that henceforth she'd have to clothe herself in conventionality. Not too onerous a price. Yet this situation with Lady Gwendolen ought to be made clear. "You were the one who broke off with her ladyship?" Stara inquired.

Marmaduke was surprised, certain he'd just explained it all. Hadn't he? She said not all, which led him to relate painstakingly every detail, more than she cared to hear, actually.

"Proposed to her ladyship. She said, 'Considering it.' But had too many conditions by half! 'By Jove,' I said to her, 'You ain't chompin' at the bit to be me wife.' She replied she never chomped on a bit of a bit. She said also considerin' Mr. Justus. Told her, if she wished Mr. Justus, I would not stand in her way. Doing the noble, don't you know. *Nobleman.* Her ladyship took umbrage. Said despite our breeding in common, we had nothing else in common. If I wanted something common, why not take you? You were wishful to be a duchess, she said. 'That's the dandy,' I said. 'If that was what she wished, I would do so.' She said, 'Do so.' And so I did."

His grace took a deep breath. Never had he talked so long. All the while Stara had been staring at him in dismay. "You asked me to marry you because Lady Gwendolen ordered you to . . . or even worse teased you to?"

The duke's bulging eyes, stuck out even more at

that. "Nothing of the sort. That is, something of the sort. But not the complete sort. If you get my meaning."

"No," Stara said, unable to sort it out. Her heart was pounding in disappointment. "I do not quite understand. You do not wish to marry me?"

The duke assured her he did. Was most anxious to. He just wished her to know that he was free of all obligations in any other quarter, so she should not feel that she had stepped in where she did not belong. Should not feel that she had o'erstepped in Lady Gwendolen's domain.

"That is not what is disturbing me in the least. Naturally, as a gentleman of the first order, I would not assume you would propose to me if otherwise obligated. But as a woman what I wish to know is . . . is your heart engaged elsewhere?"

"Me heart?"

"Yes?"

"What has that got to do with our being linked?" his grace ejaculated in shocked disapproval. "We ain't talking petticoat affairs. I'm giving you the honor to be me duchess. Mind, first thought I'd give her ladyship that honor, but she weren't worthy of it. Got the notion . . . the feeling, *you* are."

"I'm honored, your grace."

"That was me intent," he said with a smile. "Are we all set? Is everything right and tight, now."

"Tight, at least," Stara said, and his grace bowed to her in relief.

He walked once more to the door. She waited for him to turn back with another thought. He had the habit of second thoughts. She was not wrong. He was returning.

"Came to me as I was twisting the knob. You ain't taken is you? Thought that Justus fella was wild for you. Seen him following us about. Everywhere you are, his eyes are. Don't mind if you see gentlemen, after we're wed. Cicisbeos, the thing. Wouldn't like it above half if it was that Justus fellow. Need an heir. And a second son for security. After that, daresay work things out. Ain't adverse to an understanding. Understand?"

"Perfectly," Stara said, suppressing her acute disappointment. In her imaginings she'd seen his grace as loving her sufficiently so she could eventually catch some of his feelings and the two would be if not passionately joined—at least companionably so. But that was not going to be the picture. No possibility of growing into an enchanted life. It was an arrangement, as all things were in the ton.

He gave her another elegant bow, and this time he made it all the way out of the marquis's house, before turning and coming back. Stara had been rushing toward the stairs, seeking to collect her thoughts in her bedroom. The duke called her again just as she'd reached the third step. She turned and came down.

"Forgot," he explained hurriedly.

"Yes?"

He frowned. "Forgot what I forgot."

She touched his hand with compassion. "Never mind, we have much time together henceforth. I expect you'll remember it eventually."

He was pleased at that. "Righto," he said. "We have a lifetime to chat."

Stara walked up the stairs, leaving him to stare after her. She turned at the landing and saw him still staring up. She waved and he bowed.

Whether he left or not, she could not bear to see. Sometime it was best she concluded as she sat on her bed not to think of certain things.

14

Lady Gwendolen had not made an appearance. It seemed to Stara that she was deliberately avoiding her. The marquis was, as always, polite, and more than gracious. Not only did he insist on her remaining there, but that the marriage take place from his home. Which had Stara much beholden but uncertain what to respond. For the first time Stara found herself not taking charge of a significant moment in her life. Indeed, during the marquis's questioning at the dinner table, Stara was obliged to refer all matters to his grace and his grace's secretary, Mr. Walt.

Another confusion was Lady Gwendolen's seclusion which grew to the point of her now taking all her meals in her apartment. That had Stara writing a note of concern to her ladyship, but there was no response. Stara had the need to appease her friend mainly due to the guilt she felt at having won the prize—his grace. She would wager that Gwendolen had been toying with Marmaduke when she suggested Stara as a substitute and rather expected him to remain faithful. It was undoubtedly her ladyship's first try at sarcasm. More than likely she would not attempt that rickety road again.

Having a tolerable affection for her ladyship—certainly to the extent of not wishing her unhappy, Stara was affected by the duration of that withdrawal. The longer it continued, the more Stara justified herself in this manner. "She turned him down. Once Duke-duke was set free, someone else would have taken him up. He was ripe for picking!" Other assuaging thoughts were: "I'll make him a better wife than she will. I'll remember he needs to be praised for himself, not just his position, and, and mostly, I shall be so grateful."

But it was hypocritical to bemoan her act while enjoying its delicious fruits—such as the deed to Cliffview and the ruby ring, both in her possession. So Stara ceased that. Instead as the days continued, she went back to enjoying every moment of her new position. The most startling difference was in others. Witness the attitude of the servants—the butler most especially. Smithers had always treated her just on the edge of tolerance. Yet from the moment of hearing the news he hovered round wanting to know her pleasure. It boded well for her future life amidst the beau monde. After a lifetime of toadying to others, finding herself the object of such deference could not but please.

Unable to suppress the bliss within, Stara's dark eyes were aglint as she walked a full inch off the ground it seemed. Further, she caught herself chuckling continuously in anticipation of the honors in store. Henceforth others would actually bow and curtsy to *her*. And she'd have precedence at dinners. Heavens, she'd have precedence over Lady Gwendolen. Not only as a new bride, but hereafter unless a royal duchess or princess were present, Stara would lead off all the balls. More than that, she must be included in all affairs. Lady Jersey who had refused her admittance to Almack's would have to produce a voucher on the double and treat her with all due deference. Even the regent himself must honor her by soliciting a dance. This would be some appeasement for his royal highness's slight, two month's since. How often did she wince at that recollection: the overstuffed royal overlooking her curtsy and stepping onto the ballroom with Lady Gwendolen. And hadn't her ladyship preened over that! It had been Stara's lifelong dream to dance with the prince. But after his second passing her by, without even a nod to her full-blown curtsy, she no longer wished for his notice. Marcus was correct, she admitted, the regent was naught but a fat fool in a very creaky corset.

Yet despite that sour grapes consolation, in her heart Stara still yearned for at least one princely spin. Now she could attain it. As consequence of her title the regent must honor her eventually, perhaps even with a waltz.

More immediate propping up of her vanity occurred when Stara visited Lady Gwendolen's modiste. Mr. Walt, his grace's far-thinking social secretary, had not only sent the notice of the duke's engagement to the *Gazette,* but he wrote Stara a very gracious letter asking if he could accommodate her in any way. It contained the reminder that his grace had arranged for credit at several establishments so that Miss Carltons could "prepare herself for her coming prominence." Not slow to take a hint, Stara rushed to dress herself appropriately.

What a difference the treatment of plain Miss Carltons and Miss Carltons, the soon-to-be duchess of Clairidge! What bowing and curtsying on all sides from the moment she entered the establishment. As for Madame Mancon, the honor of serving this young, engaged lady almost overcame her. She, who had previously acted as if Stara's height was a gross insult to femininity, now discerned her stature was a match to her new status . . . going so far as to claim she'd known at a glance Stara was destined for *higher* position.

Stara's laughter was not the way the gentry responded to such obeisance. Catching Madame's shocked reaction, the future duchess instantly squelched her smile. But shortly all were having a most pleasurable time, for with cost no longer to be considered, there was but one common objective: to shop, shop, shop!

A ready-made dress of lace that had been prepared for a royal personage was quickly readjusted and offered to Stara. She could not resist it, especially after donning it and discovering she looked prodigiously enchanting.

Madame called in more staff to witness how supreme this dress was when worn by a lady of genuine beauty and style.

Once again Stara knew she was being toadied to as she had done to others all her life. Yet, there was some pleasure in finally being on the receiving end. One began assuming the possibility of some sincerity in the comments, she found. At least a touch of it?

But then Stara looked into their eyes. Remembering her own thoughts while doing the pandering had her acknowledging she was being falsely inflated. She hit the ground with a bump. None of it was meant, she concluded. What they were really thinking was: "I need your patronage now and will say anything to keep your goodwill and the best I can say is you don't look a positive fright!"

With opened eyes, Stara took another look at herself in the full, lace dress and concluded she looked like a doily. Promptly Stara refused it, and settled for a less ornate version. She was not yet a duchess! Her appearance must still remain true to what she intrinsically was. At that, Madame lost some of her deferential tone —suspecting Stara might not be suited to her new position of eminence. True aristocrats never had flashes of acknowledging themselves as just ordinary people. In fact, they never applied either term to themselves—ordinary or people. They were lords and ladies and everyone else was clearly there to serve and toady to them.

Nevertheless Stara was enjoying herself selecting a full wardrobe. For daytime she chose French muslin, Berlin silk and sprig muslin. For evening she stayed with either crepe or fine jaconet muslin or gauze topping a silk slip. As a young maiden, she had been forced to keep to pastels or mainly white, but as a married lady she had access to a wider palette that even included tones of gold.

At the last moment Stara was attracted by a gauze material in a rose blush shade. She had never been able to wear pale pink—that being a blond's color. But this was a deeper hue that went with her dark hair and eyes —giving her whole complexion a blooming look she felt was prodigiously potent. Two dresses were ordered in it. First a spectacular all-petaled or flounced gown suggesting a rose in bloom. The daytime dress was a matching muslin with the same rose gauze used as a filler, both in the bodice area and descending from the puffed sleeves down to her wrists, showing blushing, graceful arms within. Madame Mancot decreed flowerets of this rose gauze around the neckline and hem. But Stara vetoed that excess of bloom. The compromise was one gauze floweret at the cleavage of the bodice where the gauze met the muslin and one at each wrist, while the hem was left in its simplicity.

This very day dress Stara put on directly it arrived. Her chamber looked like a changing room with all her purchases spread out. She was expecting Marmaduke and donned this dress to present the results of her shopping. Once on, Stara immediately spotted that Madame Mancon had ignored her instructions. The neckline was all gauze flowerets. Obviously Madame expected Stara would go along with a *fait accompli,* but she did not. Rather she reached for her scissors and un-*accompli*-ed it. However, she did leave two flowerets at the center. That was all the emphasis her décolletage needed. One never ought to overemphasize the obvious. Her snipping left her with an abundance of flowerets on her dressing table. Each floweret was so beautifully fashioned, it cried out for display. So Stara stuck two in her hair, one above each temple. The overall effect, she admitted, stepping back and preening, was prodigiously charming.

While waiting for Marmaduke, Stara continued to look through several more unopened boxes and had more surprises. This time Madame had taken on herself to send along for her perusal many items Stara had not ordered or even seen. There was lingerie, nightwear and most overwhelming, a floor length ermine cape. That suggested the designer thought Miss Carltons did not know enough to order what was needed. Which peeved while the results pleased. Still if ermine capes were requirements, this certainly was a spectacular fulfillment. Lady Gwendolen's smaller white fur wrap came to mind and Stara decided what was correct for her ladyship should certainly be suitable to a duchess's style. She would keep all the additions, Stara blithely decided, in awe of her sudden spendthrift ways. Sitting on her bed, surrounded by her new purchases, feeling her life had reached an acme indeed, Stara was shaken out of her reverie at her maid's announcement of a visitor. Not to keep Marmaduke waiting, Stara jumped up and rushed to the saloon.

Thinking it would be his grace, Stara gasped when Marcus stood up.

Reluctant to see Marcus alone, she regretted not having given a general order to the staff to deny him.

He gave her the smoothest bow. Warily Stara waited for the explosion that must follow. Usually his eyes were filled with teasing lights or a passionate glow, but now there was an earnestness in his glance that disturbed her. Surely he had heard she was engaged? Why was he taking it so calmly? Was this not the final proof that she had acted correctly in accepting the duke? So much for his undying love? Heavens, she'd expected at least a bit of chagrin—he'd lost her, after all. Very properly Stara motioned him to sit on the chair across. As usual, Marcus ignored propriety and sat on the settee next to her.

"I have some rather comforting news," he said softly, taking her hand.

She took it back.

"You distract me so. You always do," he laughed with what for him was a very open, almost boyish tone. No hidden threat or dare. Just plain affection. He was continuing in the same earnest tone, "Egad, you look like a beautiful rose, just blooming. You could shatter the heart of any gentleman, even if his heart weren't already dedicated to you. Stara, my enchantress. So fresh, so lovely, so adorable, so mine!"

Stara stood up in alarm. Good heavens, he didn't know!

Marcus stood up as well, apologizing for being swayed by her "overwhelming beauty." Bashfully laughing at himself, he continued happily, "I wanted to show you this. I've been down visiting the Pinkertons and thought you'd wish to see it immediately upon my return. I came here directly to ease whatever fears you have from that corner. They admit that there is no further debt owing on your behalf. You are free, Stara, my dear girl. Never again can you be threatened in their foul manner. After actively investigating I discovered rather that they owe you a substantial sum. I could have pressed for that, but I assumed we would not wish to burden ourselves with court dealings. Best just cut them off, completely."

Stara was gazing at the legal document. A few days ago, this, *this* would have been such a relief to her. It would have meant—freedom. Freedom from debt and from having to accept Lord Stockley. Looking at Marcus's confident smile, she realized he was all expectation. Expecting what? To be embraced? To win her hand with this? Admittedly earlier he would have gone a long way toward doing so . . . despite the reservations ignited by her talk with Harriette Wilson. Dear God, what was the point of all this now? It was after the event. Too little and too late. The duke's proposal had not only freed her from all threats of her guardians, but all fears of any kind for her future.

Marcus was confused, and a strange sense of foreboding struck through him. Indeed he had been all expectation of her throwing herself into his arms. He'd even anticipated several memorable kisses. Why, to own it, he had been living on thoughts of these kisses throughout his ride back to London, stopping just to dress in his finest calling clothes. Marcus felt like a young lad—filled with ardor as he created a cravat called Love Knot—in honor of his expectation of tying the knot with Stara before his visit was over. Yet, by Jove, the scene was scarce progressing as he'd imagined. Stara was reading the paper too many times. When she finally concluded, she gave him such a furtive glance, as if in sorrow that he'd missed a major point. He was at a loss for her inexplicable behavior. Her silence and set face shattered his elation, wiping out the softness of temperament pulsing through him all these days. The sense of triumph was fast ebbing.

Stara put the paper down on the Grecian settee and turned to face him. "It was most generous of you to take time to so arrange my situation. I am most appreciative. However, I did not, you recall, give you leave to interfere in my life. Even a kindness is an intrusion without permission to act for one. Understand? You in no way stand in such a position! I refused your offer—do you not recollect?"

"Good God," he exploded, his blue eyes storming to the point of icing up. "You don't mean to tell me you did something idiotic like accepting Lord Stockley!"

"I refused Lord Stockley," she said softly.

"Then what the devil have you done!" His hands reached over and grabbed her close. Their eyes were inches apart; his embrace hard and demanding.

She wrenched away. "You are no longer at liberty to treat me with such liberties. You have correctly surmised what is generally known in London already. It appeared in the *Gazette* yesterday."

Marcus's face was set in such a fury, she backed further away. But she recollected in time that the butler always hovered close by, so she need not be alarmed. As well, she noted Marcus was reining in his temper. Almost like a magical transformation, the debonair, mocking Marcus was in control. The ignited blue eyes were hidden now under lazy half-closed lids. After this pause, he leaned back and said matter-of-factly much as an interested observer might inquire, "Whom have you honored with your hand? Since you mentioned the *Gazette,* I scarce suppose it is an immoral liaison. Those arrangements are rarely printed, just whispered. "Is it the marquis?"

His eyebrows were lifted in anticipation and cool

appraisal. Stara kept him guessing, merely responding it
was not his lordship.

Fixedly following her every expression, Marcus
still had some hope she was merely tormenting him. But
there was none of the usual banter in her tone. Obligingly the gentleman played a guessing game. With each
supposition his voice becoming more scornful. "Some
young swain? What say, since we have eliminated the
spider-shank set with the marquis, shall we try the sap-
lings? Lord Darby? Sir Percy? Come, come, Miss
Carltons, why so hesitant? Don't tell me you have discovered another One-Jewel Jack? Ah, that's it!" Marcus
exclaimed, his eyes dancing. New hope that she was
jesting revived with her silence. Yes, she was gaming
him, he concluded. Like a man in shock who'd just
been told it had all been a prank, he let out a bark of
laughter and lightly carried on, "Our dear old highwayman has been resurrected one final time, I daresay. Tiresome fellow, yet dashed difficult to dismiss. He is
arriving tonight on his horse to take you off for a life on
the road. Have I discovered your secret?"

"I am marrying the man who dispatched the highwayman and the need for all future highwaymen in my
life."

The grin on Marcus's face froze solid. A long silence followed during which that smile lost its width.
Yet she could not turn her glance from his face as it
openly revealed a range of emotions that roused her
own—shock, despair . . . loss and love. The tumult of
it reached her, splashing over. All that intensity, so
close to her and the depth of his wildness thrilled her to
trembling. But she forcibly turned her eyes away knowing she had to end all union, all connection, even of
pain. She did so by quickly, casually announcing, "I am
pledged to Marmaduke. I shall be his duchess." Unable

not to, she lifted her hand and showed him the massive ruby ring.

"Ah, now it becomes clear—who you really are at heart. Does it not, Stara, my dear one?"

"You do not have leave to use my name," she said, becoming cool herself in reaction to his arctic voice and manner. So cold, she had no recourse but to reach for the warmth of the fireplace and stand before it.

Approaching and taking the hand with the ruby ring, he held on to it so forcefully, Stara felt the ring cutting into her fingers. Yet she would not cry out. She would meet him in this challenge and stare him down. Actually Stara was pleased he was pressing so tightly. She welcomed the pain, for it cloaked the softening, shaking sensation his closeness always evoked. Now the pain kept her from swaying. The pain kept her voice hard.

"You are hurting my hand," she concluded at length, but in such an uncaring way as if she were merely informing him of an oversight.

"You have hurt my heart," he said airily, but released her hand. Before him, Stara refused to rub it. Rather she walked back to the settee and sat down. Actually, her legs would not long have held her up. For in the back of her mind, all these days, had been the dread of this scene. At least now there was the relief that it was occurring. In her imagining, she'd accepted he would be furious with her, even indifferent—she had not imagined that torn look, nor his simply saying she had hurt his heart. That look, those words reached her heart, which all along had been dutifully obeying her head. Yet now it was demanding to be heard, insisting that it too had been hurt.

Stara shook her head to silence her own feelings. Looking up, she observed Marcus had not moved from the fireplace where they had been standing. He was transformed into a statue, incapable of movement.

Unable to bear that sight, Stara looked down. The ruby ring was there on her hand, and she let it claim her attention. Doggedly she concentrated on the glow—on its seductive promise of ease and wealth and crimson velvet drapes and awnings over her bed. But the thought of the duke in bed with her disturbed the picture, and she covered up the ring and looked up anxiously again, seeking Marcus. Yet now he had his back to her, staring directly down into the fireplace.

Still in that position, Marcus began talking, almost as if addressing her in the midst of the flames.

"What could you be thinking of—you little craven? Is wealth so important that you would deny what we are feeling?" He turned at the last, and she felt her heart jump as she saw the ravaged expression. Ah, he loved her.

She rose and wanted to run out of the room. If she stayed now, she would be done for. Her happy future, her wealth, her ease would disappear.

That action was enough to encourage him. Chasing her down, he stopped her at the door—pushing her against it and then completed the entrapment by leaning against her. In a moment they were kissing with a passion that could only recollect the fire he had been looking at all this time, as if he had drunk of it and was searing her with its heat, kiss by kiss.

He pulled her entire body into the kiss, as waves from their mouths flooded down and surged round, sending sparks flying about them. She let him kiss her as she had never done before. Unable not to. And in the back of her mind, was the thought she would never again be able to enjoy such pleasure. Her response had reassured the gentleman. He was grinning as he pulled her onto his lap on a chair near the door. She allowed it, holding on with all her energy.

"You're such a fool," he whispered, "Did you really think I'd let anyone else have you. I've wanted you from the moment I first saw you. I've been patient, but only so much patience is possible, feeling as I do—as *we* do. Say it, now. Say, you love me. And always will. Say it, damn you!"

In the delicious sway of emotions she would have said anything he wished to continue it, to feed it, to climax it, but those words were, she realized as she gasped them out, the truth. "I love you," she whispered.

"And always will!" he demanded not allowing her to hide her face against his chest until she had completed the oath completely.

"And always . . . will."

"And that you are giving the duke back his ring and telling him to go to the devil!"

He said the last while holding her face between his hands and searing her with the demand. She wanted to open her lips to him and say whatever he wished, so that he would kiss her again. At all costs the fire surging through her must not be cut off—it flowed so warmly with exquisite peaks that had her yearning to float in it forever. With all her might, she attempted to say the sentence, "I'll give him back . . . the . . . ri . . ."

But the last word would not come out. He shook her to get it out, but she closed her lips and looked down, away from his compelling eyes.

Cursing, Marcus let go of her abruptly and Stara was up.

The moment she was freed of his touch, sense began to take over. For protection Stara took several steps away from him, and more as he followed.

"You are as false as a Spanish coin! Deceit in every kiss!" he exploded.

"No," Stara said weakly. "Every word I said to you was true. I do love you. And when you touch me, you can make me say whatever you will. But I was not dishonest with you. I told you from the first I wished to be the duchess!"

"Ah, points for honesty then. Do you expect as much for your deception!"

"What deception?" she asked confused, regretting his retreating into that cold, sarcastic self. Too late. He was there—Marcus, the mocker—glibly taunting.

"The deception of your lips. Of your eyes. You love, you say—but what else are you saying, that love is secondary to money? To position? Is that not final proof that rather than a lady you are simply a whore."

She jumped at the word, denying it with a flush. But he insisted on the comparison. "They offer themselves to the highest bidder. You tell me you love me but that I have been outbid. What difference between that and a ladybird?"

Stara's soft daze was instantly dispelled; replaced by fury at such a pitch it rocked through, and erupted, "What is the male version of that? Demi-beau, loose-screw, rip . . . even rake. That is you. We all sell ourselves. 'Tis the fate of all younger sons. Of all the ladies of the ton seeking to marry well. It is one of society's principal functions. Are we all dishonorable? I have been attempting to sell Stara all my life to secure her from being tossed into the streets. Only now at long last am I raised so high I'll never have to fear that again. Duke-duke has already granted me the major part of my dream: I have my *own house*. On the Isle of Wight. Surrounded by white cliffs and sands and ocean and perpetual flowers. I have my paradise on earth. The deed is upstairs in my desk." She exhaled a long, sad sigh. "Yes, I love you, but what is love but a passing sensation. You loved Violet once and then tossed her away. You loved many women in your life—and shall probably love many more. I have only loved you, and I shall probably always love you, as long as we do not commit the folly of marrying that will lead us both to regret all we have lost for a moment of pleasure."

"More than a moment . . . a lifetime of it," he said huskily.

"I do not believe that. Love is . . . ephemeral. I have seen in society how the married ladies flock to the newest rake, usually you. And their husbands, even the most admired and respected ones seek Mistress Wilson. No, I have climbed too long to back down. I am in the actual process of being handed up to the top where a coronet awaits me." With head high, facing his blue glare down, Stara concluded, "Confound it, I have eaten of the scraps of society too long to turn away from the feast. Why should I turn away—just for . . ."

"For me?" he said with a laugh. "Not much of a trade, what? Though I have turned away from countless countesses and ladies who would keep *me* in comfort— I even risked my annuity with my father to win you. And even a sizeable amount to win your freedom from the Pinkertons. All to have you happy and in my arms. Foolish beyond permission would you not say?" He was speaking lightly, with a laugh, but she could see his fists were bunched tightly in emotion. His bitter glance raked over her. Once more she was affected by the force of him, so she cried out in defense and in determination to convince them both. "You won't love me long. You are incapable of that. Lasting love is a myth."

"So you would like to believe. But if it is not? What if this is your last chance to experience a love that surpasses ordinary existence and which explains our very being on earth? Consider, one is not here just for riches or mere comfort. . . ."

"I am."

"No! You are too much of an adventuress for that. You enjoy the challenge more than the rewards. Why else would you risk your life on the highway? You'll find mere comfort a suffocation. Poor exchange for your very self. On my oath, I warrant one day you'll awaken to discover your very duchess's position has become a prison. You who now have the wit to see the ton's falsity will soon find yourself struggling to break loose. But it will be too late to win back what you have now so heartlessly thrown away. Possibly you'll be reduced to searching for it from gentleman after gentleman, only to realize love like ours does not occur every season. It comes but once a lifetime. And then you will correctly grasp you've wantonly thrown away the best of yourself—your own wild and magnificent soul."

Stara was prodigiously affected. As if a ghost of her future self had appeared before her—lost and lonely. He was winning. She could not let him . . . either by his physical touch or the glibness of his tongue. "Curse you, damn you," she exclaimed, her very body protesting, all atremble. "Oh why did you come into my life at all, when I have finally won what I have been wishing for all my life? Why do you make me need to be with you, when I have prided myself in never needing anyone? One always loses whomever one loves. It is best not to love at all than to love and lose. I know. I know. When my mother died, leaving me alone in the world, I swore I would take from everyone who was so busy taking from and tossing me aside. You say boredom and comfort are prisons. Piffle! I have faced the fear of prison itself all these months and they are not comparable!"

He started to interrupt to remind her he had freed

her of that, but she put out her hands to silence him wanting to conclude her decision. "I choose comfort. If that means waking one morning and discovering being a duchess is tedious, so be it! Better that than waking and discovering the love for which I'd tossed all away has taken off to a new lady. Yes, I love you, but I can suppress it. Doubtless I shall continue to do so—until I've wiped it and you totally from my mind and heart."

Marcus's penetrating, blue eyes looked at her with a new emotion she'd not seen in them before—pity. Shaking his head, he said in a soft tone of regret, "You are not the adventuress I hoped. You are choosing fear not daring. I have overrated you."

"Then we are fortunate you did not persuade me," she said coldly. "If you had the disillusion would have occurred too late to save us both." Her eyebrows were raised. She rose as well, signaling his dismissal.

He bowed with his usual elegance. At the last moment, he swiftly stepped up to her. The debonair, laughing Marcus she had first met had returned for their finish. "So be it. We must part. Then let us make this a well-made parting." Pulling her against him, he whispered, "One last kiss to feed on . . . all our lives apart."

She could not pull away. The well-made kiss went on and on. Her arms around his neck so tightly holding on were telling him she would remember. His kisses were answering that he would not have her ever forget —damning her with them, searing them into her memory, before he pushed her off and walked out.

Stara sat down. The room was revolving about her in the sway of emotions. Her body, nay even her soul willed her to run after him and swear love eternal. But a voice in her head whispered, "Duchess, duchess, duchess." Pressing the ringed hand against her sobbing mouth, she was scarcely aware it had cut into her lips. "Oh Marc," she groaned, "Marc!"

His face would always be there before her she knew. She accepted that although now she attempted temporarily to cover his image with other views. Of her estate on the Isle of Wight. Of the many homes. Of never being homeless again. Of peace. Of plenty. Of the horses she could ride. Of the assurance of food. Of never having to go hungry! Yes, he was correct, her days of adventuring were over. She wanted peace. She wanted ease. Dear God, she wanted to be a duchess!

If only it did not hurt so much to lose him. But she would soon make herself forget him. She had always been able to make herself do what her will wished, no matter how much her heart shirked at it. And now too, she would press on. It was like that moment on the highway, when she'd weakened at the sound of the coach. Her sensibility, her honor had called her to stop, and yet the need, the daring to reach her goal, had set her on. She'd nudged her horse on, and next moment was stopping the coach. The risk of it had given her unforgettable exhilaration. Regret came subsequently— that was true. But also there'd been joy in holding her ladyship's pearls. Until Marcus took them away. Now she had all the pearls and all the position she wanted, and he was attempting to take those away again. "Damn him to hell!" she cried out from her shaken heart.

"You spoke, m'dear?"

Stara looked up astounded. Marmaduke had been ushered in and she had not even been aware of his presence: so little effect did it have on her.

Arranging the prettiest smile on her face, Stara held out her hand to greet her fiancé.

He bowed over it. They sat together on the settee companionably, without speaking. There was a flash of realization that whereas before she had striven to fill all their pauses with bright chatter, she had now advanced or succumbed to social wordlessness. Henceforth she'd be sunk in silence herself.

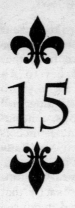

15

The London season was over, causing a mass exodus. Already door knockers were removed from town houses and furniture covered with holland spreads. The ton was flocking to country estates or watering places such as Brighton where the prince regent led the frolics or the more slumbery, modest town of Bath. And now at last society was at full leisure to assess all that had occurred that year.

First Byron, after a scandal of major proportions and a separation suit from his wife, had cast off from England and its narrow views of his life-style to self-exile on the continent. Beau Brummell's clandestine departure was still being discussed. But the grandest shock to society's self-esteem was the duke of Clairidge's engagement. For he in essence was exiling all society's ladies. After living in Lady Gwendolen's pocket for the whole season, he'd upped and chosen her beautiful companion, Stara Carltons.

The elevation of that dependent was an affront to the entire beau monde. It was one thing to have a poor companion in their midst and tolerate her to the extent of invitations to their routs, entertainments and the least exclusive balls. But quite another to have that minx, who had not even merited a voucher to Almack's, leapfrog from the fringes of their social set to the veritable top. There had to be some skulduggery! This theory was given credence by the curious, continuous silence of the lady who had clearly been destined as the rightful duchess—the diamond of their set, Lady Gwendolen.

The only possible explanation was Stara Carltons had lured his grace with her wiles! What exactly that meant, Lady Pomfort, who had pronounced it refused to specify but she was certain it had occurred. If ever there was a wily lady, it was Stara. Did not everyone recall the way she smiled at all the gentlemen? Further, she rarely, if ever, was seen to lower her lashes when talking to her many beaux. Of her fan, as well, she made scarce any use. The most inditing observation: Stara never blushed. Rather, one discarded admirer let it be known that she had seemed to understand the most shocking expressions. Marcus Justus had been heard using a certain word in her presence and she had merely shaken her head at him, without fainting on the spot.

All these gossips would have basked in self-justification if they had known that Stara actually never had fainted in her life. Nor made use of a vinaigrette. When cast down she just set her lips and carried on against either circumstance or people who threatened her. Yet upon arriving at Hillcrest, where Stara was to be wed in the fall, Stara was hard put not to swoon at the surprise awaiting her.

Originally the duke of Clairidge had made arrangements for Stara to spend the summer with his mother at the Dower House on the grounds of his own principal seat. But the marquis had stepped in, claiming himself in *parento locus*. He insisted Stara come to West-wardon, volunteering Hillcrest as the site of her actual wedding ceremony.

The awkwardness between herself and Lady Gwendolen had Stara at first refusing, preferring Mar-maduke's suggestion. But the marquis was filled with profuse assurances the invitation had been Lady Gwen-dolen's own idea. Further, to have Stara make a sudden departure from their company would give rise to the lowest form of undignified rumors that would reflect unfavorably and unflatteringly on both her ladyship and himself. Naturally Stara did not wish that. It would be a poor return for their past graciousness. Yet Stara had many a reservation, mainly that staying in her lady-ship's sphere would have her still continuing as her sat-ellite until the actual ceremony when at last Stara ascended to her proper, higher position.

It was Marmaduke's urging that tipped the deci-sion to Hillcrest. Truly he was anxious to put an end to the coldness between herself and her ladyship, but mostly he was reluctant to turn Stara over to his mother.

"Snores," Marmaduke explained.

Uncertain how that would disturb her, Stara must question that, claiming she hoped his mother would not wish to share her bed?

His grace was quick to clarify. "At table. At tea. After one game of whist. Nods off between words, ac-tually."

"Most soporific . . ." the lady concluded amused, claiming she would not be adverse to such a restful companion.

"Talks between snores," his grace amplified with so much dread, Stara was forced to acquiesce to Hill-crest. Actually that solution was inevitable. For there was one basic reason behind not only the marquis's invitation to Hillcrest, but the duke's urging her to agree and ultimately her own acceptance and that was the very bedrock of all the ton's actions—keeping up appearances. Nevertheless, Stara also sensed her ladyship had a hidden purpose, such as possibly making one last effort to wrest his grace from her companion's grasp. Of course one could not admit having such little confidence in his grace's affection. Nor give any indication of fearing a challenge. Further, Stara acknowledged she owed Lady Gwendolen the opportunity to strike back if she could. So the wedding would take place at Hillcrest.

The marquis and his daughter went ahead to their estate, ostensibly to begin preparations, but actually to allow more cooling time before the ladies met again. Stara was to remain in London a fortnight before being escorted to Westwardon in the duke's own crested carriage.

During her London time, Stara walked through the house, the garden and with a maid accompanying her through the fashionable district of Bond Street. At first she did not realize why she was so active—concluding it was anticipation. But as the image of Marcus's face continually flashed before her, she acknowledged there was someone she had to deal with, if no longer in person at least in her mind. She had to rid herself of Marcus Justus who apparently had seared himself so completely into her consciousness, she felt him still there—accompanying her on her jaunts. He walked at her elbow down the street. He laughed with her at the cartoons in the printers' windows. He escorted her back to the house and sat beside her in the library making witty asides on every sentence read. Insufferable intrusion.

Whether she was up or down, Marcus was always

before her. Once she put out her hand to touch him and was stricken to discover nothing really there, after all. What galled Stara was that he was so often in her thoughts while she was apparently no longer in his. For indeed he'd gone off somewhere without even taking leave of either her or Lady Gwendolen. Simply departed. More likely mending fences with his father. Or living with another Violet. Whatever, it was not her concern henceforth.

Happy intrusions into this wallowing were her marriage preparations. The ruby ring did not long remain solely on her fingers before being joined by a golden one with cameo stone—one of the duke's own designing. He had a hobby of creating and collecting jewels. Another presentation of his was less welcome. It was a note from the dowager duchess, thanking her for the Dunstan Collection. Every phrase was basted with begrudging condescension, clearly signaling difficulties ahead. But expecting actual rebuff, polite resentment was tolerable and probably could be overcome in the future. She contented herself with the present happiness of presents. Foremost—a collection of emeralds, also en parure—matching bracelet, necklace and earrings. Unquestionably his grace was a jewel man. He himself wore as many as style permitted a duke, which was more than anyone else. That included several rings and fobs, a jeweled quizzing-glass; a variety of jeweled stickpins that matched his outfits and snuffboxes ditto. It pleased him to find a new body on which to display his passion, and Stara was becoming more and more bedecked and bejeweled. Preferring the less gaudy pieces, Stara was forced to accept his grace's taste. Whatever she selected he would immediately dismiss with the outraged judgement, "Merest trumpery pieces." So Stara found herself possessing quite a valuable collection of gaudy if not outright vulgar gems. A tiara with canary yellow diamonds on its peaks predominated. It was presented with a matching ferronière, or a diamond pendant on her forehead held by a gold chain. When she let her hair loose and wore the full ensemble of tiara and ferronière, his grace was moved reverently to kiss her brow. He'd similarly honored her ears with a fondle when she modeled his gift of sapphire droplets. But for the several rowed pearls that reach deep into her décolletage, he restrained himself to blow a kiss modestly in that delicate direction.

Naturally all these jewels had to have golden caskets to nestle within. Other tokens of his grace's wealth if not affection were tippets and silk shawls and a collection of fragile fans. On the very day they were to depart for Westwardon, he arrived with a fur wrap for the ride. She joyfully exclaimed at its appearance, if not appropriateness, for the weather was warmish. Still, Stara kept the wrap if not on her, at least near her on the seat—forming a very comfortable cushion she could lean on and a delightful separation between herself and the slumbering duke.

At a certain turn at Westwardon, Stara could not help but recollect herself impersonating One-Jewel Jack. Just there was the place she'd stopped the carriage and had the duke, her ladyship and even Marcus at her mercy. That led to memories of her escape to the cave and Marcus's pursuit and their face to face challenge, pistol in hand, pointing at each other's head.

Delightful memory, she owned. Marcus had given many such.

Hillcrest loomed ahead in the nick of time to stop her thoughts from continuing down that dangerous path.

Another recollection intruded, but as it was not of Marcus, Stara allowed it: her first view ever of Hillcrest. She'd arrived from the penury of the Pinkertons to the

marquis's palatial residence. How awesome had been
the size of the red brick house with its wings of gray
stone. A mixture of tastes she now could fault, but then
just seemed a fantasy home in which she'd been given
her own room. Remembering her small chamber with a
fireplace that was always kept lit, she felt again as she
did then, her obligation to Lady Gwendolen. But being
wishful of making some reparation did not extend to
returning the duke. Having paid dearly by giving up her
love, Stara felt she'd more than well earned every single
new dignity. At that last Stara turned to look at his
grace who was yawning, just awakening from his nap.

"Pleasant ride," he said companionably. Stara gave
him her adoring glance he'd come to rely on. Dash it,
that set him up as naught had all his life. Enjoyed being
admired. The thought that he would have that as a constant, assured him he had made the correct choice.

Leading his intended into the estate, his grace was
pleased to see that Lady Gwendolen was no longer
playing hide-in-her-chamber. Rather she was standing
with her father to greet her guests. And, what ho! Unlike her usual indifferent expression, she was smiling.

Stara greeted the marquis with her usual respect
and turned to her ladyship. The pleasant expression,
Stara noted with relief, remained in place. But when her
ladyship went further and embraced her and the two
walked as they once did, with arms around each other's
waist, Stara was near to tears in her gratitude. This
kindness continued unabated. Rather than the usual
back bedroom, Stara was given a prominent suite that
included besides the bedchamber, a balconied sitting
room. A further mark of favor; her ladyship followed
her to that suite, chatting happily, while Stara removed
her bonnet and repaired the evidences of the journey.

At one point while brushing out her thick curls,
Stara noted in the mirror the first stiff expression on

Lady Gwendolen's face. It was possible to explain that away as Gwendolen's usual reaction to the thickness and sweep of Stara's hair. For when Stara turned, her ladyship had her new pleasant expression firmly back in place.

Again with arms around each other's waists, the two ladies descended to the waiting gentlemen. Stara felt herself truly happy and all gratitude. Thus the surprise was doubly effective and would have thrown another sort of lady off her feet. Actually the moment Stara walked into the drawing room, she sensed, off to the side a gentleman present—his back to her. He was rising and turning. Yet Stara knew who it was before her eyes verified it. "Mr. Justus," she said calmly.

Marcus bowed in his most courtly manner. His accustomed composure was only interrupted by sparks of devilry in his eyes. She should have known, she thought —more amazed with herself for being such a widgeon. Lady Gwendolen's friendliness should have alerted her. Looking about, she noted Duke-duke conversing with the marquis. Marcus was all expectancy. Obviously there was more to come. His grace emitted a "By Jove!", followed by "What say?" and "What ho!"— looking at her ladyship with strong disapproval. That was all Stara's quicksilver wits needed. Schooling her expression into complete indifference, she turned to Lady Gwendolen and inquired politely, "Am I to wish you happy?"

There was a flicker of discontent that she could not have made the announcement herself. Nevertheless Lady Gwendolen replied cheerily, "Oh yes, rather. Mr. Justus came to me and made a full confession of his long-standing love for me, and what could a lady do, but acquiesce. Mr. Justus has always been first in my heart, as I have been in his," she said with a flutter of her sparse lashes.

That loud pronouncement was accepted with a stiff upper lip by the duke, a stiff smile by the marquis, a full smile by Marcus. Only Stara did not accept it at all. "Indeed?" she questioned, turning a full glare at Mr. Justus.

"I blush to confess the depth of my affection," he said, with his usual mocking glance. "Almost, I should say, akin to yours for your fiancé," he concluded.

"Then it is deep as a well."

"Well, well. As deep as that? Small simile, Miss Carltons. Why not say rather as deep as an ocean?"

"Not much for by the sea, meself," the duke interposed, not understanding their colloquy—catching just the ending. "Said to my love, have the sea house with me blessing. Beastly sounds of the sea birds all day. Caw, caw, caw. Said to me steward, 'Too many gulls. One more and I'd call it Gull House.'"

"Only when you're in it," Marcus could not resist retorting.

Stara needlessly, speedily interrupted, lest one of the others understood. "Gulls and cormorants winging about always make me feel like a bird of a feather."

"Indeed, allow me to pluck one of your white feathers," Marcus softly bantered, "and give it to you for desertion."

Stara flinched at being labeled a coward so openly, only he was smoothly, loudly rushing on, "I collect we both have happily soared to new heights." Whereupon he kissed Lady Gwen's hand in tribute. Stara felt it on her very own skin and surreptitiously had to touch where it burned.

Pleased by his attention, her ladyship signaled Marcus to sit next to her on the settee, announcing they were to continue the very interesting conversation begun before. "We were talking of a grand tour through Europe. Mr. Justus is familiar with all the most invigorating sights. We are to remain for a fortnight in each country and conclude with a month in Italy. Or was it Greece?"

Stara's heart sank. Her desire had always been to go abroad. This was taunting indeed. Turning to Marmaduke, she reminded him they'd not yet designated the location of their wedding trip. Could they not consider Europe? But his grace was horrified at the thought of leaving home. The most he would consider was Scotland. "Got me a castle up there. Devilish fine shooting grounds. Lakes. Woods. Ghost."

"In the woods?" Stara exclaimed, caught by that last mention.

His grace reassured her the woods were free for shooting. The ghost was confined to the castle. Marval Castle." Marmaduke said turning to Lady Gwendolen. "You recall—spoke about it. Showed you a painting."

Her ladyship's eyes lit up with recognition. He mentioned with pride that it was over a hundred rooms, and she replied she had visited in that area with her father, at a place, Stallards, the estate of a relative, Lord Bolton. The marquis gave his irrelevant reminiscences of a shooting trip through Scotland, which finally meandered back to Stallards and a description of it that led to a comparison of the two estates. All three nobles fell to sizing up not only the surrounding properties but every detail of the main domains. In the middle of which, Stara finding herself not half concerned with which livery was more indicative of the region, walked to the doorway of the veranda. Looking at the garden, her thoughts reverted to Greece. What joy to see the Parthenon! Tipping her head backward, she picked up the thread of the conversation. Now Hillcrest was being counted, how many sitting rooms as compared to the duke's Scottish castle. The marquis was in a rare tweak over the duke's claiming victory, when Lady Gwendolen put in with some enthusiasm, "You are forgetting the second sitting rooms." Her father thanked her for the addition. But the duke topped all by counting all the sitting rooms in all his estates and Lady Gwendolen's eyes were getting rounder and rounder as the figure extended into the thousands, rounded out.

Stara concentrated on the sky—it was twilight. Soon the stars would come out in the thousands themselves. Marcus was at her side. "I daresay they shall be comparing chamber pots next," he whispered.

Stara could not resist laughing, but caught herself abruptly and frowned at him. "Your fiancée is also there counting her properties. Which you shall, I expect, soon be sharing. Why not count Hillcrest's silver to assure you have not sold yourself cheaply."

Marcus's face flushed but he bowed and said, "Touché." Then with his incorrigible grin added, "It appears we have both proved ourselves unprincipled adventurers who have sold our loves to the nobles. For certain we ought be counting our coming assets, but rather we are here gazing up at the stars as can the most impoverished peasant. The stars are free even to the wild highwayman as he waits for his next moment to strike. The moon is everyones and throughout the world it is shared as is the joy of love."

Stara stared at him, wondering what he was saying to her. "Are you regretting your soon-to-be wealth? Are you saying you prefer the common pleasures?"

His blue eyes lit up as if he'd swallowed a moon and it was spilling out of him. "Ah, common pleasures are indeed to my taste. The commonest of all being love. *That* pleasure I relish above all. My heart is now jumping in anticipation of that pleasure I shall shortly taste with my dear Gwendolen. In Greece. Speaking of the stars and moon, there is no moon like the one in Greece. Full gold and round as it comes down, almost inches above one's head. I have lain in the fields aside Agamemnon's tomb, walked under the Lion Gate, wandered where Helen herself must have sat, combing her beautiful, long hair while Paris planned to steal her from her husband. What sort of people are they who risk all for love? He and she plunged both their countries into a war for their passion. Do you fault them? Or envy them?"

At that moment Stara envied them. She was bemused, transported to Greece with Marcus. There they were together on a high hill. Marcus was sensing where she was going. Keeping his eyes on her so steadfastly, he continued his description of that country and soon they traveled, flew, soared together. His voice was low in her ear as he softly concluded, "Do you recall Marlowe's description of Helen? 'Was this the face that launch'd a thousand ships . . . Sweet Helen, make me immortal with a kiss.' "

Stara turned to him at that. His blue eyes were shining with the passion of his suggestion. Her own eyes were starry bright at the thought. Their blended gazes sent shivers through her soul as he concluded, "There was one face I recalled when picturing Helen." She waited breathlessly for the revelation.

He grinned at her expectancy and said blithely, "Why who else but the lady of my fob? There has never been one to equal her for perfection."

That mockery had Stara taking several steps away. She had been on a precipice, moments from stepping off into the abyss of his words and presence, when his humor recalled her to herself and had her quickly returning to her place next to her fiancé.

His grace did not look up at her presence, not having been aware of her departure.

"What are you counting now?" she asked tolerantly.

"Trees," he said, continuing his absorbed tally. Lady Gwendolen was gasping and oohing at the amount, as he went on estate by estate.

Marcus had joined them. He stood a moment and then whispered to her, "A perfect topic for a gentleman with such a wooden head."

She gave him a glare, but he silently laughed and returned to the veranda.

In her mind she was back there herself. She felt him willing her to join him. He would talk to her about Greece, or even Italy . . . but she forced herself, *willed* herself to remain at her fiancé's side.

"And now *horses!*" his grace was saying with elation.

That evening Stara found herself unable to sleep. She walked about—quite, quite cast down. Before retiring, Marcus had kissed Lady Gwendolen's hand with such fervor, her ladyship had almost floated to her bedroom. The duke had walked off, arm in arm with the marquis, counting bedrooms. He had nodded to her and she to him. Then she'd closeted herself into her chamber, attempting to wipe from memory the sight of Lady Gwendolen together with Marcus.

Of course she was jealous. Actually the newly engaged couple had left her sadly pulled, unable to swallow throughout the evening meal. Marcus had carried on vulgar attempts to catch her ladyship's glance throughout every course. Lady Gwen had continually blinked back. Before half the meal, Stara had to own herself thoroughly fed up.

Why did his doing exactly what she had done make her decision seem crass? Perhaps because she saw how it looked from the outside rather than how it felt from the inside need! Oh, it was foolish beyond permission to have assumed that Marcus would just go away and leave her to enjoy her success. She had had fleeting thoughts of sometime seeing him again and regretting her choice, but hoped she would be safely wed before.

Blushing, Stara admitted she had a secret fantasy of Marcus becoming her future cicisbeo, as the duke himself had suggested . . . which meant she had never truly accepted losing him. Ladies had often had lovers on the side—that much she knew. In some cases, such as Lady Jersey and Lady Hardwick, it was the prince regent himself. But more likely, she admitted with chagrin, it was Marcus. In the back of her mind she had clung to the possibility that someday, somehow, the two would be together—as a man and woman must be together. But all those suppositions were now harshly exploded and replaced by Marcus and Lady Gwendolen in that joined position.

Farewell all fancies. For Marcus as Lady Gwendolen's husband was not the same as a poor, heartbroken lover following her with his sad eyes begging for a crumb of her affection. In place of that dream was the horror of this summer of two couples together—a grim *pas de deux à quartre*. Unendurable, unending . . . the undoing of her ease and peace to come.

16

For a full fortnight Marcus continued to be in her presence. Stara felt like a teased child, with a comfit held just away from her lips and told it belonged to another at her side.

Marcus used his eyes like weapons. Those intense blue lights had so many messages in their sapphire depths: amusement, mockery, challenge, she could scarce parry each one. Confound those eyes! Not only did they follow her about but their every connection left a residue that kept her restless to connect again. She had to exorcise his hold, did so by keeping her head averted.

Yet on the surface, he too was evading her—devoting himself with much flourish to Lady Gwendolen. He praised her ladyship's dress, gestures and applauded every meandering remark as if it was a bon mot of the first order. Stara was only appeased by spotting a twitch round his lips. Clearly Marcus was a complete hand. Was that what he wanted then—a wife to amuse him, secret shoulder shakings on the side, twinkles belying his protestations? Yet as she was castigating Marcus for shamming through his relationship, she shamefacedly admitted, with a jolt, he was mimicking her own performance with the duke. After that realization, she was put to the blush when she caught herself with heavy compliments in her mouth and abruptly was stilled. Only to have Marmaduke, accustomed to her praise, look longingly at her and she must continue. "I'm being jolly decent to him," she assured herself, to appease her actions. All her heart wringings and conscience tugs were unnecessary. For his grace had too much confidence in his importance to assume anyone saw him as less than he saw himself. He merely needed her to go through the expected motions. Actually anything less would have been considered not keeping up her end; and anything more—"going beyond the line."

He and Lady Gwendolen were easy to gull because they demanded nothing less. Blind to all but approval, they lived in a world of it.

Still Stara had to excuse herself somewhat, for she at least wished to be sincere while Marcus operated fully in a spirit of unholy amusement. Not only was he diverted by Lady Gwendolen and Marmaduke, but even more so by her own attempts to belong and to squelch him. If only she could take life as lightly as he. Yet, yet there was an occasional flash in Marcus's eyes, suggesting he was merely a more experienced performer. That appeased—proving she was not alone in her dilemma.

Then just as Stara could not bear one more false, pandering moment of the four's sham scenes, Lady Gwendolen ended them all by taking to her bed with an infectious cold. Everyone was much alarmed, for her ladyship was the pet of the household. The marquis sent for a London specialist and could only be easy when assured it was no more than a summer cold. Nevertheless her ladyship would allow no one access to her, except her personal maid and dresser, until she was fit to be seen. That desertion left Marcus with no puppet to string along. Henceforth he concentrated wholly on disturbing Stara's smooth relationship with Duke-duke. At dinner one of the removes was a large fish with its mouth open. A natural object of humor for Marcus who quickly offered it to Stara, claiming she had an affection for cold-blooded choices. As if on cue the oblivious Marmaduke took half the fish on his plate while Marcus gleefully pronounced, "Fish of a fin, swallows his twin!"

The duke's self-importance protected him, understanding only enough to launch into a tale demonstrating his fishing prowess. At its conclusion, Marcus who had been staring at him with unnerving concentration, suddenly said softly, "Do you never conclude one of your fishes too insignificant to keep . . . and decide to throw her back?"

"Never throw back a catch. Too small, keep 'em for bait. Always make use of what one gets."

"There speaks the true aristocrat. Everything belongs to you. Never dream of sharing with the less fortunate, I expect," Marcus was now allowing a bit of anger to enter his raillery.

While Duke-duke stared in confusion, Stara jumped in at last. "His grace is known for his generosity. His cottagers are indebted to him. His villages are all well cared for. He has an open hand to all."

Marcus turned with pleasure to continue the joust with her, that having been his principal aim, since she'd been avoiding combat, "Ah, such lack of firmness suggests he might very like let a catch slip out of hand, last moment, what say?"

Stara's eyes flashed at him. "The duke has a very strong grip!"

Taken aback by his fiancée's determined defense, Marmaduke could not but second her evaluation—all the while thinking it was jolly decent of her to be so protective.

But there came a time when Duke-duke was not present to buffer for one and buffoon for the other. He'd joined the marquis in a visit to his cottagers, so Stara retired to the library waiting. When Marcus entered, she had an almost unquenchable, overwhelming desire to run to him as if he were willing her to do so. Indeed, she even took a few steps in his direction and then reversed and devoted her attention to the bookshelves.

There was a ladder for reaching the top editions. Momentarily she had a flash image of herself ascending it and missing her step, promptly being caught by Marcus. It would be a comforting ruse just to be in his arms for a blink.

"I should see through something so obvious," he said softly at her side.

Ruffled, Stara denied that reading of her thoughts, but her degree of flummox made it obvious he had hit if not on the mark, close to it.

"Why aren't you writing love notes to send up to Lady Gwen!"

"I have written my quota for today," he said, airily. "And now I am free to torment you."

"Why do you wish to do that? *I* have accepted your choosing another with perfect equanimity."

"Gammon! You are cut up, every time I kiss Lady Gwen—which is why I so often do it in your vicinity. Which calls to mind, why have I not seen his grace honor you with a single mark of affection? Is Duke-duke shy of bestowing an embrace? Have the two of you ever kissed?"

"It is scarcely your business what means of affec-

tion his grace and I indulge in. A gentleman would
never question such private matters. Certainly never
openly."

With his lazy smile, he explained he was merely
inquiring as a matter of general concern. "Just to en-
lighten us lesser mortals—how do you intend to live
without the pleasure of love? I am fully aware you have
no fondness for him beyond his title. But is that noble
even more of a fribble than he appears? Obviously he
does not love you, my girl, look to it!"

"He does love me! He's told me so. He *has* kissed
me," Stara shot back in humiliation. "He simply is too
much of a gentleman to display his affection before
other people. Frankly, I too prefer private demonstra-
tions."

Marcus's eyes were all delight at that as he thanked
her for calling him up short. "By Jove, if you wish a
private demonstration, what manner of cad am I to allow such a private moment to pass without demonstrating! Your pardon. I shall instantly remedy my
dereliction. . . ."

She stepped away from him, ordering him to keep
his distance.

"Let us cease this game playing," he said gruffly.
"You could no more remain for a lifetime in Marmaduke's company than I can in Lady Gwendolen's."

Stara remained silent, feeling his eyes on her. Reluctantly she met his glance.

"Are you capable of love?" he asked with enough
anger to alter the light touch of their duel.

"I love you," Stara admitted, incurably direct.

He laughed. Taken in surprise. "A puny sort of
love, I daresay."

"It is a genuine love," Stara continued composedly,
refusing to rise to the bait.

"No," he insisted. His voice grew hard as flint,

with sparks striking out at her. "Love is not genuine when it is admitted so . . . so indifferently. Confound your thin-milked soul!" He took a breath and then continued with less ire and just fire, "I love you to the ultimate of my being—past reason, past self-preservation, past intelligence, past waiting *any longer*. . . ."

He broke off as the door opened. The footman came to light the candles. The couple waited in silence until he'd concluded and departed. In the candlelight Stara rose and let her finger trail over a stalk of hard wax, stopping just short of the flame.

"We cannot discuss here what we must," he said gruffly. "Where can we meet alone?"

"There's no purpose. . . ." she faltered.

"The cottage—where you dropped your cache, my lady highwayman!"

"That cottage has been let."

He prevented her slipping out from the door by blocking her escape with his tall form lounging against the knob. "Where shall we meet?" he demanded, but Stara was shaking her head. "You don't dare!" he taunted.

Looking at his mocking gaze, the lady felt that destructive surge in her veins to meet a challenge, to risk, to conquer . . . to dare.

"By the waterfall," she said with a small, breathless laugh. "The cave."

Both their eyes kindled with the memory of their original meeting there.

Throwing back his head and laughing, Marcus instantly stepped aside taking her pledged parole.

The next morning Stara was already dressed in her new black riding outfit that fit her form in such a fashion that it became more daring than even a low-cut gown. Its ebony color made the whiteness of her skin more remarkable. Her hat had a visor brim. It was severe, but that was contrasted by her wearing her hair loose and long.

Neither Stara nor Marcus had spoken after making their morning appointment. Actually Stara had a difficult night. She gave herself over fifty reasons to fail the appointment. Everyone was summarily dismissed. The heart has its own reasons and arguments.

Having arrived ahead of him, Stara waited outside the cave, facing the waterfall. The warmth of the day made the cascading water seem so refreshing, she had a desire to disrobe completely and toss herself under. Her urges would undoubtedly destroy her, she told herself severely. Nevertheless, she walked through the bank of the stream, ruining the shine of her boots. The train of her riding outfit was tucked over her arm keeping it high and dry as she reached the opening of the dark, cool cave.

He was not there, which regrettably gave time for second thoughts. As an adventurous lady she'd long philosophized if one thought too much about an action, one never accomplished anything. But next moment she heard sounds at the cave's entrance and was relieved all leisure for reconsidering was passed. What was to occur was beginning.

Not wanting to be spotted so easily, making a challenging game of their encounter, Stara walked further into the cave, but keeping in the outer chamber.

It was a small cavern. Not far from here were larger limestone excavations, spacious enough to hold streams and lakes in their depths. This one she'd fully explored with a lantern until she knew its every twist and turn. It had three passages that turned back to the beginning and one that continued into the heart or the inner chamber and beyond. The deep center was cold and black and filled with hanging stalactites. But today she did not have her lantern, nor was she wearing a cape to keep out the cold so she remained in the front. It was tolerably comfortable there, due to many a split in the stone where the sun broke through. Even from the wide mouth, sunlight and sun rays spilled in. To the side and above in this anterior chamber, she'd previously discovered an extending ledge situated directly under a hole in the roof. Of such proportions was the hole, the sunlight spilled down in a focused stream, pooling up there. Sitting directly under made one feel as if one were outside in the warmth, while being hidden in a secret place. Indeed so sequestered was this spot she could not be observed from below unless she leaned over . . . or stood up.

To that special ledge Stara climbed and settled herself to wait. Above she saw a slice of blue sky. Below it was variegated shades of light and dark through which abruptly one moving shadow emitted a stream of curses.

"Where the blazes are you?"

Unmistakably Marcus's loverlike tones, she concluded with a smile.

"Look for me," she called out, her voice echoing.

The sun was throwing a halo around Stara as she leaned over a ledge above him. Her hair spilled down long and glowing. In an instant he was there and had her in his arms. The ledge was narrow. Both began to slip.

"You could have chosen a less precarious position."

"We *are* in a precarious position," she said calmly.

"*You* are," he mocked, making clear what was always known, that women suffered for any discretion rather than the gentlemen involved. "Lady Gwendolen would not criticize me for trysting with you. Rather she'd fault you as a hoyden. As would all society, in faith."

"That is correct. I am the one risking all. Yet I accept the risk for the reward. Aren't you here to pleasure me?" Her voice was all laughter at his shock. No gentleman, even one as open and seemingly unflappable as Marcus could accept direct talk from a lady. She deliberately kept outfacing him, making her point even more pointed, "Rather like a ladybird yourself, I daresay."

"Good God, I've never . . ."

"Been reduced to a mere instrument of pleasure? Like Violet? How does the reversal feel? Indeed is not *pleasure* your objective in life? What else do you want from *me*?"

"If that's what you think . . ." he began, but she was carrying on with a low vibrant voice. "If you really cared for me, you would have left me alone, knowing that I'd find it difficult to resist you."

"Confound your logic! Why should I leave you alone? Why make it easy for you to continue with your mistake! You know you have to turn down the duke and come to me. Your coming to me now proves that."

"No," Stara said frankly. "It only proves that my wanting was stronger than my will. It also proves what you've always known about me. I'm an adventuress . . . taking a chance for the wild dare of the moment. You knew I could not completely refuse this meeting with you. So now I am here. What do you want?"

"You know what I want," he said gruffly, leaning down. He reached for her hands, kissing first one palm and then the other. Then he pressed both saluted palms against her face as if transferring the kisses. She felt them on her skin. Then Marcus kissed the front of her hands on her face and between her fingers. She allowed that just for curiosity's sake, she told herself, wondering where he would go next.

He went to her lips with his lips. Obviously his

original aim. Kiss after kiss. She allowed herself to be
controlled by him physically, as she'd so often imagined
at night. Their lips were so long together they began
breathing as one. She was learning what it felt like to be
so meshed into another the blending became a complete
comfort. All the loneliness she'd ever felt since her
mother was gone was being filled up—every empty, lost
spot found and touched and soothed and joined. At one
point her eyes flickered open and Stara saw an intense,
blue world above, as if the sky had come down and was
threatening to flood over, to crash into her. But she
wanted it to crash . . . to finish her off—finish something that was tossing her wildly about. A storm was
loose in her. In both.

"I say, Mr. Justus, is this the place?"

It was the high-pitched voice of Marmaduke Melton, the seventh duke of Clairidge. Clearly the fastidi-
ous lord was not finding the cave up to his level. He did
not trust his riding garb to the muck about him, and
thus must walk on tiptoe and with eyes down. He had a
horror at the thought the closest stalactite might touch
his attire. The coat after all was by Weston, and he
would lief it have no spelunking souvenirs on its sleeves
or shoulders. He called again for Marcus—which made
clear to Stara his appearance was by appointment. Instantly she moved back, hiding in the cold shadows.
Rapidly her senses cooled as the realization sunk in.
Her shock deepened at the dimensions of this obvious
trap—for the duke, but more ignobly for herself!

"You traitorous thatchgallows . . . you cad of the
first order!" she said, her voice low but weighted with
betrayal. "This great moment of love, I gather, was
mere bait to keep me here long enough to be exposed.
You are worse than the Pinkertons! Just like them, you
are seeking to get what you can from me, regardless if I

wander in despair ever after! What a widgeon I was to have any feeling for you."

"Control yourself," he responded softly, matter-of-factly explaining, "This had to be done. You would not be turned from your destructive path by mere words. Since you did not have the fortitude to break with the duke, I simply arranged for the duke to break with you. I'm going to call . . . to show him we are here . . . in a compromising position."

His voice throughout was expressionless, each word spoken lost more and more volume until stillness took over.

"Yes," Stara whispered, "you are beginning to hear how infamous your plan sounds when said openly, are you not? Well, call out, man! If that is your aim? Or is it dawning on you that one cannot win another by such a sham? If I am not willing to give up Duke-duke, your stratagems shall not force me. As for his grace, I shall simply cry out that you have gammoned me into coming here. He will believe it. I've proven to you before about both the duke and Lady Gwendolen that they will always believe what puts them in the least disgraceful position. I'll call to him to rescue me. He wishes always to appear as my hero. Go ahead! Do your worse! I am prepared to foil you! All you've achieved is my contempt!"

Marcus gave her a polite bow and shied away, quickly climbing down. Below, the duke was calling out at intervals. Marcus approached him. In the shadows he led him back toward the entrance, all the while rapidly explaining his mistake. He had not found a stack of jewels on which he wished the duke's opinion. Rather they were mere trumpery pieces.

At the cave's entrance, his grace stopped, refusing to be pushed out. He had not come alone. His groom was there.

"What say, Mr. Justus. I do not enjoy such flummery. Did you or did you not find some interesting jewels? And if you did, why not bring 'em me? Why urge our meeting here? Got a notion you mean me harm. Brought me man here to protect me. Fischer, search the cave. See if there are any ruffians here!"

"You're jesting!" Marcus exclaimed. "Or rather I was jesting. It is all naught. You are perfectly safe, my good fellow. Merely walk out of the cave and ride back to Hillcrest."

"You are an adventurer, egad!" Marmaduke exclaimed. "With an ace up your sleeve, I warrant. Brought me here to rob me! Notice you ain't bought her ladyship a ring. Your pockets are to let! Lady Gwendolen's got high expectations. Don't settle for ordinary jewels. Not like me lovely Miss Carltons who ain't likely to take a pet at anything. Hard to please her ladyship. Chap like you needs lots of blunt. Were you intending to hold me ransom?"

So preposterous was that, Marcus had to laugh aloud. His sound echoed in the cave. Some of the righteous assurance went out of his grace. Yet he would not easily relinquish his conclusions. Indeed once Marmaduke put himself to the fatigue of thinking out a problem, he generally held to it buckle and thong. Had to be some kind of skulduggery here which he would scotch. Brought his man. It was his plan to expose Mr. Justus and prove him unworthy of her ladyship, and he intended to carry on with it. Lady Gwendolen ought not allow herself to be linked to such a ruffian. Two more servants were waiting with the horses. He called them to the cave. Fischer was already advancing with a lantern into the cave.

Marcus attempted to look amused and indifferent. Yet his heart feared. Even at his most jealous and most desperate, he would not have wished Stara to undergo so public a humiliation. His expression continued inscrutable, very much as when he held a losing hand at cards. "My dear fellow, you are perfectly free to search this entire area, with an army if that is your wish, but I can only say, you have not only jumped to an unwarranted conclusion, but are rather overwrought. Too much claret at dinner last night? Brandy afterward? A hair of the dog this morning? The mind boggles at the tale you have concocted. I vow you must be a reader of these Gothic romances! How else to explain such . . . idiocy. Unless it is your natural bent?"

Laughing and walking calmly past his grace with all apparent disinterest in the search, Marcus left the cave. The attitude of amusement had his grace reconsidering, following Marcus out onto the bank. The waterfall was making so much noise, he could hardly hear Marcus's continued chatter, but he could tell the blasted fellow was finding it all vastly amusing. Marmaduke was prepared to call off his men when he took another look at Marcus. Fellow was not going to outbluff him. "Make a thorough search, there!" he called out, and sat down on a rock to wait.

Marcus's heart was beating. Any moment he expected to hear a cry, to see Stara being dragged out by his underling. Despite the distasteful manner, if she were discovered, it certainly would complete his original plan. Yet he no longer believed in it himself, now that he was awake from the wild torments of his night's longing, during which he'd concocted this mad scheme. Rather he must arrange a story to exculpate the lady. He would have to throw himself upon the sword to save Stara's reputation. Otherwise he'd lose any possibility of her ever accepting him. He must prove himself worthy of her. The only way to do that was to show his love was strong enough to allow her to make her own choice. Never at a loss for long, Marcus had his new tale at a ready. He would confess to having abducted Stara against her will and brought her here to show the duke and have him free her at a price. That story would doubtless disgrace him and his new found relationship with his father, and might even lead to a stay at Newgate. Yet he could do no less than protect Stara.

"I say, your grace," Marcus called, still with his amused smile. "I confess I do have something of yours in there. But I wish to explain that I took it against its will. That I myself forcibly . . ."

He stopped speaking abruptly as the duke's man returned empty-handed.

Egad, Marcus exhaled in profound relief. His usual devil-may-care attitude was back in full force and he could not stop himself from laughing! That wondrous minx! She knew a way out! Yes, he recollected, she'd once gone into the cave and yet somehow doubled back and appeared outside the entrance. Must be a side portal, leading to the top. Best get these fellows some distance away from the area.

No sooner thought of then acted. Marcus jumped onto his horse and drew them away. Hastily the duke ordered his menials after him. Even his grace was rushing to mount. All were away in a racket of hooves and oaths and shouts of "Halt!" Then silence. Except for a light laugh as Stara emerged from behind the waterfall. Having heard all, and realizing Marcus was going to disgrace himself to save her, she lost some of the fury that his original deception had sparked in her. Whistling for her horse, she mounted. Her hair, splattered by the waterfall, dried in the wind as it streamed behind her. Her knowledge of the shortest routes assured she would be at Hillcrest before the rest, which she was. Just barely. The duke was catching Marcus in the stable, while Stara, having returned her horse to the hands, was slipping out.

"Gammoned you for good, your grace," Marcus was crying. "We've had a jolly lively morning, what?"

Flummoxed and fuming his grace exclaimed, "This was all a jest! For what purpose? Oddsblood?"

"Merely to while away a dull morning. Some fun, eh? I thought as a gentleman who had encountered One-Jewel Jack, you must be finding the days beastly boring! Gave you a faux adventure. Are you not grateful to me?"

His grace remembered his position and that of his adversary and concluded he was not worthy of his challenge. Nor would he risk his life over a mere prank. With all the disdain of his breeding he exclaimed, "Touched in the upper works, by Jove. Not worthy of her ladyship." Stalking away, he turned and gave vent to his wrath, spitting out, "Obviously a *second* son!" He could have tossed back no worse insult. Satisfied, his grace left the field of combat. No duel. No fisticuffs could have leveled the fellow better. And his grace sniffed in self-congratulation.

Stara relaxed. All her limbs atremble. Marcus had emerged unscathed. As had she. All was as before. Except for her regret. If she had been caught, she would have been free to go with Marcus without having to make the decision herself to give up the duke. It might have been best if she had not hidden. For then it might have all been fait accompli, while now the decision was once more hers.

17

It *was two days since Stara had, in effect,*
locked herself in her chambers and refused to come out.
Her excuse to the others was perfectly acceptable—she
had caught Lady Gwendolen's indisposition and was
resting. But Marcus was alarmed, annoyed and even
concerned. She could be showing displeasure with him
by this unwillingness to be in his sight. Or she could be
fearful of her own feelings and wished to stay hidden
and unchallenged until in sufficient control to carry on
with her decision to be a duchess.

Marcus sent many a message through Stara's maid,
receiving the same reply each time. "Miss says she am
doing better and will see everyone when she is cooped."

"Cooped?"

"That be what she said, sir," and Daisy bowed.

"But she is cooped up now . . ." Marcus began,
and then it hit him, "Did she say *recouped*?"

The maid looked confused. He offered her the
flowers he had picked and a note of apology.

Lady Gwendolen's maid was passing and reported Mr. Justus's having given flowers to Miss Carltons.

The next morning one of the ladies was down for breakfast with the gentlemen. It was Lady Gwendolen. Her face looked whiter than usual, but her eyes were alive with some kind of feeling. Marcus sensed it was anger, although he was unaware of the cause. He attempted his usual gallantries, but she kept staring at him with almost a piercing glare.

"I did not receive flowers from you, Mr. Justus—even though they would have come from my own garden and required merely an order from you to the gardener."

Marcus just about to take a sip of coffee, paused at that reprimand and almost blushed, but he brazened it out instead. "Naturally I would not send you flowers, your ladyship, that would be too puny a tribute for the feelings I have for you."

The duke looked up and put in his two pence. "Posies please ladies. Sent a bunch to Miss Carltons each day she took to her bed. Puts a cheer in the room, me mother always said."

"Yes," Lady Gwendolen said emphatically, keeping her eyes on Marcus with disdain.

"I have sent you many a note," Marcus said nobly.

"Not the last two days," she responded sharply.

"Since you had not responded, I feared I was fatiguing you," he attempted to skirt the issue.

Lady Gwendolen was inexorable. "Yet, I understand from my maid, you sent a note *and* flowers to Stara."

"What ho!" the duke reacted, putting down his steak bone.

Marcus remained calm, finishing his biscuit and wiping his hands on a damask napkin before responding casually, "Yes, I did. Felt myself remiss in not having sent her a single note during her convalescence. Unlike my constant attentions to your ladyship."

Lady Gwendolen was confused, not certain whether to accept that or not. She had been in such a pucker over her maid's report. Actually she had made an appearance while still not satisfied she was fit to be seen. Her anger had sustained her, but now, seeing the matter-of-fact attitude of her intended, she felt perhaps both she and her maid had overreacted. Keeping her eyes on him a moment longer, she still did not sense an iota of guilt. In fact, at one point while spotting her unswerving stare, Marcus merely held up a piece of kipper, as if in salute to her. She blinked rapidly at that, uncertain whether she was being insulted or honored. But following hard upon his gesture came his urging her to eat—that she needed sustenance after her long bout with illness. The last was said with concern enough to appease her ladyship, sufficient to believe what she wanted to believe—that no one pledged to her could possibly be pledging himself to another at the same time.

His grace catching the drift of the gentleman's concern about her ladyship, inquired, "Off your feed?"

When Lady Gwen admitted this to be the case, he commented, "Never had that problem."

"Your generous proportions attest to that," Marcus could not resist inserting, a twinkle in his eye. "But her ladyship is ethereally delicate."

Much struck by that description of herself, Lady Gwendolen ceased eating, for appearing less corporeal was rather difficult while swallowing. "I have been told I am as delicate as Lady Caroline Lamb," she said smugly.

Marcus was quick to second that, while Marmaduke took a moment to recollect that Lamb lady and upon doing so, exclaimed, "Dicked in the nob, I daresay."

"Who is!" her ladyship demanded.

"Lamb woman—cut herself in a ballroom, dressed as a page . . ."

Marcus was amused. "That was the lady's way of showing her devotion to Lord Byron. I have found ladies can be quite overcome when in the throes of *amour.*"

"Not ladylike," the duke mumbled.

"Indeed not," her ladyship replied. "There is a limit to how much one's emotions should control one. Propriety ought be observed even in the most private emotions. Actually, especially in the most private emotions."

"Righto."

The two nobles stared at each other in approval, and continued to make a good meal.

It was Marcus who put down his fork and stared, aghast. While Lady Gwen's passionate inclinations were of minimal interest, Marmaduke's could not but concern since Stara was to be their object.

"Correct me, but as a point of clarity, your grace, you believe one should have *no* private emotions? Or one should have them, but not demonstrate them before others?"

The duke shot a suspicious stare at the blue, taunting eyes. "Ain't your business what I believe about those matters. Ain't going to have any private feelings for you. Or before you."

"Quite right," her ladyship approved.

"Just as a matter of discussion. . . ."

"Not gonna discuss such matters. And if I were gonna. Wouldn't with you. Wouldn't with anybody, by Jove! Give anyone a look with me glass and put 'em in their place."

"But we are amongst friends here, are we not? I'm interested in the way you think," Marcus pressed, sitting back and peeling an apple with the same precision he was peeling away at the glossy skin of his grace.

"See here, Justus, we ain't gonna continue these games. Got a weird humor. Getting me to ride across the country for a jest. Not my kind of amusement, don't you know? You is a damned jokester! Privileged to be invited to table—should be entertaining afterward. See through your levity. To the loose-screw beneath, by the by. Enough to give you the go-by if not her ladyship's intended!"

Marcus was astonished at the degree of anger coming from his grace. With a raised eyebrow, he considered if his grace were quite the fool he thought him. Very possibly no one could quite be that. Beastly uncivil these nobles—thinking they could ring a peal over anyone and at will reduce one to staff! Marcus was a second from calling his grace to account when he reminded himself that man-milliner was not worth either his sword, fist or repartee.

The role of the jester had often been his. Beginning from the days at his father's table when he was always below the salt, he had constantly set the table if not on a roar, rather on a rile with his unruly breaking of the rules. His father, the earl, and his brother, the viscount, were so conscious of their consequence, Marcus almost viscerally rebelled against them and all they represented. That explained his attraction to a fellow nonconformist, a lady who similarly saw through society's high-in-the-instep airs.

The duke was still eyeing him guardedly, expecting a response and Marcus shook himself from thinking of Stara to give him one. "Very well, your grace," he began with a tolerant smile, "I'll just assume you have no feelings at all for anyone or anything. And save my breath to cool my porridge."

"We ain't got porridge, do we?" Marmaduke inserted, his main interest in life distracting him. "Hey there, Smithers, is there porridge?"

The butler assured him that while there was not, he could immediately have cook make some, unless his grace would be satisfied with another kidney? His grace was mollified with that, after glancing suspiciously at Marcus's setting for porridge and observing none, concluded the man was joshing him again. "Damn gabster," he muttered and fell to, demolishing the two kidneys quickly offered.

That led Marcus to reevaluate his grace again, assuming he had not underestimated him, after all. Her ladyship was also accepting a kidney. Marcus put down his fork and sat back, wondering how Stara could countenance marriage to this fool . . . wishing she'd been here at table to smile at Marmaduke's alarm at not being offered first dibs of all there was, even if it was something as inconsequential as gruel. Actually Marcus was just wishing she were here merely to look at her. Oft simply seeing her beautifully sculpted features assuaged him. He would so enjoy taking her to Greece and having her stand aside a marble Aphrodite and overshadow that stone symmetry by her own perfection —an Aphrodite in the flesh and warmth.

In the midst of that soft reverie, Marcus took a quick drink of coffee and burned himself. While the gentleman was not attending, the servant had refilled his cup. Observing the incident, her ladyship castigated the servant with a sharp tone for not having added or at least offered cream. Immediately Smithers apologized for his staff, while Marcus was graciously turning it aside. Yet her ladyship would not allow that.

"Please do not interfere with my discipline of the

staff! He should have added the cream. That is his duty."

"Quite right," the duke inserted. "Me man has saved me from many a burn. Oft reminds me when there's something at table that disagrees with me. Adds the sauce just as I like it."

"Does he feed you as well?"

The duke stared menacingly at the laughing gentleman across from him. Attempting to think of a reply, he was spared that mental activity by an interruption. A footman was handing a note to the butler, who considered it of sufficient import to interrupt his grace. Marmaduke opened it with one hand while with the other he finished off his tepid coffee.

"Egad!" he exclaimed.

"Too hot?" Marcus could not resist throwing in, adding, "Where was your man with the cream?"

His grace did not rise to the bait; his face was white, his eyes popping. The letter had obviously thrown him into the devil of a pucker.

"What is it, Marmaduke?" her ladyship asked in concern.

He read the letter again from the beginning while his two fellow diners exchanged glances of confusion.

"Egad!" the duke exclaimed again.

"Can you possible be more . . . explanatory?"

The duke stared at Marcus. "Blast the man!"

"Me?"

"Blast that One-Jewel Jack fellow!"

Marcus's eyebrow went up at that. "Really, I thought you had already done so."

"Had. But he's got himself accomplices!"

"Are they after you again?" Marcus inserted, rolling that thought in his mind with some pleasure.

"After me intended!"

"What the devil do you mean!" Marcus was all

concern now. "Speak man! Is somebody threatening Stara?"

Slowly the duke began to read the letter again. At which point Marcus, cursing him, rose and snatched the missive out of his hands, giving it a quick perusal.

Ere the duke had finished objecting, Marcus had acted. He'd run up the stairs to Stara's room. She was not there. Her maid, Daisy, explained her mistress had gone riding very early this morning and not returned. Rushing to the stables he found her horse still missing. It was shockingly past time for a lady to still be riding, unless something had gone amiss.

His eyes hard, Marcus returned to the small dining room to report the results.

The duke shook his head. Lady Gwendolen wished it explained to her. After his fashion, his grace did so. "They've got Miss Carltons. Want ransom. Blighters threaten not to return her else. I'm to take it them."

"I should not do that," Lady Gwendolen said calmly, undisturbed by the danger to her one-time friend and companion.

"No?" his grace asked hopefully.

"Certainly not. Why else do we have servants? Send the amount required through Smithers here."

Smithers serving more coffee, nearly spilled it, almost ready to deny that privilege, when Marcus interfered.

"You lily-livered, cocksure fribble! They want you in exchange for having killed their leader. You must rush and give yourself up!"

The duke uncertain before—now that Marcus was telling him what to do, immediately felt free to decide the opposite. "Can't appear meself. I'm the one they got a grudge against. Body for body—it says. Not my body, egad."

"You'd rather it was Stara's!"

The duke looked down at the letter he was reading for tenth consecutive time. "The ruffians won't hurt her. Woman, what? Besides it's me they want and me money. Give 'em the money, they release her, what? Best thing to do."

"Indeed."

Aghast, Marcus turned to Lady Gwendolen, disbelieving she had approved Marmaduke's cowardly conclusions.

"Why should his grace risk his life? It is typical of Stara to go riding off in the morning without a groom. Stands to reason someday she would find herself in a broil. Just as one must expect blisters from riding without one's gloves. I do not see why Marmaduke should become involved."

The duke smiled at her and rose to send a message to Mr. Walt, his astute and speedy secretary, to arrange for the money.

Marcus would not be dismissed, saying brusquely, " 'Tis not Stara's fault you killed the blighter. That was your action, my good man. Be a man and find your woman. Rescue her, by Jove."

Ignoring Marcus's shouting, the duke handed his note to a footman. "I have instructed Mr. Walt to get it done on the dot. Letter says not to inform Bow Street on threat of dear Miss Carltons's life. Else I'd set the Bow Street Runners onto the villains. Their job, after all. If no one else will deliver the money, I expect Mr. Walt will. Very knacky knowing man, James."

"You pigeon-hearted blackguard! You curst rum touch! *I'll* deliver the ransom and rescue her! By heavens, that the life of a woman of such worth should depend on you! At least I'll do all possible to assure her immediate safety and return!"

"I forbid you to go," her ladyship interrupted, running up to him. "We have servants, stewards for such

assignments. Furthermore, I do not understand this devotion to Stara! Are you or are you not in love with me,
first and foremost? I shall need you by my side during
this difficult time. Naturally I am unnerved. After all,
One-Jewel Jack was enamored of me. Indeed, I expect it
was me they wished to abduct, but they knew I was
inaccessible, being too much of a lady to ride alone.
Yes, undoubtedly I was their original object."

"You ain't read the letter," the duke inserted helpfully, setting her straight. "It's *me* they want. Cause I
killed that footpad."

"Then obviously both of you should give your-
selves up in her stead. Stara has done nothing to be the
one suffering now!"

"Heavens," her ladyship objected. "Are you seriously assuming I would allow myself to be even in the
same room with highwaymen and that sort of person!
Nor do I believe his grace should so lower himself!"

"Righto."

"You're both . . . a disgrace to not only your
sexes but to your very humanity! Here's a beautiful caring, lively, irreplaceable lady in dire straits and you two
talk of position! To the blazes with both of you!"

"Mr. Justus! How dare you speak to me in those
terms. I warn you I feel your entire attitude is one I
cannot approve of. And if you intend to risk your life
for a mere companion of mine, I shall know where you
heart is and be forced to end our engagement on the
spot!"

Bitterness overflowing him, Marcus allowed a
scornful laugh and then snapped, "I shall go. And you
can go to the devil!"

The duke was horrified, demanding an apology.
Her ladyship's turning to his grace for protection had
him quick to challenge Marcus. "I'm pretty handy with
me pistols. If you care to meet me!"

"You would risk your life in a duel with me, but not to save your fiancée!" Marcus exclaimed, storming around the room.

"It's a matter of code," the duke said, haughtily.

"Well, I shall be delighted to blast your head off the moment I return with Stara safely in my arms!"

"You understand, Mr. Justus," her ladyship inserted with frigid tones, "that decision on your part has ended our relationship. As of this moment!"

A mighty laugh of despair and disgust shook Marcus. "It's rather clear. The two of you are so perfect together. Two pudding-hearted wimps. I don't think Stara would consider your code as sufficient reason for your abandoning her."

"I shall not cry off," the duke said, with pride. "However, if her ladyship no longer feels you are her choice. And in the event Miss Carltons decides I am not hers. Shall make a push for Lady Gwendolen."

"I believe we can assume that Stara has already shown herself not worthy, Marmaduke, by risking herself with her early morning jaunts. If she truly honored her position as your fiancée, she'd have been more circumspect—in deference to you! But obviously she is not bred to the responsibilities of our high position." (The duke had to agree to that.) "Therefore," her ladyship airily jumped to conclude, "we can resume our original engagement as originally discussed before being interfered with by Stara's maneuvers."

"By Jove," the duke exclaimed. "Never thought of it that way. Egad, what a position! You feel, your ladyship, a prior claim to me?"

"I do indeed."

Pleased at the thought that two ladies were anxious for him, the duke dwelled on it in pleasure. "Can't escape it," he concluded. "Prior rights is prior rights. Not one to stand on points, but her ladyship's title enti-

tles her to first consideration of me. Shall have to make
arrangements with Miss Carltons. Blister me, not certain how. But I will, I daresay."

"Very simple, Marmaduke," her ladyship responded, relying as usual on inconsistencies when all
else failed to achieve her wish. "You simply explain to
Stara you had misunderstood our arrangement. Stands
to reason you cannot be wed to two ladies. Obviously I
have precedence in all things, why not in this? Offer her
a home. Yes, Stara was always wild to have a house.
Two houses, if she wishes! Thus I expect we can appease her."

The duke was delighted with that resolution or actually with having someone else solve his dilemma for
him. His forte was execution not conception. "Gave her
Cliffview on Wight. Mere island place though," he recalled, and then frowned while his mind sifted through
his possessions. Finally he hit one he was prepared to
part with. "Worthing Hall—that's all the way in York-
shire. Not apt to visit that."

"Worthing Hall is sufficient, I expect," her ladyship concluded.

Lady Gwen enjoyed this form of negotiation—
when the other party was not present and thus not able
to protest. But she did recall some of Stara's dreams and
graciously put one on the table. "Stara has a prodigious
desire for a London town house. Yet we should not
wish her to be so present in our presence. Best give her
the estate in Richmond, which is close to London, but
not directly there. And an income, as well as Worthing
Hall." Lady Gwendolen dismissed all other claims by
Stara with quite an exaggerated shrugging of her shoulders. "That should more than end all your obligations!
I daresay you will be considered generous by all the ton.
We must give her some compensation for losing such a
prize as yourself." (The duke looked gratified at that

and in full agreement) "but at the same time we must not appear as if we were buying her off! That would demean both us and dear Stara herself. Still we must make her willing to give the appearance of being the one to break off."

The two continued along this line for some moments. They enjoyed discussions of this ilk, whether counting properties or rearranging properties to satisfy propriety. The duke was nothing loath to contribute Richmond to the pot. Even upped the offer to include a hunting lodge—claiming one could not do without one of those. Her ladyship reminded him Stara was not hunting-mad and he compromised with another remote area estate in Cornwall. It was as if he were checking off all the possible discards. That was perfectly agreeable to the lady. All the while Marcus was staring at them in a range of emotions from astonishment to disgust to wrath, exploding, "So much for your feelings for the lady!"

The duke was insulted by that. "Have feelings for her. Wouldn't be giving her all these estates and the income for them. Jewels too. Lady looks dashed lovely in me jewels. Pleasure to see her in them. Want her to keep 'em. Designed them especially for her. Pity if she were not to grace them." His eyes glazed over at the image of the beauteous Stara bedecked with his selections. He regretted not being the one to be escorting her when she showed them off. Actually for a moment he was regretting Stara. He glanced at her ladyship whose eyes were implacable and at Marcus's face of contempt. "Blast it, can I help it if her ladyship has a prior commitment to me! Can't cut meself in half. Like to. Like Miss Carltons. Kind of face I like."

That last was too much for Marcus's determined sangfroid, "Ye Gods, she has the kind of face an entire world would like! Would honor. Would carve into works of art!" He struggled with his rage. "While you've got the kind of face I would like to land a facer right this moment."

"I am not known for my expertise with me fives, as you are, sir. Nor am I such a fire-eater. But you shan't find me backward for a sparring match, if you demand it!"

"I wouldn't soil my hands—with either of you! While you're both playing 'least favorite property' to facilitate your futures is there no concern the lady may not have a future? No concern—double-blast your souls—what she might be suffering at this very moment at the hands of these . . . ruffians? Isn't that gnawing, tearing image slightly disturbing to anyone else but me!"

"It appears you have strong feelings for my fiancée," the duke objected in his most top-lofty tones. "Call you to account for that! Blister me, she is engaged to me, don't you know."

"I thought you'd just given her the slip—you and your new fiancée here!"

The duke looked in confusion at her ladyship. His position so uncertain, he did not know where to stand. So he sat down at the breakfast table again. Her ladyship sat down as well.

"The situation has been resolved to all our satisfactions," her ladyship said softly and decisively. "You apparently have always loved Stara, have you not?" she pronounced, daring him to refute that. He did not. "Just so," she continued. "Therefore, I gather you must be delighted at this resolution. Further, you are indebted as well to his grace for giving you the opportunity to rescue the lady you . . . eh, love. And thus win her from his grace. The duke shall further arrange for both of you to live a life of plenty and ease. What then is the purpose of enacting us this Cheltenham tragedy?

It is all settled." Turning, she gave her hand to the confused duke of Clairidge. He put down his forkful of steak and took up to his mouth her ladyship's fingers for a perfunctory salute that satisfied both and settled all.

Marcus was furious at his own bolt of relief at this resolution. In essence it was exactly what he had been pushing for these months past. Disgusted with all three of them, he exclaimed scornfully, "It's jolly fine for us all! I expect Stara might have something to say about this situation—that is assuming she returns alive and unharmed." His voice sank at this reminder and he could only mumble, "What does any of this matter? I can only think of rescuing her before it's too late!"

"If it is," Lady Gwendolen replied placidly, "then I expect this entire discussion was unnecessary. His grace shall be free in any event."

Marcus stared at her in speechless shock. Then, "Is it possible you are as shallow as you appear!"

"I say," the duke interposed. "Are you insulting my fiancée?"

"Which one?"

"Did you call her ladyship shallow?"

"I did."

"Well," the duke thought about it. "Is that an insult?" He turned toward her ladyship.

"We have ended the discussion, Marmaduke. It is all settled. What do we wait for, but the funds that shall be arriving. The rest, the rescue and such, I expect is of concern merely to Mr. Justus, here. We can, if you wish, go for a stroll for digestive purposes."

His grace was quick to rise and extend his hand. The lady took it.

"I hope you never can digest this morning's work," Marcus said bitterly. "In your joyous reconciliation, I hope you have an occasional thought for the suffering of a lady in dire threat because she has been of use to you both!"

The duke appeared concerned at that and ready to respond, but her ladyship pressed his hand and said coldly. "I cannot think of a lady who can handle the situation better. Stara is very resourceful. And you are very efficient. I am certain both of you shall be able to fight your way out of this dilemma. Further," she smiled languidly, "both of you shall doubtless conclude it all a jolly adventure as you emerge triumphant. In which case we shall be pleased to come to your wedding, as we shall honor you both by inviting you to ours."

And with a joint nod of dismissal to Marcus, the two nobles walked out into her ladyship's prize rose garden, stopping to hail and inhale the Lady Gwendolen rose, still triumphantly aflower, bloom after bloom.

18

Aching, bristling to be acting, finally Marcus was off to the appointed place. Strapped onto the back of his black hunter, he had a small leather bag containing the quickly arranged ransom. Also hanging on the saddle was a holster, large enough to accommodate Marcus's deadly dueling pistol with a ten-inch barrel and silver sights.

His face grew grimmer as he rode ahead for an hour through Hillcrest's Home Woods all the way to the other side. Deeming himself no longer in sight of any of the duke's nor the marquis's men, he stopped to alter his outfit.

Earlier the marquis, upon returning from visiting a neighbor and being made acquainted with Stara's dilemma, reacted as one would hope a decent person would. Marcus was appeased to see not only concern but genuine caring, even a tear in the old gray eyes as he prayed that Marcus would rescue the lady. He wished to send some of his own men with him, and even volunteered to ride a pace himself. Marcus was full in his gratitude, but the letter had stressed Hillcrest was being watched. Any sign of accompaniment would mean the end of the safe transfer.

With grand effrontery the duke came to the stable, and had the gall to wish him well. Yet this morning his grace's attitude was less callous. He must explain himself to Mr. Justus, he began. During the discussion with her ladyship he'd been persuaded he was taking the correct position. But today he had awakened and found he was not easy in his mind over the conclusion. Actually, he was willing to join forces with Mr. Justus.

After having spent so much time egging on this lord toward this very decision, Marcus found himself resenting the intrusion. Quickly he gave him the same excuse he had just given the marquis, and Marmaduke was relieved he did not have to follow through on his gesture. Rather his grace after repeating his well wishes volunteered the very pistol that had ended the life of One-Jewel Jack.

Marcus had laughed at the size of it. "You could not have gotten a man at any distance with that toy," he exclaimed. "Further, I discussed the issue with the Runners who had the culprit's body. It was a blunderbuss that did him in. I expect one of your outriders finished him off."

The duke was silent. "If you knew that why did you not tell . . . the ladies?"

"I do not believe that one gentleman should betray another," he said gallantly, and the duke was humble in his gratitude.

"But you understand why I felt I could not rescue the lady. My aim has always been . . . eh, shaky."

Marcus had nodded, not wishing any further delay for exculpation. "Time is of the essence, your grace," he said impatiently.

The lord quickly agreed, waving him off. It needed

only Lady Gwen to come running after and volunteer her services. But of course that did not occur. Heavens, what was he thinking, her ladyship never arose before noon. A life threat to her dearest friend could scarcely be considered of sufficient importance to alter her routine.

The transformation being completed, Marcus was menacing in his black breeches, tall boots and a coat of several capes, also in black. In the pocket of the coat was a black mask he would don the last moment before entering the appointed place. But sufficient camouflage came from his large-brimmed, black slouch hat with its rather revealing single authentic jewel on the side. Clearly a signature.

Now he allowed his horse to let loose and gallop out its restlessness. In fact, he leaned over its neck and urged Black Jewel on. In a short time they had eaten up the straight roads. Black Jewel had not had a run like this in a while. He was enjoying himself, and if Marcus had not such a serious mission, he too would have found pleasure in being out on the road again, ready to risk all. But he reined in Black Jewel, directing him to canter, so he would not miss the turn. Remembering the instructions, Marcus concluded from here the fields had to be transversed until one reached a common, and then a road to a hill. He and his horse took all easily, accustomed to long runs even over hills and across glens while being pursued. Guiding his animal to trot on, Marcus rose and fell easily in the saddle, not using his spurs. Black Jewel never needed that treatment. A word or two, even a whisper, and he knew what his master wished.

Checking the direction once more, Marcus saw himself close to his destination, so therefore he swung out of the saddle to give Black Jewel a rest before the last spring forward. Meanwhile Marcus was placing his mask over his eyes. Focusing on the distance, he concentrated on the extensive acreage of woods ahead. There in the dense midst would be the meeting place. He attempted to quash the dread he had been feeling since first hearing of Stara's plight. What if he were unable to rescue her? What if through some failure, delay, miscalculation on his part he lost forever the woman he loved. Yesterday, unable to wait for the duke's ransom to arrive, he had taken what money he had and what he could collect from the duke and marquis and ridden off to the meeting place ahead of time. No one was there. Nor had anyone arrived, although Marcus waited through most of the night. Cursing the abductors and life itself, Marcus finally had to admit his action had been pointless. He returned, sunk in a brown study, to Hillcrest. A change of clothes, some ale and he was mounting again. He'd at least been cautious enough to save Black Jewel for the appointed time, and taking up the ransom he'd set off again this morning. Yet the same anguish pursued him; thoughts that hugged his back like weights he could not shake off. Was she alive? Had she been hurt! He knew her spirit was strong enough to withstand the trauma of the event. But if they had hurt her in other ways! They were low-bred ruffians—associates of an impostor. Cowards who attempted to revenge themselves on a lady for their leader's demise! Let them be prepared then, in faith! For he would show them how a genuine adventurous gentleman would handle them and their presumptions. Other maddening thoughts would intrude! The gnawing possibility that the beautiful dark-haired Stara had had her dignity and honor affronted! In that case he would relish shooting each one of them—finishing off by carving out their hearts! At that vow, Marcus checked his sheathed knife. He'd refused to take a sword. A duel was only possible with one of equal class. Nor would he give any of these lowlifes even a chance for a fair fight. He would cut them down on sight!

Swinging back up on his horse, Marcus's face was grimmer yet. His heart paced to the exact rhythm of his horse. The words both heart and hooves were saying were prayers for Stara's safety. "Stara, my love! Stara, my heart!"

Black Jewel was galloping now, eating up the road. In a blink the woods had been reached. Marcus caught his breath with hope that this time he could meet the abductors face on! Threading through the trees, Marcus carefully noted the signs. The money was to be left by the large oak tree on the second turn up ahead.

He dismounted and placed the leather pouch in full view. Then, as instructed, he rode away. But as not instructed, he waited a while and doubled back. Slipping off Black Jewel, with pistol drawn, he made his way 'twixt the trees back to the meeting place.

The pouch was still there. Marcus's lips curled at this repeat of his last night's despair! Would he have to wait again for naught! Was it all a blasted trick! Or even a trap? Or worse, had he been spotted yesterday and the footpads were now concluding the bargain had been broken and acted accordingly? His heart labored in rapid beat. Yet he could do naught but wait some more. In an hour of silence Marcus had not made scarce a movement. Then he shuddered and stiffened as someone approached. Steadily, Marcus lifted his pistol in position.

A fellow in a dark cape stopped at the appointed tree. Marcus waited for that man's cohorts. He counted the minutes. Forced himself to hold back until assured no others were arriving. None came. With a measured, light step Marcus revealed himself. But the figure was too concerned with retrieving the pouch and rushing on to turn round and notice he'd been observed. It would be a chase, egad! Marcus attempted to keep up, to keep close, to keep each step muffled. Eyes glowing with the hunt, Marcus was triumphant at the thought the knave was leading him to Stara's hiding place.

On through the woods, they went. The leader was swift and certain in his steps. Marcus was quiet, stopping when the man did. Then of a sudden, the dark gloom of the woods was over. First one and then the other slipped out of the woods onto the road where the sun was ablaze, especially on the high rocks ahead.

Confound his effrontery! Did the knave have the audacity to walk openly? Was his horse close by? Would he reach it and gallop off while Marcus's animal was still tied to a tree in the heart of the woods! But the man with the ransom did not signal a horse. Nor was there either horse or man waiting for him. Rather he turned toward some rocks, approaching them on a sudden run, slipping round a boulder—beyond which he disappeared.

Marcus let out a string of oaths, trying to choke them still. He rushed toward the rocks, scouring the area. No sign, anywhere.

In the name of heaven, he groaned—had he lost the culprit? After waiting, tracking, spotting and reaching this point, dear God, had he lost him, and thus lost Stara! But Marcus was too experienced an adventurer to succumb to regrets. That way one never succeeded. At the moment of one's worst blunder, one simply carried on, and a solution usually presented itself. Eyes sharp, Marcus glanced about. Retraced his steps. Came again from another direction. And another. Then repeated his first attempt. Desperation flooded over him as this time he wasn't being given a sign, after all.

Thunder 'n' turf! He needed no help. He would make his own sign. He would take apart every rock in the area, if needs be. Pounding and stroking the rocks around, Marcus found a small crevice and quickly followed that until the schism began to spread. Yes, by gad, it was leading to an alcove wide enough for a thin figure to slip through. Obviously the blighter had ducked into that! As there was no other way he could have so promptly disappeared, Marcus pushed his way through the tight fit.

Within it was all shadows. So dense, Marcus stumbled immediately on several stairs cut out of the rocks. He caught himself by holding on to the cold stone at the sides. Each step it grew darker, which had Marcus blasting himself for not having a lantern. Yet how could one assume the need of one? Through touch he made his way down the stairs. It had been so warm outside Marcus had been overheated in his cape, but now he wrapped it round as the cold penetrated.

At the bottom he paused, attempting to assess the situation. This area had several caves with dangerous interior terrain—crevasses, lakes. How could he search without light when each step was a risk. Yet confound the risk—he was here for rescue. He must step on and step quickly. Shortly, thankfully, his eyes grew more accustomed to the dark, so he struck out boldly and hit flat against a wall. Cursing, Marcus was forced to stop. The image of Stara bound and besieged set him off again. Movement regardless of direction was better than standing in place. That had always been his credo. So he moved. Again the image of Stara's face wet with tears almost unmanned him, slowed his steps. He called himself to account. This was not the way to succeed on an adventure. He'd been in enough to know the more one carried on with all confidence, the more certain one was of success.

Coolly, Marcus put away his emotions, his love for her, all thoughts of Stara at all. He was merely exploring, he told himself. The beating of his heart no longer occluded other sounds. He heard a noise. With a joyous gasp he recognized footsteps ahead. With all confident speed, he kept close behind. The sounds seemed to be ascending. Marcus noticed the rise under his feet. He too was elevating. A few more steps had him at an arched doorway. Passing through without pause, he found himself in an anterior chamber where there was light sufficient to see ahead. The light came none too soon, for he was standing on a projecting ledge. Gingerly Marcus moved back against the arched wall.

Now he could take time to gaze about and note from whence the light came. There were holes in the roof through which the sun was slipping in, revealing the narrowness of his platform. One step more and he would have fallen into the open area below. Looking down at the chamber, he was struck by a sense of familiarity. That gnawed. Then by gad, he recognized it. He'd been in it before! Only this time he'd come through the back area to the front. Even if he had not recollected that place, he instantly recognized the person who had been leading him. For the person below at that very moment removed a cloak. And then a hat. Long dark hair fell about her person.

"Stara! Blast you!" his voice thundered through the space.

Stara turned with a laugh.

"Ah, Marcus, you took your time about coming for me, didn't you?"

He made a mad dash around the ledge to the steps leading him down toward her. Stara was obligingly advancing, when of a sudden she stepped back. The man approaching was dressed as One-Jewel Jack—mask and all. Her face was white at the fear it was not Marcus after all.

The two figures confronted each other.

Marcus laughed that lazy, easy laugh of his that usually gave a jolt of anger or amusement or more often pleasure to her heart. Slowly, with a mocking grin, he removed his mask and came toward her.

In relief, in joy, in a flood of love, Stara clapped her hands and propelled her body toward him. Marcus grabbed her in his arms for a long satisfying embrace.

Feeling the joyful thudding of his familiar heart, Stara kept her face burrowed in his chest. He had both arms squeezing her in the tightest most triumphant hug she'd ever felt, and he'd ever given. Close together, they rested.

In the midst of their joint elation, Marcus was whispering anxiously, "Confound it, you're not hurt? Are you? In *any* way? But what the devil is this game you're playing? And with whom?"

Stara stroked his cheek. "I knew you would be the one to come to my rescue. How did you persuade the duke to give up his opportunity to finish the Jewel group?"

Marcus allowed a laugh of derision, which had her exclaiming, "Don't tell me he was afraid to come!" At his amused assent, she frowned like a disappointed child learning of the foibles of the adults. "Oh how deflating! How . . . disappointing. I had hoped there would be some struggle to be my champion. My knight ready to risk all to save me!"

"*Duke,* not a knight! Dukes, according to his grace, and indeed to Lady Gwendolen, need not bother with rescuing and such. Why do they have menials?"

"You cannot mean it? My rescue a mere job for the servants! Oh, that . . . fribble! That I ever let him kiss my lips! And Lady Gwendolen endorsed that?"

Marcus was busy staring at her beautiful face. The light from the top of the cave showed her eyes glowing in a combination of fury at being betrayed and yet mischief at the trick she had pulled. He understood what she had done, but not why she had done it.

"You wrote the letter?" he demanded with as much tolerance as he could muster in view of the agony he'd been put through.

"I did! Wasn't that a brilliant stroke?"

"Depending on your aim," he said guardedly, his eyes coldly seeking the truth.

"But you know the reason. While reconsidering the future in my rooms, I realized with a start how much I regretted your scheme having gone awry. Its success would have meant my having lost the duke without having to actually give him up on my own. Thus, all would have been made easy for me. I could go where my heart wished me to go."

"And that was . . ."

She threw back her head in laughter. "Why to you, of course."

"Wouldn't it have been somewhat less convoluted and dare I say honest to admit, as I did, that you wanted me and simply turn down his grace?"

"Poo! Pale stuff that. Much more adventurous this way, would you not say?"

"Is it not possible," he said with still a glint of suspicion, "that you were hoping his grace would come to your rescue? Was this not one last test of not only your feelings but of your suitors?"

"Heavens, no. I had no question you would come. You are the adventurer. It's my belief actually that Duke-duke did not even shoot at One-Jewel Jack. After all, you'll recall I was the highwayman myself, and I saw his eyes when I challenged him. Probably all a hum. That entire tale. Very likely Sir Percy did him in."

"No, it was the duke's outriders. Fellow was shot with a blunderbuss."

"Ah, well, just as I expected. I assumed he would

suggest sending his men along. I even hoped since the object was supposedly something dearer to him than his pocketbook, *he* might come as well. But I was certain you would lead it. I intended to wait and drop you a clue to make you my first rescuer who would thus win me. I had a rather pretty story to tell of my escape . . . of my being forced to help them, lest they shoot the duke! Oh, I had plenty of tales. But when I saw one lone figure, I knew it was you. So I didn't need any more flummery!" Her eyes were filled with the excitement of it all. She was still holding on to his hands in all confidence, as she joyfully concluded her tale. "Actually it was so much simpler that none of them came. Realizing you were alone, I had to merely make certain you picked up my trail to our special place. For a moment when you first entered the cave you went the wrong way and I came back and made some noises so you could pick up on me."

"Did you, by Jove!" he said, affronted. So much for his pride in his trailing ability. Ruefully, he exclaimed, "There ends all my credit for being a first oars stalker! But now, Miss Carltons, that I have meekly followed you to the cave, and we are here together, and further you have your ransom money, might I be so inquisitive as to inquire what your next object is?"

Stara realized she should not have mentioned helping him. To make amends she inserted quickly. "Of course you found the entrance yourself. No mean trick that! And you were so quiet in your steps, I was afeared you were not following. You are an intrepid hunter, indeed!"

"Without the flummery," Marcus said, his eyes demanding naught but the truth. "I can survive without the layers of gammon you give his grace. Tell me now, with no more fiddle-faddle—why did you cast this elaborate scheme?"

Stara was pleased to keep him still waiting. With a teasing grin for him to follow after, she climbed back up to the sunlit ledge, where they had embraced before. There she patted the hard rock on her side in invitation. He joined her, beginning to see the humor in her daring, especially when she said eagerly, "I feel we were interrupted last time by the duke. I thought we could meet here and plan our future. It was with a prodigious amount of regret that I surrendered all the delightful security I'd won. I intend to hold the ransom as a type of dowry from the duke. Not setting it more than tolerably high, I have no compunction about keeping it. I certainly hope you do not intend to return it him—as you did the jewels."

"Yes, I shall return it him."

Stara groaned and was attempting to persuade him against that when he shushed her with the demand, "Your heart is always attached to funds. Why then did you give up wealth of major proportions for this pittance?"

"You are vain enough without my replying to that!"

"Answer, minx!"

Stara sighed and admitted she could not give up his kisses. "Despite the risk that someday, with your history, you might very well drop me to find another Violet. That fear held me back for some time. As well as my one desperate need, I might even jolly well say ache to have a home. Note, I'm giving up Cliffview which is quite a sacrifice—one of some magnitude, in faith. Keep that in mind in the eventuality you decide to stray. Also, that I am rather handy with a pistol. Recollect that. And further that while not the authentic One-Jewel Jack, I was at least a fair approximation. Be warned."

He was unable to hold back from kissing her then. Madcap! Wild, adorable, daring scamp! The more she

showed her love for security the more he felt the glory
of her having tossed it away for him. He was humbled
by her sacrifice, and yet could only nod at her as if she
could have done no less. For in truth, neither of them
could have acted differently. They had been linked together from the beginning. He had kept her in his
thoughts nigh unto every moment they were apart, so
that despite any degree of space, they were always close
together, in essence. She had disappointed him when
she did not admit this linkage between them—ran off
for titles and jewels. Yet her coming back, especially
since she'd cut all ties to society that she'd spent so
many years spinning, assuaged him to the depth of his
heart.

Marcus had her in his arms and he held her there,
admitting the need after the days, nay, weeks of missing
her. His embrace had such vigor she felt herself surging
with him. Together. Bound. The total abandonment of
each to each.

"You are my hero," she said, with a contented
sigh, cuddling against him like a kitten.

He pulled back her head to look in her eyes. "Tell
me. Say it clearly before me. Marcus Justus, I love only
you."

"Doubly so now, since you are my rescuer."

"You do not regret the loss of the duke?"

"Not likely! Not after he refused to snatch me
from the clutches of the vile varmints who'd absconded
with me!"

"From yourself, you mean," he said with a laugh.

"Well, his grace was not aware of that! Nor were
you. I expect you would have faced down an entire
mob of men for me!" she said contentedly. But a sudden thought left her at a standstill. Shocked her into her
demanding, "I say, why did you come alone if you were
expecting a group? And why dressed as One-Jewel

Jack? You could not have expected to fool his cohorts, for they would have known he is dead."

Her eyes blinked rapidly as she sharply drew in her breath and said, "Unless . . ."

While her eyes rounded at her conclusion, he merely grinned and handed her the fob he always wore.

19

"*Look closely at the face carved there,*" he suggested helpfully.

She did. Then frowned. "From the scant glimpses I've had of it before, I always thought it bore some little resemblance to me. But then so did Lady Gwen think it looked like *her*. And other ladies saw resemblances as well."

"Piffle the lot of them! It is, I own, an *exact* copy from the original. Or yourself."

Her eyes danced in delight. "But how! When? You had this fob before you met me at the balls. Unless you'd seen me previously without my knowledge?"

"I'd seen you previously. And you'd seen me previously. A bit over four years, actually. You were in a carriage of young ladies on their way to Miss Lavadale's school. We had a very meaningful exchange. You leaned out the window and waved to me as the moonlight flooded your face. It stayed in my mind during the years of travel. I had this carved at my direction—from that memory."

Clutching the carving, she was thoroughly aghast by that revelation. "You are One-Jewel Jack!" Stara exclaimed. "I knew I recognized the feeling when you first kissed me on the balcony! It was just like my dreams of the kiss we shared on the highway. Heavens, this means I never loved anybody else my whole life but you!"

"I cannot say as much," One-Jewel Jack admitted ruefully, his eyes dancing, as he swore, "Nevertheless the beauty of your face remained with me—permanently drawn in my memory."

"Drawn and quartered into your fob, eh?" Stara gibed. And then recollecting the first time they met on the road, she sighed and admitted. "That experience certainly was what inspired me to impersonate you when at Point Non Plus. It was a jolly delight to resurrect you. For apparently you always had a place in my heart. But how is it possible you remembered me, a mere school girl, and after so many?"

"You were unique among the ladies I held up," he said with a grin.

"Because I had not one jewel to contribute?"

"Because you were a jewel in yourself. And I took the greatest jewel from you or your first kiss. There was so much delight in that moment for me, and you were laughing throughout—not the slightest bit frightened. As I rode away, I wanted to keep that memory. That is why I had this carved, so you'd always be with me."

Stara looked down at the fob, recollecting all the times she'd watched him admiring it, and was awash with sudden resentment. "I say, I wish I'd known all along it was me you were ogling! I certainly would have given you a set-down!"

Marcus let out a whoop at that, but Stara insisted, "But did you recognize me that first night on the balcony of the ballroom?"

"No. I did not. Yet the feeling was the same . . . my heart knew. As if I'd found you at last."

"For me too," Stara whispered, and he must stop and kiss her several times to ease their longtime longing. It roused it instead. Stara backed off, wanting the full delight of the story explained to her, as a child wishes to hear every detail of a favorite bedtime tale. "Tell me all! Such as, well, when exactly did you know I was the girl of the fob?"

"Shortly after that night," he replied, with affectionate willingness to tell her any bedtime tale she wished as long as she remained so soft and dear and loving in his arms. At her demand for more specifics, he roused himself from the feel of her and said appeasingly, "Ah yes, my wild delight, one glance at you recalled my first view. Whereupon I checked the uncanny resemblance with the carving. Then certain facts added to make the connection positive—such as your having gone to Miss Lavadale's school. Any remaining doubt was dismissed upon your impersonating One-Jewel Jack and subsequently admitting you'd had a meeting with the original. Then your hold over me was explained. At once I knew I must no longer play fast and loose with you. I must make you my own."

More details were requested such as his feelings, being the authentic One-Jewel Jack, when she appeared as that gentleman. Grinning, Marcus admitted she'd justly given him a taste of his own medicine. "Not jolly pleasant being taken unaware at pistol point. Not the adventure I assumed it was. But when I spotted you through that disguise, the experience turned delightful after all. My principal thought was how alike we intrinsically were."

"Indeed," she said with a sigh. And then a new alarm struck, "But at whom did the duke shoot? Not you?"

"If it had been me, his grace would have gone to his reward. Obviously you were not the only person impersonating me. In truth, One-Jewel Jack had been retired while I was on the continent. It was the invention of a younger man. I had no intention of carrying on with that game. I discovered more effective ways to twit society from within. But your impersonation, blast you, brought him back in fashion—especially with her ladyship spreading the story that the highwayman was a romantic swain of hers—obviously at your instigation."

Stara grinned her acknowledgment. "Yes, I had a jolly time transmitting my girlish daydreams of One-Jewel Jack to Lady Gwendolen. Overdid it, actually! She became so enamored of my highwayman, I resented it. But you must have been delighted at how popular the fellow became—every lady's secret passion."

"The devil you say! After you altered a daring adventurous fellow into a comic, loverlike sot? Nor did I thank you for his popularity when I'd long since abandoned that persona, and scarce wished more impersonators popping up—especially after I'd reconciled with my father."

Stara was making soft little sounds against his chest, but he wasn't certain whether they were regrets for the discomfort she'd caused him or amusement. In any case he accepted it as consolation and stroked her long, loosed hair, giving vent to his own fantasies.

"But," she whispered, sharing an intimate glance and laugh, "it was rather a lark—was it not? Giving the wealthy a bit of their comeuppance?"

"Yes. Actually my life down that road began as a lark. As well it was retaliation against my father and brother for their top-lofty, hard-nosed attitude toward me and all who were less titled."

"Were you ne'er frightened of being caught? I own

I was! Even in this escapade, I dreaded being uncovered ere I'd carried it to fulfillment."

"Gratifying to know you shared a particle of my agony these last days," he inserted, still not completely having forgiven her gammoning him so effectively. But Stara was entranced by the confession of his past. "Did you never see yourself as swinging on a scaffold?" Her face was white at that possibility for her love, and had her visibly shuddering. That concern could not help but appease. Laughing, he ruefully admitted, "Those visions would intrude. But actually made all more of a challenge. Saw myself rather like Robin Hood—spreading the fruits of my efforts to the road people. There are so many living by the wayside. We, in our estates and ballrooms and riding by in closed carriages rarely see the truth of it. English souls reduced to groveling for existence. Ye Gods, how could one see families without a home or meal and not wish to redistribute a bit? A single fob tossed their way changed their entire lives."

Stara hugged him at that expression, wishing she could have been on the road with him. "Perhaps we can still do it," she exclaimed with her usual spark. "We need not be One-Jewel Jack. Rather make new personas and between us change all England!"

He dissuaded her. "At first it was a bit of all right to find myself a legend. But living on the road one suffers the loneliness and the hunger and the sadness of an outlaw. There is the excitement that one might be caught, but then, each carriage did not hold fat lords gloating over their plenty. The ladies particularly I regretted alarming. So I began the legend of One-Jewel—that they might feel even my plundering was a compliment. I found a lady will give one near anything as long as she sees it as a tribute to herself."

"As did Lady Gwendolen," Stara agreed. "Curious, when I was One-Jewel Jack and saw her appeased by the compliment, it just increased my disrespect."

A quick look at Marcus had her aware that she'd correctly interpreted the slight quiver in his voice, he was near to laughing. She demanded an explanation of it which with a great deal of nonchalance he gave, letting her know that to a gentleman, ladies gave other rewards, which were quite delightful.

In the midst of his chuckling Stara felt her feathers ruffled, "What do you mean? I hope you did not take liberties! But of course you did. You did so with me as a young school girl. Widgeon that I was, I thought I was unique. And now I hear it was your usual practice! Oh drat!"

This was the Stara Marcus had become accustomed to. Sweet and adorable one moment—yet firing up and getting wild as a hornet the next. Now she was jumping away from him. And striding out of the cave to the waterfall. He'd belittled a very cherished memory.

Calling out, rushing after, Marcus caught up just as Stara ducked behind the falling water. She was adroit at moving through that curtain of wet, knowing just when to lean against the cave and inch her way. Marcus stumbled back and forth and emerged drenched. His clumsiness had her stopping to giggle. Then considerately, she reached toward and led him safely under and around the waterfall. A few steps up and they were platformed like royalty, above all, looking down at the cascading water. The sun's warmth was not quick enough. So obligingly, Stara used her scarf to dry his dripping locks. Leaning over, her long hair trailed over his face and throat and chest—causing a symphony of sensation on his skin. He reveled in it. So much so, he could not help but push the scarf away and take up handfuls of her locks to dry and soothe his damp skin. That became so pleasurable for them both, they forgot the practical purpose as they stroked each other from dry to inflamed.

"We shall tumble off here into the water again," Stara warned, pulling away.

"That will be cooling," he said, with a smile.

"Yes, but we ought welcome the heat. We shall need a great deal of it when winter comes, and you and I are out in the cold on the road."

"You have given up much for me," he said with pride.

"Do not remind me," she responded, half with a laugh, half a groan. "If you had not made me give back Lady Gwen's pink pearls—we might have lived for some time on that. Or if only that impostor had not been killed, we might've reverted to type to collect some income."

"Pure fustian! We are no longer outside the law. We are deucedly respectable, my love. Did I not tell you One-Jewel Jack's execution was in motion? I was set to unearth the root for I could scarce allow all these ragamuffin appendages to keep sprouting. Yes, including you. Egad, when I discovered I'd been played by a *lady*, I was dashed near knocked acock. However, you at least had more style than that misguided menial who played me to death and was blasted off by his grace's men at first entrance! What a demeaning end for One-Jewel Jack, a gentleman of some distinction. Would I had acted sooner with the honorable demise I had arranged ere that bungler stepped in."

"Bungler? The duke or the impostor?"

"Both."

"Speaking of the former, do you think I'm obligated to return his ring?" Stara queried with some regret.

Marcus considered telling her about the generosity of his grace and even her ladyship. Yet at this lovely, languorous moment he was not certain he wished her to have warm feelings for anyone but himself. Reluctantly, but valiantly, he informed her she was not as impoverished as assumed. "You missed quite an edifying scene between our two nobles. It began with Lady Gwen judging my rescuing you was a lack of devotion to her. Frankly, her ultimatum was: either I stay with her or she'd break our engagement. Unlike certain people who dawdled about a similar commitment, you'll note, without hesitation I chose you. Thereupon, her ladyship concluded the duke had a prior commitment to her. It was quite an education in logic how she convinced him *you'd* cried off by being abducted! No more than a few sentences were required. Yet as a gentleman and somewhat shamefaced, he was nothing loath to recompense you with the manor in the English Channel. . . ."

"A home! . . . a home!" Stara interrupted. He followed her running back down to the clearing before the cave. There in a less precarious position she had proper space to give vent to her delight. Taking his hand she had him whirling with her. He could not help laughing along, although he resented that he was not the one to give her that joy. "God in heaven," she was continuing, "we shall have a home. That was the only thing I was regretting . . . just a bit," she added hurriedly, not to overset her heart's love.

"You shall always have a home. That *I* shall swear! But chiefly your home shall be in my heart. There can be, I vow, no greater security nor . . . haven."

Sighing, Stara relaxed against his heart, but continued happily with her dreams, "We shall have a decidedly comfortable life on our Isle of Wight. Actually, if you'll recollect, it is a perfect location in case we ever become bored and wish to take a turn for smuggling."

Marcus guffawed at that, entranced by the way his daring adventuress's mind worked, calling her incorrigible. Further he let her know that he had discussed his situation with his father and brother, and they had agreed he was worthy of being reinstated, even if he married his heart's love and not Lady Gwendolen. "I pretended that the duke had cut me out due to his standing, and since that is what they expect in life, they understood. Further I discovered," and his eyes twinkled with satisfaction, "my brother did not actually wish me to marry a lady of higher status than his wife, a mere baronet's daughter. So the annuity is made secure. And my mother's estate."

"Goodness gracious!" Stara exclaimed. "Are you roasting me? We have *two* estates!"

"More than that, if you wish to accept them. Lady Gwendolen spoke of one in Richmond, I believe, but I was so distraught at the time, one hardly had time to negotiate. Nor do I think we need or ought take more. . . . There was also the mention of some jewels he had made to your specifications. That is," Marcus said coldly with a suggestion of an offended sniff, "if you prefer his offerings to the mere fob I have for you."

Stara was in a stunned wonder. "We can have all that *and* each other as well? But is that fair? I was certain I'd have to give up *something* in life. At first I was giving up my love to achieve security or the duke. Then when I chose you, I was giving up my security for love. How is it possible that now we have both? Surely it is too much! Too wondrous! Are there really such happy endings? Or shall we return and find his grace is threatening me as the Pinkertons threatened me all my life . . . keeping me always hopping."

Marcus swept the lady into his arms, assuring her she need never be frightened. Never again need go adventuring. Indeed, his only request was that she give up adventuring, for he could not risk losing her again, as he feared he'd done when hearing of her abduction.

After several kisses of reassurance, Stara wondered however what would have happened to them, if she had not been adventurous this time and abducted herself. "I daresay we should have had to marry our nobles, after all?"

"Nonsense. You were merely premature. I had resolved to don my highwayman outfit for one last time and take you away from his grace and keep you away until you realized you and I were meant to be together."

Stara's face was filled with regret at that lost treat. "Dash it! I would have so much enjoyed that! Oh botheration! If only I had waited." Her groans of regret were so continuous, her loved one was forced to promise a grand abduction directly they were married. In fact he was willing to make it an annual occurrence in celebration of their marriage.

"It all ended as I planned," Stara said happily in the midst of their continuous embrace.

"You are the very devil of a manipulating adventuress!"

"Gammon. After admitting you were the real One-Jewel Jack, what face have you to call *me* an adventuress! Although I admit I take it as a compliment. Actually, if it were not for my manipulating and adventuring, I would not have won what I wished all along. You."

Marcus could not find fault with that conclusion. He could only obligingly amend, "You are a wild, adventuring lady after my own heart," and kissed her so many times, she was wild indeed.

Stara, the lady adventuress, rested in her true lover's arms, having gotten all she wished in life at last: a home, income, true love and an adventuring gentleman she could manage, after all. As long as she did so with all her heart.

COMING NEXT MONTH

HIGHLAND LOVE SONG by Constance O'Banyon
From the bestselling author of *Forever My Love* comes a sweeping and mesmerizing continuation of the DeWinter legacy begun in *Song of the Nightingale*. In this story, set against the splendor of nineteenth-century Scotland, innocent Lady Arrian DeWinter is abducted by Lord Warrick Glencarin, laird of Clan Drummond—the man of her dreams and the deadly enemy of her fiancé.

MY OWN TRUE LOVE by Susan Sizemore
A captivating time-travel romance from the author of *Wings of the Storm*. When Sara Dayny received a silver ring set with a citrine stone, she had no idea that it was magical. But by some quirk of fate she was transferred to early nineteenth-century London and found a brooding and bitter man who needed her love.

ANOTHER LIFE by Doreen Owens Malek
Award-winning author Doreen Owens Malek takes a steamy look behind the scenes of daytime television in this fast-paced romantic thriller. Budding young attorney Juliet Mason is frustrated with her job and pressured by a boyfriend she doesn't want to marry. Then she gets assigned to defend handsome leading actor Tim Garfield, who may be the most wonderful man she's ever met—or the most dangerous.

SHADOWS IN THE WIND by Carolyn Lampman
The enthralling story of the Cantrell family continues in Book II of the Cheyenne Trilogy. When Stephanie awakened on Cole Cantrell's ranch, she had no idea who she was. The only clues to her identity were a mysterious note and an intricate gold wedding band. Feeling responsible for her, Cole insisted she stay with him until her memory returned. But as love blossomed between them, could they escape the shadows of the past?

DIAMOND by Sharon Sala
Book I of the Gambler's Daughters Trilogy. Diamond Houston has always dreamed of becoming a country and western singer. After her father's death, she follows her heart and her instincts to Nashville with legendary country star, Jesse Eagle. There she learns that even for a life of show biz, she must gamble with her soul.

KILEY'S STORM by Suzanne Elizabeth
Daniella "Dannie" Storm thought she had enough trouble on her hands when her father found gold in the local creek and everyone in Shady Gulch, Colorado began to fight over it. But when Marshal Jake Kiley rode into town to settle the matter, she realized that her problems had only just begun—especially her strong attraction to him.

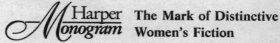 **Harper Monogram** The Mark of Distinctive Women's Fiction

YESTERDAY'S SHADOWS
by Marianne Willman

Bettany Howard was a young orphan traveling west searching for the father who left her years ago. Wolf Star was a Cheyenne brave who longed to know who abandoned him—a white child with a jeweled talisman. Fate decreed they'd meet and try to seize the passion promised. 0-06-104044-4

MIDNIGHT ROSE by Patricia Hagan

From the rolling plantations of Richmond to the underground slave movement of Philadelphia, Erin Sterling and Ryan Youngblood would pursue their wild, breathless passion and finally surrender to the promise of a bold and unexpected love. 0-06-104023-1

WINTER TAPESTRY
by Kathy Lynn Emerson

Cordell vows to revenge the murder of her father. Roger Allington is honor bound to protect his friend's daughter but has no liking for her reckless ways. Yet his heart tells him he must pursue this beauty through a maze of plots to win her love and ignite their smoldering passion.
0-06-100220-8